A FEW WORDS ABOUT THE STORY FROM THE AUTHOR

I live in Perth, Western Australia, with my partner Kerryn, Jake and Alfie the dog. Three other children (Tom, Bill, and Lucy) have long since flown the nest. Whilst the story portrayed in this novel is a work of fiction, two of the main characters are based on friends of mine who live in Perth. Their criminal exploits described in this tale are entirely the product of my imagination. In developing the story line and secondary characters, I may have inadvertently, or otherwise, drawn on some real events and experiences of my own.

During my four years in Nairobi, I worked in several countries in East Africa, including Uganda. Employed by one of the then 'Big Six' consultancy firms, I was engaged on a project which evaluated the practice and efficacy of delivering primary school textbooks into regional Uganda. The key recommendation to the United States Government was that future funding would be best applied in developing educational facilities and enhancing the skills of teaching staff, rather than donating books which were often unused.

I hope you enjoy reading the story as much as I did when writing it and being passionate about football, could not resist the opportunity to relive a match I played in during my time in Uganda.

MOT LUFC and up the Subiaco Shakers!

Paul Coates 2024

A FEW WORDS ABOUT THE STORY FROM THE AUTHOR

TAKE A GOOD LOOK AT YOURSELF

by Paul Coates

First Edition.

© 2024 Paul Coates.

No part of this publication may be reproduced or transmitted in any form or by any means, electronic or mechanical, including photocopy, recording, or any information storage and retrieval system, without permission in writing from the publisher.

This is a work of fiction. Names, characters, places, and incidents either are the products of the author's imagination or are used fictitiously. Any resemblance to actual persons, living or dead, businesses, companies, events, or locales is entirely coincidental.

Cover design, editing and typesetting by
Karren 'Wren' Payne

All rights reserved.

ISBN 978-0-6455637-2-6

"I am the Lord, thy God … thou shalt not steal."
Source: Exodus, the Bible

"For I know I have plans for you … plans to prosper."
Source: Jeremiah, the Bible

"If there is a God, his plan is very similar to someone not having a plan." **Source: Eddie Izzard**

"Two wrongs don't make a right ... and no, Paul, three won't either." **Source: Patricia Coates when disciplining son. Scarborough, North Yorkshire 1967.**

FOREWORD

// EXTRACT FROM WORLD BANK REPORT (PAGE 25)

TITLE: WHERE HAVE ALL THE TEXTBOOKS GONE?
SUBJECT: TOWARDS SUSTAINABLE PROVISION OF TEACHING AND
LEARNING MATERIALS IN SUB SAHARAN AFRICA
AUTHOR: TONY READ, WORLD BANK

"Research has also revealed that the delivery of textbooks to schools does not necessarily imply that textbooks are used in the classroom. Kalibbala, writing on the implementation of USAID funded support for primary school education in Uganda, commented;

"Current textbook utilisation levels in schools are very low. It was erroneously assumed by past textbook provision programmes that textbook provision was synonymous with utilisation, and that once books were delivered to schools they would be read by students. However, many new books remain unused in school cupboards and stores."

1

ONE DEATH AND A NEAR MISS

SEEKING REFUGE FROM both the heat and errant balls launched by a slow trickle of recreational golfers, two kangaroos bask in the shade of the trees along the fairway of the seventh hole. They look up to the sky, drawn by the sound of a Qantas Airbus 380 heading southwards, two hundred kilometres from home. Oblivious to the cry of "FORE", they barely notice a small, lethal, white ball rocket past their heads at great speed, missing them by inches. Nor do they hear the word 'bugger', uttered by an irritable retiree coming to the realisation that he has probably lost his third ball of the round, with twelve holes still to play.

Majestically, the Airbus begins its descent and is soon drifting towards the runway. Jam packed, the plane is full of excited passengers, either arriving at a new destination or coming home from foreign lands.

It is 40°c outside and another five degrees hotter in the storage facility at Sydney airport. Puzzled, Bluey Edwards scratches his head, which has a fine covering of close-cropped ginger stubble. He stares at a large crate, perplexed. Returning to his office, he scrambles through an untidy pile of paperwork on his desk but cannot find what he is looking for, so re-enters the main warehouse. Once more, standing in front of the mystery crate, he scratches his head and subconsciously tugs up his trousers which have submitted to gravity and slipped below his belly. After re-reading the details on the blue paper docket, taped to the crate in a clear polythene wallet, he calls over to his foreman.

"Hey, Brenton mate, what's this doing here?"

"What's what doing here?"

"This bloody crate right in front of me. What do yer think I'm talking about?"

Joining his boss, the foreman inspects the crate, wiping sweat from his forehead with his sleeve. "Dunno mate, I haven't a clue." Then, squinting at the crate, he adds, "It's got USAID stamped on it."

"Well bugger me, I'm working with Sherlock bloody Holmes. I can see that, you muppet. The manifest that's taped to it says it should have gone to Uganda via Kenya. So, what the hell is it doing here? I thought this sort of stuff normally goes through Jacko's warehouse."

"Dunno boss. Yeah. No. I dunno."

"Yer 'dunno' a lot, do ya Brenton? How could you miss an effing crate this size?"

About to respond with another 'dunno', Brenton manages to verbally change direction in the nick of time.

"Sorry boss, what do you want me to do?"

"Yer could start by doing your sodding job," answers Bluey, raising his arms in exasperation.

"Do you want me to give them a call, boss?"

"Naw mate. As usual, I'll 'ave to sort out the mess. I'll give the yanks a call," responds Bluey, huffily, and marches back to his office. Before he enters, he stops, turns to the foreman and shouts back.

"Mate, this 'aint good enough. You need to pick up yer game and take a good look at yourself."

* * *

Shouting above the engine noise of the Lockheed C-130 Hercules, the captain reports his position to ground control.

"This is November Lima Two Zero One, reporting in. Mission successful. We're almost at the northeast Rwandan border and have dropped off all the equipment and supplies to the Tutsis rebels. Current position means we'll be shortly crossing into Uganda airspace, and we should be back at Entebbe Airport in a couple of hours."

"Received. Keep safe, see you soon. Over and out," came back the response from ground control.

Frowning, after examining the dials, the captain turns to the co-pilot.

"Fuel looks low but should be enough to get back. I'm a bit surprised though. Thought we'd have more as we've got rid of all the weight after the drop off. It doesn't make sense."

"Not quite, Captain."

"Whaddya mean, not quite?"

"There's a large crate still in the back. It's full of books," explains the co-pilot.

"What the hell are we doing with a load of goddamn books. Go back there and see what Hank has to say."

The co-pilot unstraps his seat and makes his way to the main cargo area. A minute later, following a short exchange with Hank, he returns and straps himself back into the seat, before addressing the captain.

"Hank says he thinks we're supposed to drop it in Uganda. The supervisor in the loading bay said all the information would be in the documentation. It's an USAID package, but there are no instructions in the written orders as to where we've got to drop them."

With a reddening complexion, the captain scowls in frustration. "Goddamn. What the hell is going on? Get on the radio. Use the one in the back. Ask Ground Control where we are supposed to drop them."

It was a fruitless and frustrating five minute conversation with the staff in Ground Control. Nobody was aware of the existence of the crate, let alone its planned destination. Eventually the supervisor comes onto the radio to offer his advice, with a very clear caveat that he would take no responsibility for the outcome if they decided to follow his suggestion. Returning to his seat, the co-pilot repeats his conversation, verbatim, which elicits the expected response from the captain.

"Are you goddamn kidding me? Goddamn pen pushers. Tell Hank we are getting short of fuel and to drop it as soon as possible. Tell him we've just crossed the Ugandan border."

Once more the co-pilot unstraps and returns to the cargo area, to deliver the instructions. Five minutes later, he returns to the cockpit to report back. "All done, Captain."

Shaking his head, the captain replies, "Goddamn Washington, seat shining, paper shuffling, pen pushing sons of bitches. They all need to take a good hard look at themselves."

* * *

Children run around excitedly, barefoot, kicking up the orange-brown soil. Shielding their eyes from the unrelenting sun, they look up to the sky and watch the plane disappear into the distance. They dance around the crate and others crawl under the parachute, laughing and wrestling with each other. Elders from the village approach and berate the children, who scatter and run away to avoid the wrath and punishment from the adults.

Three men stand near the crate, inspecting it. A pool of blood has soaked into the ground, darkening the soil. The source of the blood is evident, pooled around two legs jutting out from underneath the cargo.

One of the elders addresses the leader. "It's American, Chief Masika."

"I can see that Eze. More books. We do not need more books. I thought that had been agreed after the mzungus from Price Waterhouse came here." Shaking his head whilst staring at the two lifeless legs and the blood soddened ground surrounding them, he adds, "They will pay for this."

"I agree Chief, I think these American mzungus need to take a good look at themselves."

* * *

Flicking through a golf brochure in his expansive airy office in Kampala, Ambassador Sexton Bagley gives an annoyed 'tut' when his phone rings. Petulantly, he snatches the receiver from the cradle.

"I have told you Martha, I do not want any calls for the next hour."

"Sorry Ambassador, but it's Bruce Patterson from the Australian embassy. He said the matter is urgent."

"Oh! Brucey Patterson. Very well, put him through."

An Australian accent greets the Ambassador, causing him to smile. "G'day Sexton. How's it hanging?"

"Good day Bruce, always a pleasure. What can I do for you and the Australian Government?"

"Mate, it's more a case of what I've already done for you. You owe me one hundred dollars."

"Do enlighten me," replies Bagley, smirking.

"I've just got back from Kabale. You may know it.

It's a small town in the Rubirizi District. Anyway, I met the head man, Chief Masika, and I can tell you he's not a happy little Chieftain. He's got a bone to pick with you."

"How could he? I've never met the man."

"I know. It is more an unhappiness regarding Americans generally, rather than you personally," explains Patterson.

"Bloody cheek. They get millions of dollars of aid from us every year. We are proud of USAID and our humanitarian work here, not to mention strengthening their democratic governance amidst their tinpot dictators."

"Yeah mate, save the speeches for your embassy receptions. Not sure about the governance bit though, given the record of your lot. As for tinpot dictators, old Donald Trump could give 'em a run for their money."

Ignoring the comment, Bagley asks, "So, what's the bloody problem?"

"Well, you know your very American habit of dropping things on foreign countries. In this instance, not bombs, but parachuting large crates of textbooks into remote villages. I'm talking about your primary education initiative to supply their schools."

"Yes, of course I know what you're talking about. But I thought we'd discontinued that."

"Apparently, there was one final drop of a crate that was left behind at Sydney airport. Your boys must have missed it when collecting the last consignment that arrived in Entebbe Airport a few weeks ago. Anyway, this last crate was picked up by your lads in the Airforce and subsequently dropped on a village near Kabale town."

"You are joking?"

"No mate. I know you lot have a propensity to bomb the buggery out of foreign nations, but it seems you get more casualties from the crates, than you do from your bombs."

"Very bloody funny, Patterson."

"Cheers. And no worries, I've squared it with Chief Masika. I slipped him a hundred dollars compensation. You know how they love hard currency over here."

"What, only a hundred dollars compensation, for killing one of his villagers?"

"No mate. The crate landed on one of his goats and one hundred dollars, American not Australian dollars I might add, is the going price that we foreigners must pay for a goat. Especially if it's the Chief's goat. The locals pay a fraction of that price, of course."

Laughing with relief, Bagley says, "Well, it seems I do owe you a drink or two. I'll meet you at the Sheraton around six."

"No worries, mate," replies Patterson, and adds, before ending the call, "maybe your lot need to take a good look at yourselves."

* * *

// EMAIL TO HEAD OF USAID CENTER FOR EDUCATION FROM DEPUTY ADMINISTRATOR

As you are aware, one of our chosen interventions for supporting primary education in remote communities in the African continent is the provision of educational materials, primarily books. Given inaccessibility issues, the practice of book drops (parachuting large crates into remote areas) has been standard operational practice. This is now being discontinued for the following reasons:

A review of our primary education interventions, conducted independently by Price Waterhouse, has revealed that book drops are ineffective. The culture of Ugandan tribes appears to result in the failure to use the books as intended. These are treated as a gift and, as a matter of respect, the crates are left unopened. In fact, an unintended effect is that these tribes devote valuable, and scarce resources to build sheds to safely store the unopened crates.

Book drops have resulted in four fatalities in the last three years, with unsuspecting villagers being crushed to death. The review by Price Waterhouse also found that the standard of teaching in remote, rural areas is generally extremely low.

Therefore, future funds will be devoted to building teacher training colleges, which will be strategically located in regional centers and initially run by American educationalists.

The pilot project will be delivered in the Western Ugandan District of Rubirizi, located some 364 kilometers from the capital, Kampala. This innovative scheme will be undertaken in collaboration with our counterparts and longstanding partners from the Australian Department of Foreign Affairs and Trade. They will be sending a team of skilled construction experts (bricklayers, plumbers, electricians etc.) to ensure the building works are completed quickly and to western safety standards. USAID will be supplying all the materials.

Omer Stanforth
Deputy Administrator
Global HQ
Washington

TWO DEATHS (ONE JUST PLAIN UNLUCKY)

FOURTEEN KILOMETRES SOUTH of central Sydney, a hundred-acre property houses several listed buildings, all constructed in the early 1900s. Its entry in the New South Wales Heritage Register describes the location as *'having a strong visual impact on the surrounding landscape whose original buildings are of a unified scale and materials resulting in a harmonious appearance.'* The description of the notorious site in Malabar would prompt its inhabitants to laugh and scoff at the irony of the florid pretentious language in the guide. None of the residents live there voluntarily and, for most, their stay is temporary. A few never leave alive, their final exit being in a wooden box. To a man, they all wish they had never had the pleasure of an extended stay at the Long Bay Correctional Complex.

Inevitably, the long history of Long Bay boasts residents whose notoriety is well documented. 'Alumni' includes Roger Rogerson, the former corrupt police detective who received life imprisonment for murder, drug trafficking and perverting the course of justice. Equally as notorious, Ivan Milat, the convicted serial killer, spent the rest of his life in the facility. Most of the one thousand inmates live in relative anonymity, serving sentences ranging from life to a few months. Convictions range from murder and armed robbery to conscientious objection. In short, Long Bay, which deals with the full scope of what the law considers to be criminal activity, is home to an eclectic mix of offenders.

One of those offenders, Boof Arkins, adopts the most innocent expression that he can muster, as he sits at a large imposing jarrah desk, facing Governor Hanson. Sat to the side of the Governor, is the General Manager of the facility, Ray 'Boomer' Jessop. Smiling inwardly, Boof is amused at the amateurish attempt of the 'Good cop, bad cop' routine. He scratches his bony forearm and constantly smooths back his widow's peak, as he sincerely answers each question. His prison clothes hung apologetically from his thin body.

Although both Hanson and Jessop successfully climbed high up the correctional services career ladder, they arrived via hugely different routes and backgrounds. An alumnus of Geelong Grammar, Hanson had been fast tracked through the system assisted in his journey by various family connections. Despite having to deal with, what his Barrister father termed, the detritus of society, he had rarely got his hands dirty on his speedy route to the top. On the other hand, Jessop, brought up in Sydney's western suburbs, had negotiated his pathway through underfunded and violent schools near his childhood home. Somehow, against all the odds and in contrast to many ex-students of Jessop's secondary school, his chosen career fell on the right side of the law. Working through the ranks of the prison service, Jessop had arrived at the top. Hanson relied heavily on Jessop's worldliness to keep things running smoothly, even if his methods and approach seemed, on occasion, a bit rough around the edges.

Thirty minutes of questions, cajoling, urging, and prompting had not shed any further light on the circumstances surrounding the death of Boof's cellmate. The identity of the perpetrator was not in dispute, being caught on the prison CCTV system entering the cell. He was apprehended shortly afterwards in the showers, trying to cleanse himself still covered in blood. His shank was discarded on the shower floor. Having been allowed compassionate supervised leave to attend his mother's funeral, Boof was not even on site during the assault and murder. Unable to secure any information from the perpetrator, the Governor was hopeful that Boof, who lived daily in close proximity to the victim, may have some thoughts on the motive for the killing. It turned out to be a fruitless exercise, at least as far as the Governor was concerned. For Boof, it broke the monotony of his routine life in a small cell.

Sighing in disappointment, the Governor allows Boof to return to his cell in time for the dinner session. Once Boof has left and is out of earshot, the Governor turns to Jessop.

"I don't know what to make of it, Jessop. Seems to me he's telling the truth. But it's hard to tell."

"I agree sir, but he's a shifty little bugger."

"Yes, he certainly seems to have, what the criminal element calls, street smarts. Tell me something, why is he called Boof? Isn't that the name given to those who are a bit thick? You know, 'Boofhead' and all that. I have to say he doesn't come across as stupid."

"He isn't sir. Too crafty by half in my opinion. Boof is also a name that the inmates give to those with a propensity to conceal items up their arse, sir."

"Sorry?" asks Hanson, not quite believing what he is being told.

"It's called Boofing, sir."

"Boofing?"

"Yes, sir. It's also called hooping, plugging, butt chugging ..."

Screwing his eyes in disgust, Hanson replies curtly, "Yes, thank you Jessop, I think I've got the picture."

"Yes, sir."

"And what, pray tell, would our friend endeavour to hide up his rectum?"

"So far, sir, he has been caught with drugs, cash and a mobile phone".

"Surely not all at once? The man can barely be sixty kilos soaking wet."

"No, sir."

"Well bugger me!" exclaimed Hanson.

"I'd rather not sir," replies Jessop, fully confident the comment will go above the Governor's head.

Although the Governor and Jessop were none the wiser, Boof, on the other hand, suspects that he has a fair idea of what led to the demise of his ex-cell mate. With his own release date imminent, he intends to use this information to his own advantage and, if his hunch is right, the financial reward will be substantial.

During their three months sharing a cell, Boof, and the now deceased Smithy, had developed a friendship and shared many stories. Most were true, give or take the occasional stretching of facts for dramatic effect. One tale grasped Boof's attention and not just because the circumstances seemed so left field as to stretch credibility. If it was true, his cellmate would become a very rich man once he had served his time at His Majesty's pleasure. Despite challenging Smithy's story, Boof's cellmate stood firm regarding its veracity. Gradually, Smithy introduced the idea that Boof could be included in the deal if he was willing to help. Facing an initially sceptical and dismissive Boof, Smithy was adamant, and raised the subject with increasing frequency as their release dates approached. Smithy was due out two weeks before his cell mate, but he insisted that he would wait if Boof gave him the nod. Smithy needed someone he could trust and was certain that Boof was the man. Boof noticed that, as the day of his cellmate's release drew near, Smithy became increasingly anxious. It was as if he knew he was in danger and Boof wondered whether this was connected to the hidden stash that he intended to raid when released.

But now, poor old Smithy would never get his pay day. Perhaps, Boof would.

Back in his cell, Boof sits staring across the small space at the now vacant bed opposite, pondering his deceased cellmate's tale. He had checked Smithy's drawers, but the guards had already cleared out his belongings. All that remains as evidence of his cellmate is a few faded droplets of blood staining the floor, which the clean-up operation and scrubbing has failed to eradicate. Not all hope was lost. Boof has one more card to play and is patiently waiting for the guards to complete their final rounds before the lights go out.

Playing over Smithy's story in his mind, Boof trawls the recesses of his memory. His interest is in a piece of paper that Smithy waved in front of him one might, and he is sure Smithy said it was a specific colour. But what colour? This paper is critical to getting hold of the cash.

A barking voice from the doorway snaps Boof out of his dreamy thoughts, dragging him back into the physical reality of his cell. "Right Boof, I'm closing the door now and it's lights out in five." The guard stares at Boof expectantly, awaiting a response.

"Righto boss," replies Boof, in a deferential tone.

Creeping out of bed and pressing his ear against the door, he listens to the footsteps of the guard, which echo down the corridor. Once Boof hears the guard's final instruction to old Pete, who occupies the cell at the end, he retreats from his cell door. The coast is clear. After jumping onto Smithy's bed, he flicks off the plastic cover on top of the bedpost and carefully edges his middle finger down the hollow metal leg. He finds nothing in the first one and then tries the leg that is jammed against the cell wall. Feeling paper, his heart begins to race. He carefully manoeuvres his skinny finger to avoid pushing the paper further down and out of reach. Trapping it between his middle finger and the wall of the bed leg, he slowly edges the paper up until enough appears at the top for him to pinch the corner and draw it out. *It's blue, that was the bloody colour Smithy said it was, blue* thinks Boof. A broad smile of triumph reveals a small gap in the middle of his bottom teeth.

Back on his own bed, Boof reads, and re-reads, the document. He ponders its contents. *It looks like old Smithy wasn't bullshitting after all*, he thinks. *The cunning old bastard, who'd have thought it? Either that or it's some sort of massive piss take.* But he knew Smithy. Smithy was not the piss taking type.

With his own release date imminent, Boof mulls over Smithy's story. On the one hand it was hard to believe. On the other hand, it was even harder to believe that Smithy would be capable of making up such a story. Especially a story as involved as this one. According to Smithy, the drug smuggling venture was a smoothly run, lucrative enterprise. Smithy was a minor cog in an exceptionally large machine at the Australian end of the operations. A mere delivery boy.

Prior to his incarceration for an unrelated minor offence, Smithy had gradually pieced together the main elements of the operation. Chatting to other equally as small cogs in the machinery, he eventually pieced it all together.

With evident self-satisfaction, he enjoyed sharing what he had learnt, during long conversations in their cell. One of the most important airports in the east African region, Nairobi, is used as a transit point for drug smuggling. It has good connections with west Africa and the heroin producing countries in South-West and Southeast Asia. In recent times, the police have made inroads into disrupting the supply chain. Increased seizures of heroin with Nigerian connections bound for Uganda, Tanzania and Kenya put growing pressure on producers, distributors, and dealers alike. International law enforcement agencies were getting more adept and those involved on the other side of the law were getting progressively more nervous and suspicious.

The head of the operation based on the east coast of Australia is Hakan Yilmaz. Drugs would flow into various east coast locations and channelled through a very efficient network of distributors and dealers. Due to the simmering distrust between each player in the international drug dealing chain and the developing sophistication of the authorities in tracking movements of funds through cyberspace, cash, once more, became king. Payment to the African link of the chain would be made in cash, which was smuggled back in the direction from where the drugs came. African crime lords demanded cash payment in hard currency, either American or Australian dollars. Given the increased attention and ultimate success of the authorities in making seizures, the syndicates sought increasingly inventive ways of transporting the drugs into Australia and the payment in cash back to the African continent.

Smithy was a 'gopher' with limited involvement in the smuggling operation. Delivering packages to a designated contact point at a nominated warehouse in the airport was the limit of his job. Curiosity, however, got the better of him. It was curiosity that eventually killed the cat.

Smithy learnt that large consignments of cash were periodically being smuggled in a particularly audacious way, courtesy of the US Military and the United States Government. Schoolbooks published in Australia were sent to Uganda as part of an international aid program primarily funded by the American agency, USAID. The drug money would be hidden in the middle of a crate of schoolbooks by airport staff working on the payroll of Hakan Yilmaz. It was one of a consignment of twenty crates to be delivered to schools in Uganda by USAID. Only nineteen would arrive at their intended destination. This remaining crate would be 'inadvertently' left behind in Sydney and hidden by Yilmaz's men at the airport. Later, the missing crate would be 'discovered' and sent separately on a private commercial airline via Nairobi Airport, to rectify the supposed administrative error.

It would never reach Uganda, because the operatives in Kenya would ensure it was lost in their system. With the branded paperwork of the United States Government attached to the crate, it would slip as easily through customs as a hot knife through butter. It virtually had diplomatic status. Providing an 'official' turned up with the appropriate paperwork, no questions would be asked. Statistically, over fifteen per cent of consignments at Nairobi airport were misplaced or simply stolen. Nobody would devote much time and resources to investigating the loss of a crate of schoolbooks.

With unfettered hubris, Smithy told Boof about his scheme to get rich.

The smuggling operation ensured the "cash" crate would be stored separately from the other nineteen and hidden away. Therefore when all the crates were collected and loaded onto the plane by American officials, it would be left behind. Once the main consignment had left the airport, the smugglers would wait a few days before sending the cash crate to Kenya. Smithy's plan was to make sure that, for this consignment, the smugglers are going to be disappointed. Smithy and his mate, Spit Jeffries, who also worked at the airport, had hatched a plan to move the 'cash' crate to an entirely different warehouse. Their theory was that the drug smugglers, when they discovered the crate was missing, would assume it had been found by the Americans and taken with the rest of the consignment. Whoever the gangsters came looking for, both Smithy and Spit would be in the clear. Smithy was just a bit part player and not involved in operations inside the facility. He delivered packages and left. Spit was simply an unknown quantity, just a bona fide airport worker earning a living with no involvement whatsoever in anything illegal.

All Spit had to do was to move the crate on his forklift to another warehouse during a quiet moment on his night shift. The plan went without a hitch. The crate was successfully relocated by Spit to a secluded dark corner of a neighbouring warehouse, with no written record of its transfer to the new location.

After a few days, when they are sure the coast is clear, they plan to collect the crate and live happily ever after, in Bali, on the proceeds. Both Smithy and Spit would spend the remainder of their lives doing what they loved most, eating, drinking and surfing.

Following the tale with intense interest, Boof struggled to understand why Smithy was taking the risk of sharing the story with him. He was unclear as to why Boof wanted him involved. As far as he could tell, Smithy and his mate had it all worked out.

Once he heard the final part of Smithy's tale the fog lifted and it all became clear. Fate intervened. Spit became an unfortunate entry in the annual Australian Bureau of Statistics publication. That year, 192,463 deaths were registered, and Spit was the third fatality in New South Wales and one of sixty five recorded deaths resulting from a shark attack. This left Smithy as the sole beneficiary, but in need of a partner he could trust to help him get to the loot. It was, at least, a two-man job and there was more than enough cash to share and see them through a very comfortable carefree life on the Indonesian island.

For many nights, Boof had pondered Smithy's proposal. On the verge of giving his cellmate the green light (with some reservations) a fortunate stroke of serendipity for Boof, if not Smithy, had purged his lingering doubts. Concerned as to whether Smithy could be trusted to keep his mouth shut, Boof feared that the loose tongue of his cellmate might bring the drug smugglers knocking on his door. Notoriously, Smithy was known for being incapable of keeping a secret and liked to brag. It seemed to him that, with the demise of Smithy and Spit, no-one except himself knew about the relocated crate. Better still, there was nothing to connect it to him and he now had the blue manifest document in his possession.

* * *

"Lighter, cigarettes, wallet containing sixty-five dollars, mobile phone, key ring with three keys attached. Sign 'ere please," says the prison officer responsible for Boof's discharge.

Boof gathers up the items and pockets them after signing the paperwork. "Cheers Mister Hardy. I'll be seeing you."

"I have no doubt of that, Boof, although the basic idea is to reduce recidivism."

"Eh!" replies Boof

"What I am saying is, that although I have no doubt that we will see you again, the purpose of prison is to stop us seeing you again. The basic theory is that your time spent here is intended to discourage you from repeating the same mistakes."

"No Mister Hardy, I'm done. It's the straight and narrow for me now."

"Really?" asks Hardy, with an exaggerated squint of scepticism.

"Yep, really."

"If you say so Boof, but don't worry, we'll keep your bed warm just in case. And … we'll see you soon." Laughing sardonically, Hardy presses a button beside his desk which causes a loud jarring buzzing sound to emit from the exit door indicating that the lock is released. "See you soon," repeats Hardy.

"Wanker," mutters Boof under his breath as he re-enters the free world, shielding his eyes from the intense glaring sun.

3

DAMO

RANDWICK DISTRICT RUGBY Union Football Club had just won its second successive Australian Club Championship against one of their long-term rivals, the Manley Marlins and the post-match changing room is buzzing with laughter and good humour. Everyone is in good spirits, with one notable exception.

"What the hell was that mate?"

"What was what, Link?"

"And don't farking keep calling me Link."

"Sorry mate, it's become a bit of a habit," replies Damo, with no hint of an apology in his tone.

"So, what the hell was that?" asks Link.

"What?"

"That last Try, you greedy bastard. Why didn't you lay it off to me? I could 'ave scored. It was my big moment."

"What are you whinging about mate, I scored, didn't I?"

"Yeah, but you were lucky. You had two men to beat. I was in the clear," complains Link.

"Mate, you were ten yards from the try line and you've got hands made of grease. If you managed to avoid dropping the ball, that would have been the longest run you've made all season. Anyways, you'd 'ave got caught by that brick shithouse Māori."

"I haven't scored this season and it was my best chance all year. Not only that, but it's also a bloody Final. It could've been my moment of glory. We were twenty points ahead mate, yer could've given it to me."

"Mate, you're a bloody prop, for God's sake. It's not what you're there for. You're the battering ram. Stamp on people or be stamped on. That's what you do. I mean look at you, you've got a face like a sack of spuds. A face that positively invites being stood on."

"Fuck off, why are all you poncy centres such a bunch of wankers?" counters Link, with a rhetorical question.

Laughing, Damo replies, tidying the side parting of his hair. "We all have our roles mate. Look at me, I've a responsibility to maintain these good looks, run like a cheetah and score the tries. I'm afraid in the looks and speed department you missed the bus a few years ago. It's genetics mate, you were just unlucky."

Sulkily, Link strips off the rest of his muddy kit, wraps a towel around his waist and heads for the shower.

Pete 'Beaver' Cape has recently joined the club and after watching the exchange with some amusement, sidles up to Damo.

"Hey mate, I've been meaning to ask. Why do you call him Link?"

"Well mate, 'cause he's the Missing Link. Look at him for God's sake."

* * *

The rugby club was Damo's second family, and filled the gaps left by his family at home. Growing up, he was not blessed with a story book domestic environment.

The youngest of three boys, Damo had not known his father even when he was present in the home. Distant and irascible, the family patriarch checked out from family duties shortly after Damo started Junior School.

It was no bad thing; his father was abusive, and it was down to his mother to clean up the mess, which she did as best she could. One day, his eldest brother, Col, who grew into the size of a barn, decided that they, and particularly his mother, had suffered enough. From what Andy, his other brother, told Damo, it all happened quickly. It was midweek and Damo was at school rugby training, but the others were at home. Andy was in the kitchen working his way through a ham sandwich during the incident, so did not see what happened firsthand. Hearing a brief exchange of words followed by a dull smack, Andy ran into the living room to find Col, then just twenty, standing over his father who was lying, unconscious, on the floor. His mother, in tears, looked down at her prone husband with a mixture of horror and relief.

The following day his father left and years of anxiety, caused by constant worry, evaporated from his mother. Her previously careworn face immediately looked ten years younger. She wore, for the first time in years, a beatific smile as if the weight of the world had been lifted off her shoulders.

Unfortunately, her newfound happiness was short lived and trouble, once more, darkened the doors of the household. Putting to use his unusual size and ferocity, Col chose a pathway after school that led him directly to jail. Not discouraged by a prison sentence for assault, Col graduated to burglary, and it was this that brought Damo's two separate lives, rugby and his home, together.

One of the second-row forwards, Ned Kenny, is Head of the NSW police division that deals with serious crime. Ned's nickname is 'Speed' because the six-foot eleven-inch giant of a man, is not known for his sprinting ability on the field. His brain is significantly faster than his body, hence his success in the police force. A propensity for

Damo to lose his socks, which frequently drove Coach Jones to despair combined with Speed's chosen career, is the unlikely catalyst that causes his two separate worlds to collide.

Often, Damo would open his kitbag in the dressing room and find he had forgotten his socks. On the day of a preliminary final, Damo opens his kit bag and duly announces that his socks have, once more, gone missing. He asks if anyone has a spare pair. Hearing this, the temper of Coach Jones explodes. Jones is an old school screaming, spitting, fire and brimstone coach. Lost sock circumstances merited the dropping of Damo's first name.

"Holden, you bloody idiot. How many times do I have to warn you? They won't let you play unless you have the correct kit."

The coach has a habit of selecting two or three players each game who would benefit from an inspirational message. He would scribble words on a piece of A4 paper and tape it to the locker door of the chosen players. Damo, who is sitting on the bench resting his back on his locker door, flinches and then swerves to avoid the coach's blow. Slamming the heel of his hand against his intended target, which is Damo's locker door rather than his head, the coach plants his face one inch from Damo's. They are nose to nose and Damo, who can smell yesterday's dinner on the coach's breath, waits for the lecture.

"Look what I've written on your bloody door. Look what I've written. What I've written is what I want from you, Holden. THAT'S WHAT I WANT FROM YOU. GEDDIT?"

Three words are clumsily printed, in the coach's handwriting, on a piece of paper taped to Damo's locker door. Although he had already seen and read it, he reflexively turns to examine it again, to appease the coach. In fact, it is one word, repeated three times. The coach shouts out the words, covering Damo's face in spittle. Unfazed, Damo is the most sanguine player in the team and is unmoved by the Coach's normal method of motivation. He is, however, blessed, or some would say cursed, with a smart mouth.

"Yeah boss, I read it," he replies calmly.

Looking at Damo expectantly, the coach asks the same question that he always asks of the player who has been fortunate enough to be selected for one of his special notes. "Well then, what did you think of it when you read it?"

Sat on the bench opposite, Speed holds his breath. He knows the situation is unlikely to end well.

Looking directly into the eyes of the coach, Damo says, "To be honest, I did think that it's a bit repetitive. Yer know, with the same word being written three times. But that's not what struck me first."

Oblivious to the sarcasm, the coach replies, "Good. Good. So, you idiot, what did strike you first?"

"That there are actually two m's in commitment. Not one."

Tense silence swamps the locker room. Twenty fully grown, large muscular men, all ready to wreak physical havoc on the opposition, turn into a class of nervous schoolboys waiting for the headmaster to explode and hand out corporal punishment. Coach Jones is still processing what he has heard when 'Speed' lumbers up to Damo, purposely creating an imposing physical barrier between his teammate and the coach.

"Here ya go," says Speed, throwing a pair of socks into Damo's lap. "I've found yer socks."

The coach's complexion had turned puce. Anger rendering him unable to reply verbally, he balls his fists. Fortunately for Damo and the Coach, Speed's intervention has largely diffused the situation. Leaning around the side of Speed, whose bulk still dominates their space, Coach Jones gives a final warning which enables him to save face and have the last word.

"Count yerself bloody lucky Holden. Yer teammate's saved yer bacon." Looking up at Speed, who is towering above him, the coach nods. "Cheers Speed, good work."

Coach Jones marches out of the changing room and the team files after him like contrite schoolchildren. A couple of players shoot Damo a reproachful look but, by the time they return to the changing rooms after beating the Rats, Warringah Rugby Club, all is forgotten in the jubilation of making the Grand Final. Luckily for Damo, he scored a try and had a reasonable game, thereby avoiding further post-match attention from the coach.

In the club bar, the true significance of the missing socks becomes clear. It is not until Damo, one of the smallest players in the team, sidles up to Speed, that he hears some unwelcome news. Club socks are about to precipitate the collision of Damo's, erstwhile, quite separate worlds.

"Just wanted to say cheers mate," says Damo, passing over a glass of beer, which becomes engulfed in Speed's hand.

"No problem, mate," comes back Speed's reply.

Seeing that Speed was not going to offer any further explanation or information, Damo asks the obvious question.

"Where did you find the socks, mate?"

During the pause, whilst Speed takes a long drink from his glass, Damo perceives hesitancy in his teammate. Carefully placing the now half empty pint glass on the bar, an embarrassed Speed looks at Damo.

"I got them from your brother."

"Whaddya mean? Which brother? Andy?"

"No, the other one, Colin."

"I'm not following you mate," said Damo, quizzically.

"He was caught with an accomplice inside a jewellery store, in the city centre."

"Buying what?"

"It was after hours, Damo. He was wearing the socks, your socks, over his hands. I assume he was trying to avoid leaving any fingerprints."

"Are you kidding me?"

"Yeah, no. 'Fraid not. He's in custody. I didn't want to burden you with it before the game."

"What'll happen to him?"

"He'll probably end up back in Long Bay given his previous record, but at least this time there wasn't any violence. No-one got hurt. Just straightforward burglary. He even came quietly, which must be a first, given his record."

"I suppose you'll need the socks back then."

"Yep, I suppose they're evidence. Better get yourself another pair and remember to bring them to the next game. It's a Grand Final, so no mess ups."

* * *

Driving a concrete truck by day and working as security on the door of a Coogee nightclub over the weekend, provides Damo with a liveable source of income. Now a regular fixture at Selina's, it was the first bar he was taken to by his brothers on his eighteenth birthday. Unlike his wild older brothers, Damo was a self-titled 'squarehead.' He avoided trouble, tried to stay on the straight and narrow and, at eighteen, was still a little naïve. On his first ever night in the club, he was set up with an attractive vision of a human in a short dress who put an arm around Damo's shoulders and placed the other hand on his knee. Despite feeling embarrassed and uncomfortable, he allowed his new companion to grab his hand and place it just below the hemline of the skirt. With increasing boldness, fuelled by his first experience of alcohol and loud verbal encouragement from his brothers, Damo slid his hand under the skirt but froze when it brushed against an unexpected lump. His brothers exploded with laughter when his companion's voice deepened, exclaiming, "Surely you knew?"

Damo screamed "NO," jumping off his seat in horror, to renewed guffaws from the group.

Ten years later, wiser, and far more worldly, he is running security on the door. At five foot eleven, Damo is small compared to the other four bouncers who dwarf him. Two are from the Randwick squad and two are Pacific islanders, who play for the local Rugby League club. All of them are colossal and expert 'knuckle' men. Between them, they have developed a system for dealing with troublemakers, who are full of liquid courage or fuelled by drugs or both. When it starts to kick off, Damo would go in first to attempt to reason with all involved parties before angry words escalate into angrier punches. Most of the time Damo, taking his affable 'Mister Reasonable' approach, has sufficient charm and diplomacy to successfully diffuse tense situations. He has a talent for de-escalation, for reasoning, for getting people on his side.

If Damo's chat does not resolve the problem, then the bouncers move into gear. Typically, the sequence of events follows a well-worn, familiar path. Damo politely explains to the unruly clientele that they must either quieten down or leave. On occasion, Damo's request is met with a flat refusal. They would tend to look him up and down, decide he was not the biggest bear in the woods and issue the same sort of challenge, which usually goes like "Are you gonna make us then?" Smiling, Damo would point to his team of imposing door attendants and explain that he would not be making them leave, but the guys behind him would. He asks them to reconsider their position. Occasionally, testosterone and macho male pride has travelled well beyond the point of no return and no quarter is given. The boys would move in, and the outcome was always the same. A short exchange would result in cut eyebrows, broken teeth, and noses. And, usually, lots of blood.

Beaten, the troublemakers would be escorted to the refrigerated keg room, which is so cold that it arrests the bleeding, until the ambulance arrives. When the paramedics are ready, the punters would be escorted back through the club to the ambulance. The warmth of the nightclub would often re-invigorate the bleeding wounds, and the paramedics would have to work quickly to stem the flow, before carting them off to hospital. Rarely were the police called. Rarely did those involved in the altercation lodge a complaint.

If Damo ever got dragged into the foray, he could handle himself, but his philosophy was based on one simple doctrine. Why have a pack of big dogs and bark yourself. Afterall, he has his rugged good looks to maintain. What Damo sees in the mirror each day is at odds with the rest of the world. When spruced up, he thought he did have the look of Matt Damon. His teammates clearly did not share his optimistic interpretation of the image reflected in the mirror. As the team's scrum half, a physics teacher, would point out, everything in the world is relative according to Einstein. Relative to the likes of Link, Damo did have movie star looks. But very few people looked like Link.

4

EARL

"WHAT THE HELL was that mate?"

"What was what, Dean?" replies Earl.

Pointing to a man and his son walking down the street, Dean answers his brother. "That Earl, that. He's a neighbour and a mate for God's sake. What were you thinking?"

Turning back to face them, the neighbour calls back. "Hey Earl, let that be a lesson to you."

Earl and Dean burst out laughing at the ironic humour, unlike the man's son who rubs his neck and scowls back at them.

"Yer see," says Earl, chuckling, "it's all good."

"Mate, they came round for a laugh. The kid had his new jiu jitsu suit on and he'd just come back from his first lesson with your trainer. It was your bloody recommendation, and he was feeling pleased with himself, wanting to show you what he'd learnt. He challenged you to a grapple, not a sodding MMA bout."

"Yeah, I know. I'm not bloody stupid."

"Mate! It was supposed to be a friendly play-fight."

"Yeah, I know. And it was."

"Jesus, you went at him pretty bloody hard," explains Dean.

"Naw, I didn't."

"Mate, you had him in a double leg hook, with a rear naked joke."

"Yeah, but I didn't squeeze hard," mutters Earl, defensively.

"Mate, he nearly passed out, he's a kid for God's sake. You're not sorting out meatheads and drunks at yer club now. You need to take a good look at yourself."

"Look. I admit I get a little competitive … when fighting."

"COMPETITIVE! The kid is ten years old. Lucky his old man knows you and can see the funny side. Yer could be back in Long Bay for assault of a minor."

Beneath the simmering aggression, there is a larrikin inside Earl, struggling to get out. Engaged in an ongoing battle of practical jokes with his neighbour, whose son he had almost choked to unconsciousness, the larrikin escaped on occasion, but it does not always sit comfortably with him. When he smiles, revealing slightly crooked front teeth, the recipient of his outward bonhomie is often left with a feeling of unease. Is Earl really joking and or is he going to rip your head off? It was hard to tell with that menacing smile and the reputation that preceded him.

His neighbour, who he referred to as 'that fucking POM', is blissfully unaware of his past. The 'POM' struck up a friendship after engaging in banter in the street when he first arrived from England. Fresh off the boat, the POM did not possess the local knowledge of Earl's history. Knowledge that prompted some other residents in the street to give him a wider berth.

Earl, like Damo, held down two jobs. One they had in common. Security on the door of a nightclub. In Earl's case, the club was called the Lemon Tree owned by Darren Chilton, a notorious businessman. Always dressed in black, with dyed jet-black hair and a closely shaved goatee beard, Chilton was a recognized local 'celebrity' whose business interests are, what a local newspaper once described as, 'murky'. On occasion, to protect these interests, the services of Earl are called upon. It is a topic that Earl never discussed with anyone. Not even his brother or his best mate, Damo. What Earl knew, stayed well and truly in the vault.

His other job is FIFO (Fly in Fly out). The name is given to workers who travel to remote areas, usually mines, and remain on site for several weeks before returning home for a break. He is working on a three and two. Three solid weeks working on site and two off back at home. So, every few weeks he would return for some rest and recreation, in between any 'business' he is asked to conduct on Chilton's behalf. On the mine site he supervises the maintenance teams to ensure the smooth running of all the plant and machinery used to extract Lithium. He works at the only Lithium mine outside Western Australia, based in the Northern Territory near Darwin. After five years, the novelty of the work, and the four-hour flight from Sydney, has well and truly worn off. He is getting no younger and wants out. Somewhere he can surf whenever the mood takes him. His dilemma is that FIFO workers are very well compensated and, if he stops, the money will be missed.

* * *

Maroubra beach is one of Earl's favourite surfing spots. Its name is derived from an Aboriginal word meaning 'like thunder' describing the sound of the waves pounding on the kilometre-long expanse of white sand. Regular swells make the beach a place for seasoned surfers and the locals, like Earl, get very territorial when interlopers congest the waves.

After two hours in the water, Earl bobs, waiting expectantly for the next wave. It will be, he decides, his last of the day. Finally, it comes, he paddles furiously, breathing heavily, rises onto his feet and takes the wave at its peak, riding it all the way onto the beach. Satisfied, he purposely falls into the shallow water and, exhausted, drags his board and himself out of the ocean. Trudging through the sand, he can still hear the roar and crash of the waves behind him.

His mind is clear, he is wrapped up in his own world. Forgetting work for the last two hours, he has been bobbing on the swell, ducking some waves and riding those that break perfectly for him. All his worries are temporarily cleared from his mind. But Fate brings a fresh unexpected, though temporary, problem. A sharp, aggressive voice snaps him out of his semi-meditative state. Turning back towards the water, Earl sees a black-haired surfer, with olive skin and a swathe of tattoos, jogging towards him. The surfer drops his board onto the sand and then sprints until he is face to face with Earl.

"Yo bro, what the fuck were you doing?"

Puzzled, Earl places his board on the sand and faces the surfer. Two hours of meditative calm have already instantly dissolved, replaced by rising red mist which he is trying to keep under control.

"Yeah you. That's right, you. You pasty ginger twat," shouts the surfer, as he faces up to Earl.

"What's yer problem?" asks Earl evenly, through gritted teeth. His expression transforms into what his friends call, 'the Earl stare'. Glassy eyed, a flat tone and something between a smile and a grimace. It is usually a portent of a swift violent response.

"You mate, you're the fucking problem. You're an idiot, you dropped in on me. You did it just then. No apology, nothing. Whaddya got to say fer yerself?"

"Firstly, I'm not your mate and second, I didn't drop

in on you. You'd already missed the wave by a mile. You were too slow."

"Only because I had to pull out when you took it, you useless twat."

The 'Earl stare' hardens imperceptibly. "That's twice you've called me that. Don't risk a third."

At six foot three, the surfer towers over the shorter Earl, which gives him false confidence that the older bloke in front of him can be easily taught a lesson. Disdainfully, he looks at Earl, shifting his gaze up and down. He decides that the 'old ginger twat' is easy meat.

Keeping a close eye on the increasingly agitated body language of the surfer, Earl studies his adversary's neck tattoo, noting that it is the insignia of a local gang.

Squaring up, the surfer shuffles from side to side, angry, agitated, fists balled, gorged veins bulging from his neck. "Oh yeah, you ginger twat, what are you going to ....."

A short, vicious, powerful uppercut leaves the surfer's unfinished question forever hanging in the air. Nevertheless, the surfer had got his answer. Staring at his adversary, Earl appraises the condition of the semi-conscious figure, lying face down on the sand. Once he hears a groan, he turns and walks casually off the beach, onto the paved walkway and towards his battered maroon Ute in the car park. He throws the board in the back, places a towel on the front seat and sits on it.

Driving back to his bungalow, he listens to music on Rock FM in silence. Earl is not a sing-along type of guy.

Turning into his street, he parks a few yards short of his home and winds down his window. Chuckling to himself, he reaches over into the glove compartment and grabs an egg box. He takes out both remaining eggs and throws them against the front door of the POM's house. They smash and immediately trickle down. The radiant heat on the door, from the blisteringly hot day, cooks the eggs almost immediately, leaving a satisfying white streak.

Laughing out loud, he restarts the vehicle and drives a few yards further down the street. Still wiping tears of mirth from his eyes with his free hand, he turns into his driveway and parks near his front door. Chuckling, he climbs down from the vehicle and feels an unfamiliar texture under his thongs and an unpleasant viscous liquid creeping between his toes. He examines his feet and then looks down the drive. Except for a couple of survivors, most of the eggs had been crushed under the wheels of his car. "That fucking POM," he mutters, but allows himself a smile.

Having showered and exchanged his shorts and tee shirt for chinos and a linen shirt, Earl grabs a bite to eat before setting off to his shift at the Lemon Tree. He walks through the door a few minutes early and is immediately accosted by the manager who informs him that the boss wants to see him. A quick response inviting him 'to come in' answers his knock on the office door at the back of the club. He slumps onto the leather chesterfield sofa placed along the left wall. Behind his desk, Chilton turns his swivel chair at an angle, to address his visitor.

"How's it going Earl? Glad to be back to civilization?"

"Yep," replies Earl.

"When did you get back?"

"Yesterday."

"Was it a good flight?"

"Yep."

"For fucks sake, Earl, you need to shut up and let me speak," says Chilton sarcastically, "what's with the mono syllabic answers?"

"Sorry boss, I'm a bit knackered, been on the water all day."

"Down at Maroubra?"

"Yep, having a surf at the beach."

"And, from what I hear, a bit of boxing practice."

"Sorry? Whaddya mean?"

"I've had a call from Hakan Yilmaz."

"Oh yeah, what did he want?"

"'Oh yeah' indeed. You seem to have assaulted one of his men. Worse still, it's his nephew. His mate saw you in action and recognised you. Your reputation precedes you."

"He was on his own," replies Earl, evenly.

"Apparently not. His mate was surfing with him, he was in the ocean and says he saw you take an unprovoked swing at Kemal."

"Who?"

"The one you decked."

"Well, if his mate was in the ocean, he couldn't have possibly heard what this idiot said to me. So, he can't know it was unprovoked."

"Were you provoked?"

"Yeah, he called me a ginger twat. In fact, he called me a twat three times. The third time was after I had given him fair warning. He was giving me a load of shit. Reckoned I was dropping in on him. Which I wasn't, incidentally. So, just so we're clear, I'm not apologising."

"No need Earl. I did on your behalf, to keep the peace. I told Hakan that you would be spoken to, and I would ensure that it won't happen again."

"No worries."

"So, consider yourself spoken to and do not let it fucking happen again."

"If you want to apologise, that's up to you. But as far as I'm concerned, he can shove his apology up his arse. He deserved it. And while you're at it, as for the likelihood of it happening again, I can tell you it won't. It won't, providing that lanky streak of piss doesn't mouth off to me."

Respectful of one of his most valuable and trustworthy employees, Chilton reads the room and uncharacteristically lets Earl's petulance ride. In truth, he was secretly pleased with what transpired. Hakan's nephew had been in the club a couple of times, shouting the odds and playing the gangster. Riding on his uncle's reputation. On both occasions Earl had been away, working at the Lithium mine. *Better to have the trouble and confrontation away from the club, than in it*, thinks Chilton. He did not mind the additional bonus that young Kemal's card had been marked.

Departing, after a dismissive wave from Chiltern, Earl joins the other bouncers at the door. Seething at the mild rap on the knuckles, he struggles to hold his anger in check. Wisely, he stations himself to the rear of the door, instead of upfront. He needs separation from the public that night, to avoid venting his angst on the first unfortunate troublemaker who comes along. Fortunately, for all involved, it turns out to be a quiet night and Earl excuses himself halfway through the shift, leaving the team to see out the rest of the night until closing. His last trip up to the mine site had been exhausting and he is looking forward to his two weeks back home. Resting and surfing.

Hooting loudly as he passes his neighbour's house, Earl chuckles at the thought of waking up the POM. That thought immediately rouses his suspicion and he flicks on the headlights to full beam when he turns into his own driveway. No sign of any more mischief.

Settled on his couch with a beer, he watches a college football game. Although a Geelong footy fan, he became interested in American football when his nephew got a spot for a college team in North Carolina. Now COVID is well and truly consigned to history, he is planning to go over, even if it meant having to spend more time with his brother, Dean.

Fiercely proud of his eldest son Mac, Dean lectures and moans endlessly about the pandemic and its impact on their life. Dean and his long-suffering wife, Lynne, were unable to travel to see Mac's first season. Spending hours on the internet, Dean would quote death rates, infection rates and any other statistics he could find to give credence to his battery of COVID conspiracy theories. Earl had to listen to the same old rubbish every time he saw his brother and the endless ranting became tiresome. He could hear Dean's ranting, echoing in his mind.

It got to the point where Earl had stopped going round to his brother's house. Those who lived in the household, Lynne, and Fergus, the forgotten other son who resided in Mac's shadow, were beginning to climb the walls. When the vaccinations eventually came and Government restrictions relaxed, Earl hoped for a return to normality. Unconvinced, Dean saw it as a pyrrhic victory, happily pointing out that the vaccine did nothing to prevent infection.

Roused from his stupor by an insistent buzzing, Earl picks up his mobile which is vibrating on the scratched, low wooden table. Most of his furniture had seen better days. He looks at the screen and sees it is his best mate. An upbeat voice filters into Earl's right ear.

"Mate, you're back then, I take it. How are you?"

"I'm good Damo, and you?"

"Pumped mate, pumped. We won the Granny."

"The Grand Final, well done mate. It's late and I'm knackered. Whaddya want?"

"Nice Mate. Real nice. With that cheerful, happy-go-lucky manner, you should be a children's entertainer. Balloons, red nose, clown costume, big shoes, and all that," replies Damo, sarcastically.

"Mate, I'm talking to the only clown in this conversation," counters Earl.

"Okay mate. Just checking in. Are you up for a frothy or two tomorrow night?"

"Yeah mate, sure. See you at the Dog at around six, if that suits?"

"Done mate, I'll let you get your beauty sleep. God knows you could do with it," chuckles Damo.

"Yeah, well mate, just don't forget your wallet this time. It's like a bloody onion."

"Eh. Whaddya mean?" asks Damo,

"Whenever you open it, you cry," replies Earl, ending the call.

5

THE DOG

PLACED UNINVITINGLY ON a corner block of a busy intersection in Randwick is the Dog, which its website optimistically describes as a surrogate living room for the local community. With dozens of taps pumping a wide range of beers, the marketing pitch informs you that it is the ultimate place to round up the gang. At six o'clock on a Monday evening there were not any gangs to be seen. The pub was practically empty. Damo sits with two beers in front of him waiting for his mate and, seeing Earl enter, waves him over. He pushes a glass of beer across the table towards Earl and points to the stool opposite.

"Cheers Damo."

"Cheers mate," responds Damo.

Earl sits and lifts his beer in one fluid movement. Both men take a large pull of their drink before setting down the glass. Wiping the froth from his mouth, Earl starts the conversation. "So how did you do in your Grand Final? Sorry I missed it, but I had to do a few extra days in Darwin."

"No worries, mate. Yep, as I said, we won. It was pretty much a repeat of last year. Same opponent, same sort of score, with yours truly getting the best try of the game. What about you?" asks Damo

"Nothing much to report other than I've had a gutful of mining, flying in and out and all the shit that goes with it. There's plenty of work up at the Lithium mine if you're ever interested but they're all nuts up there. They're not right," says Earl, tapping his freckled forehead. "They all earn good money and come home to blow it on drink, women, Utes and jet-skis."

"Jet skis?"

"Yep. Look at all the idiots shooting round the bay every weekend and I'd bet you more than half of them are FIFO. What else are they going to blow their cash on?"

"Drugs?" ventures Damo.

"No mate, we all get tested before going on site. They'd lose their jobs."

"So, if you've had a gutful mate, what's your plan?" asks Damo.

"Don't have one yet, but whatever it is I'm looking for easy money and a lot of it. Getting too old to be grafting in forty plus degrees or, when I'm back here, dealing with pissed up weekend warriors who are looking to take my head off. I need to break this cycle. I need a change."

"Well mate if you find something that's easy and good money then count me in. I feel the same way."

Over the next hour the two friends chat and joke as the pub gradually fills with other patrons. Try as they might, they fail to come up with a viable plan to get rich quickly. Most of their ideas belong in dreamland and the more realistic ones seem unlikely to get the sort of money they are looking for. But they need not have worried as a plan was heading, full pelt, towards them. Their moment of pure serendipity arrives in the form of an unexpected guest who sidles up to them.

"Earl mate, how are you doing?"

Feeling a tap on his shoulder, Earl turns on his stool to find a familiar face staring down at him.

"Mind if I join you?"

Nodding and pointing to a spare stool at the table, Earl invites the newcomer to take a seat and then looks over to Damo.

"Damo, this is Boof. Boof this is Damo." The two shake hands and they all clink their glasses and say 'cheers'. Damo looks over to Earl and raises his eyebrows seeking an explanation of the connection between his friend and Boof.

"I've known Boof for a few years Damo, we have a mutual employer, Darren Chilton."

"Oh, I see," responds Damo, who did not really, but made several assumptions which he kept to himself based on the Chilton connection.

"So how long have you been away?" asks Earl, euphemistically.

Boof looks over to Damo then back at Earl, unsure of how to respond. "A while, just got out yesterday," he finally answers.

"It's alright Boof, Damo here knows my history," assures Earl.

"So, what were you in for Boof?" asks Damo.

"Nothing much Damo, they reckon that I'd breached my probation conditions, but I'm out for good now."

Knowing better than to dig any deeper, Damo changes the subject. "So, what's your plan now Boof?"

Boof is vague, telling Damo he has an idea but does not elaborate. After a few more beers, the three are relaxed and happily laughing, joking, avoiding serious topics. With the evening wearing on, Earl gets the growing impression that Boof has something on his mind that he wants to share. When Damo excuses himself to use the toilet, Earl's suspicion is immediately confirmed. He watches Boof lean over the table to check that Damo has disappeared around the corner of the bar and out of sight and earshot.

"Mate, I was meaning to look you up. I've got a proposal to put to you."

With a piqued interest, Earl encourages Boof to explain, but his friend is reticent.

"Best we discuss it in private, mate, wagging his thumb towards the direction of the toilets. I've no idea if your mate can be trusted."

"Mate, he can, but obviously it depends on what you have in mind. He's not exactly a choirboy but if it involves hurting people, it would be a 'no'. But that isn't exactly your game either, is it?"

"Naw. But it's a funny old one and will be plenty worthwhile for two, or even three, if your mate's up for it."

"I take it from all the secrecy that it isn't legal?"

"Well, as I say, it's a funny one. It isn't black and white. It's a grey area, an ethical conundrum," says Boof, stroking back his black widow's peak. A habit he had when deep in thought.

"Ethical conundrum? Big words for you Boof. What the hell have you been doing in Long Bay? Courses on moral farking philosophy?"

"As a matter of fact, I have."

"You must be joking. You, studying philosophy. You're taking the piss," replies Earl, incredulous.

"Mate, it wasn't a course or anything like that. Just a talk, what the Governor called a seminar. A real weirdo he is. Not yer usual Governor. A posh bloke from one of those private schools. You know the type. Privileged, a bit of a naïve dickhead. Educated, but no common sense." Boof sips his beer and continues. "Anyway, he told us that he thought the inmates would benefit from a lecture on the principles of morals. He said it might make us rethink how we behave when we get out. All of us in the seminar were about to finish our time and we were his pet pilot project.

Told us it might help reduce recidivism. Whatever that means.

"Recidivism?"

"Yep, he's into Kant."

"Sounds like he's one," replies Earl, sarcastically.

"No mate. He talked about some German philosopher bloke called Kant. Went on about goodwill, which this Kant geezer says should drive our behaviour."

"What, he expected you all to become do-gooders overnight?"

"To be honest I didn't really understand any of it. None of us did. But the sandwiches and cakes afterwards were good, and we got extra time out of the cell." Boof nods over to the corner of the pub. "Anyway, your mate is coming back, do you want me to discuss it here or not?"

Earl looks over his shoulder and sees Damo weaving through the crowded bar. "Well mate, if it's not illegal, or at least it's borderline and doesn't involve beating anyone up …. and there's a few dollars in it, then, knock yerself out. We were discussing ideas earlier but drew a blank. Let's hear it, we'd both be interested."

Seeking more reassurance, Boof asks, pointing towards the fast-approaching Damo, "And you're sure he's trustworthy?"

"One hundred percent mate. In fact, one hundred and ten percent compared to the idiots you normally get involved with."

Taking a seat, Damo looks to Earl and then to Boof. "You two look guilty, have you been talking about me?" he jokes.

"As a matter of fact, mate, we have," replies Earl.

* * *

Earlier the same evening, Kemal arrives at Sydney airport with instructions from his uncle, Hakan, to locate the crate of schoolbooks and then make sure that arrangements are made to ship it to their contact in Nairobi. That morning Hakan had received an unwelcome call from his man at the airport, Jacko, informing him that the crate could not be located. Surviving the initial tirade from Hakan, Jacko then received an equally unwelcome threat that, if the crate has been lost, it will not be the only thing that Jacko would be missing. Subconsciously, Jacko cupped his testicles.

With no small degree of trepidation, Jacko awaits Kemal's arrival. Kemal assumes the task is going to be straightforward and he will be back in time to fulfil his own personal arrangements and plans for the evening. His assumption proves to be wide of the mark.

A heated discussion takes place in Jacko's small office at the corner of the storage facility. Explaining that the consignment was collected on the scheduled date and that the records confirm that only nineteen of the twenty crates were transported, Jacko is sure that Hakan's crate must remain somewhere at the airport. Frustrated that the discussion is going nowhere, Kemal snaps. Leaping from his chair he leans across the small desk and Jacko receives a spray.

"I am not interested in your fucking stories or what your paperwork has printed on it. Take me to where the crates were located."

Wiping spittle from his face, Jacko replies nervously. "Well I can do that of course, but I can assure you they are not there."

"Just take me there."

Leaving his office, with Kemal breathing down his neck, Jacko strides over to the corner of the warehouse. He stops and points to a stack of crates.

"They don't look like books," snaps Kemal.

"They're not. These are disposable nappies."

"What?" asks Kemal, confused.

"Nappies, diapers or whatever you want to call them," explains Jacko.

"Why are you showing me these things? Are you mocking me?" snarls Kemal.

"Because this is the spot where we stored the book crates, until they were shipped out. Obviously, this is a busy working facility, and a lot of cargo has come and gone from this area. You asked me to show you where the books were. This is where they were," explains Jacko, pointing to the area.

"Was our crate stored with the others here?"

"Yes. At least it was when it first arrived, but we moved it over there," replies Jacko pointing to the far corner of the store. It was hidden behind those boxes so it wouldn't be spotted and accidentally taken with the rest."

They walk over and Kemal circles a stack of boxes positioned in the area.

Filling the uncomfortable silence as Kemal glowers wordlessly at the boxes, Jacko tries to explain the situation in a desperate attempt to be helpful. "These are disposable beakers, you know, for coffee vending machines. Our crate was behind where the beakers are now. Obviously, at the time, other boxes were there. Not the beakers. It was garden furniture."

They search the whole warehouse together, which Jacko knew was a fool's errand having already searched it twice after Hakan's phone call. For the time being Jacko is happy that Kemal is occupied, hopeful that the young gangster will calm down in the time it takes to satisfy himself that the books are no longer in the warehouse. Fruitlessly, Kemal prowls around the facility and questions staff. Noone admits to remembering the crate, noone can shed any light on the mystery. Back in the office, Jacko shrugs, facing an angry Kemal.

"I told you, it's not there. They must have found it and taken it with the rest."

"But you said it was hidden," says Kemal.

"It was. I checked that personally. Maybe they wandered around the place and spotted it."

"They?"

"The men who collected all the other crates. The Americans. Look, I don't know. I can't explain it. I'm just guessing."

Waving for Jacko to be quiet, Kemal makes a call to Hakan whilst walking over to the far corner of the office. From his desk, Jacko can hear the muffled sound of Kemal's uncle shouting down the mobile phone. Nervously awaiting the outcome of the call, Jacko shuffles paperwork on his desk, pretending he is busy. Hearing the conversation end, he looks up.

"My uncle wants to know if there is a similar warehouse nearby. He wonders if it could have been taken elsewhere?"

"There's only one other warehouse which carries out the same function as this one. It's run by Bluey."

"Who the fuck is Bluey?"

"Bluey Edwards. But I'm telling you, there's no record of an inter facility transfer. There would be paperwork. Transfers are rare. The last time it happened was over eighteen months ago according to the ledger. It's only done when space is becoming an issue at either facility. Neither warehouse gets that full nowadays, since we both had extensions built."

Disinterested in Jacko's laboured explanation, Kemal barks an order. "Take me there. My uncle wants everywhere searched."

"You're wasting your time."

"Just do it," says Kemal, pointing to the entrance.

In the other warehouse, Jacko is greeted by Bluey as he walks through the main entrance.

"Jacko mate. We rarely see you cowboys in Indian territory,' announces Bluey. His tone is welcoming and friendly, but he eyes Jacko's companion suspiciously. From Bluey's facial expression, Jacko could tell he had taken an instant dislike to Kemal. Attempting to defuse the situation, Jacko gives a cheery introduction.

"Nice to see you, Bluey. This bloke here, Kemal, is a nephew of a friend of mine. It's a bit embarrassing but it looks like we may have misplaced his uncle's consignment. We've searched the place from top to bottom, but no luck. Slim chance, I know, but wondered if you had seen it."

"Unlikely Jacko, we run a tight ship over here, everything is accounted for."

"I know mate, but thought I'd ask."

"What was it Jacko? It might jog my memory."

"It was a crate of books for kids."

"What like nursery rhymes or fairytales?"

"Schoolbooks," interrupts Kemal irritably, rapidly losing patience.

Glaring at Kemal, Bluey responds.

"As I said to Jacko here, son, we run a tight ship. And for the record I can't remember ever seeing any schoolbooks in here. So, I'm afraid you've had a wasted journey. Looks like you'll have to put in an insurance claim."

"How about you let us have a look 'round ourselves?" It was nearer an order than a request and from that point onwards, if Bluey harboured any thoughts of co-operating, they disappeared like a ship in the mist.

At six foot two he matched Kemal for height but has twenty years and twenty kilos on the young gangster. At the height of his powers, Bluey played front row for the Beasties, the Eastern Suburbs Rugby Union Club. His reputation as a fierce competitive player with white line fever preceded him and few players of opposing teams looked forward to confronting him on the pitch. Although older and mellowed, he was not about to allow some kid, barely out of nappies, to shout the odds. Straightening to face Kemal, who had moved a step forward trying to intimidate the store man, Bluey gave him a grin snatched straight from his footballing days, when he was known as the smiling assassin.

"Maybe your mummy needs to wash your ears at bath time son. But let me repeat myself. We don't have your books, so you're either going to have to look elsewhere or put in an insurance claim with my mate Jacko 'ere. So, if there's nothing else, I'm a busy man and would be grateful if you'd now piss off out of my warehouse."

Now seething, Kemal is scrambling to regain, psychologically, the upper hand. At the same time, he reflects on his recent experience on the beach and decides that he can not afford to lose face for a second time that week. Getting involved in, and losing, another fight would not impress his uncle. If he causes a problem and then returns empty handed, he will have made matters much worse.

Calling back to Bluey, who has turned away and is retreating into the depths of his warehouse, Kemal shouts, "Just make sure if you find them that you tell Jacko." Kemal tries to make it sound like an order, but is ignored. Bluey does not even turn to acknowledge Kemal. Tugging on Kemal's sleeve, Jacko indicates they should leave.

Back behind his desk, Bluey works his way through the day's paperwork. Grateful for a distraction, he answers a knock on his office door and his offsider, Brenton, comes in and takes a seat.

"What was Jacko doing over here boss? Not seen him in ages."

"He said he'd lost a crate. Wouldn't be the first, won't be the last. He was with the owner. Some pissant little wannabe gangster by the look of him, up to mischief."

"What was in the crate?" asks Brenton.

"I think he wanted that crate we found. The one with the schoolbooks in it. Y'know, the one that the yanks forgot about, but collected after I called them."

"Did you tell Jacko and this gangster bloke that?"

"No Brenton. You can take it from me, he was no bloody textbook salesman. Frankly, if he's kosher and it's already been transported to where it should have gone, then Jacko and Al Capone's little problem has been solved. That is, if the crate was his to begin with. Which I doubt. Besides, as they say in those old films, I didn't like the cut of his jib."

"Jib?"

"Never mind Brenton. Bottom line is, he's a wrong 'un. He's getting nothing from me. Sent him packing, I did. And if he does come back and speaks to you, you say the same. You've never seen them. Understand?"

"Yes boss."

* * *

Back at the Dog, Damo is intrigued.

"Me? You were talking about me? My favourite topic. Tell me more. Were you discussing my good looks, sparkling wit, sporting prowess or immense intelligence?"

"Did you say good looks?" snipes Earl.

"Yep, reckon I'd fit in nicely in the centre pages of an Yves St Laurent catalogue."

"You've as much chance of modelling as I have," retorts Earl.

"Yeah. No. Mate, I think in your case we would be talking about the Target Catalogue," replies Damo. "So tell me what you were talking about, if not my good looks. Sporting skills? Intelligence?

"No mate. None of those. It's something more realistic. It's whether you are trustworthy. Your ability to keep things in the vault. I told Boof that you're very trustworthy," replies Earl.

Damo looks over to Boof and asks, "Trustworthy? Keeping things in the vault? Sounds dodgy. Is it legal?"

Before Boof responds, Earl chips in. "Boof here thinks it's a moral conundrum."

"Eh?" asks Damo, confused.

"A sort of grey area," explains Earl.

"Eh?" repeats Damo.

"If it's gonna stay in the vault, then let me explain," suggests Boof.

Smiling, Damo replies. "Mate, the vault door is open, ready to take in your proposal and, when you've finished, the door will be slammed shut. That's a guarantee, whether I choose to be involved, or not."

Boof looks over to Earl, who responds with a nod of reassurance. Boof leans forward over the table to ensure privacy, not that they could be overheard given the noise in the now raucous bar. The two friends mirror Boof's body language and also edge forward to listen in. Still wary, Boof explains the broad principles but avoids details. No names, no dates, and no places. Most of the questions fired at him are batted back with deliberately vague answers.

"There you are lads. I know you're keen to get more specifics, but I reckon I've given you enough to decide whether you want to be in or out. Have a think about it, but we need to act fast so I'm gonna need a decision after you've thought about it overnight."

"Sounds as those there are some serious characters involved. People you would not want to piss off," says Damo.

"True, but the beauty of this is that there is nothing to connect us to it. Those who nicked the money are pushing up daisies."

"Isn't that, in itself, a cause for concern?" asks Damo.

"One died from a shark attack and the other was murdered in prison."

Earl intervenes. "That's what Damo's saying, Boof. Wasn't he shanked because of it?"

"I doubt it mate. If that was the reason, they'd have waited until he was out so they could use their powers of persuasion to tell them where he'd hidden the money," answers Boof. "Killing him means either it is connected, and they now know where the money is."

"Or?" asks Damo.

"Or it was nothing to do with this. Crims get the shiv all the time inside, just for looking at the wrong person, in the wrong way at the wrong time," replies Boof.

"Shiv?" asks Damo.

"Yeah mate, shank, shiv, a homemade blade," explains Earl.

Rising from his seat, Boof says, "Anyway boys, I'm going to leave you both to it, so you can discuss it in peace. Give me a call tomorrow, Earl, and let me know."

"No worries."

Once Boof has gone, they resume their discussion.

"What do you think Damo? It's a lot of money, if

Boof's guess is right. No more graft. A comfortable rest of our life awaits if we pull it off. I'm not even sure it's illegal. If it is, they aren't gonna go running to the cops to complain that their drug money has been stolen. Are they?"

"I think you have a lot of 'ifs' in there, Earl," replies Damo.

"True, so you're not up for it then?"

"I didn't say that mate. I have to say that following your mate's argument from that kraut philosopher bloke, about morality ..."

"Kant?" asks Earl.

"Yep him. There is a moral principle here which means we should do it."

"Go on," chuckles Earl. "I can't wait to hear how nicking a few million dollars earned through the misery of drug addicts and young kids can be justified. Especially by a kraut."

"Mate, this was your problem in class when we were kids. You don't listen. You don't pay attention. As explained by Professor Boof, the esteemed criminal intellectual, Mister Kant said an act is moral if the intention is good." Damo sits back and takes a sip of his beer, the picture of smug satisfaction.

"Mate, we are stealing money. Taking someone else's money, for our own benefit. Obviously, our years in school together with the Marist Brothers were wasted on you. How about, thou shalt not steal?" Now Earl sits back and takes a drink with equal satisfaction.

Leaning forward, Damo delivers his final argument. "Mate, we are relieving the drug traffickers of significant assets. Less money in the system to ruin the lives of addicts and kids. If that's our motive, who cares if we also make a few bucks into the bargain. Afterall, we're taking a risk and we'll have done society a great good." Damo looks expectantly at Earl, who sits quietly, his brow furrowed, scratching his head covered with slightly greying, red hair.

With a widening smile, revealing a gap next to his front teeth, Earl gives his answer. "Mate, I do think you may have an exceptionally good point there. I'm in."

"Good man, so am I," replies Damo.

A MAN AND HIS MONKEY

EARLIER THAT MORNING Earl called Boof to talk about the proposal and told him they are both interested. Still cautious, Boof questioned Earl about Damo. Was he trustworthy? Was he committed? Satisfied by Earls assurance, Boof suggested they meet in a local café owned by a friend. A booth at the back is reserved for them by the owner, to give them a bit of privacy.

"Looks like someone's dropped a few bits of fruit into a dog bowl full of sawdust. What the hell are you eating, Boof?" asks Earl, as he chomps through his bacon and egg panini.

"It's an acai bowl. Extremely healthy."

"You've only been out of pokey for a few days and you're already up with the trends. Very impressive," says Damo, who, unable to find any dish with a sausage as the main ingredient, just elects for a cup of coffee.

Patiently waiting for Boof to finish his bowl, Damo appraises his new business partner thinking that the pale skinned, thin apparition in front of him needs as much healthy food as he can get. Not to mention a good dose of vitamin D from the Sydney sun. Earl's belch announces the end of his panini.

A non-binary server approaches the table and seeks permission to clear the plates. Damo looks at the server suspiciously unsure how to address the staff member so opts for a neutral "yes thanks." Once they are alone

Boof puts meat on the bones of the information that he gave them the previous night and then waits patiently to ask questions.

"So, we're not sure how big the crate is, but you reckon a sixteen-footer van should be enough?" asks Damo.

"Yeah, more than enough. I'm sure that's what Smithy said he had," replies Boof.

"What worries me," says Earl, "is that this is official US Government cargo and what's going to persuade the airport staff to hand it over to us three. Would you hand it over to the likes of us? I know I wouldn't."

"I've got overalls for all of us, so we'll look official. They've got a logo of the American flag on the sleeve. I got them from Jimbo's Fancy Dress."

"For fucks sake," says Earl.

"No mate, don't worry. They're part of a costume."

"For what?" asks Earl.

"Tom Cruise in Top Gun. We won't wear the plastic Top Gun sunglasses that come with them, of course."

"Are you kidding me?" says Damo.

"It's all good mate. I'm not relying on the Top Gun suits. They are just what you call, useful background. You know, make us all look kosher. But mate, don't worry, I've got this."

Boof holds up his blue manifest copy. "This, my friends, is the lottery ticket. This is the golden ticket that takes us into Willy Wonka's chocolate factory. There'll be a matching copy taped to the crate. They'll check the details, retain this copy for their records and they'll be happy. Their paperwork will be in order and Bob's your uncle. Off we will go taking a load of schoolbooks with a few million dollars packed in the middle. It's a beauty."

"Where did you get that?" asks Earl, pointing to the manifest document.

"From my cell mate, Smithy. I searched for it after the guards cleaned out his stuff.

"How come they didn't take it?"

"He'd hidden it in his bedpost."

"How did you get it out when you were discharged? Everyone gets searched and this docket has Smithy's name on it. Didn't they ask what yer doing with stuff from the bloke murdered in your cell?" asks Earl, staring at the manifest copy that Boof had passed to him.

"Kept it safe in a cigar tube. Hidden in place they wouldn't look."

"You're kidding me. Your name's Boof, I'd have thought that's the first place they'd look for anything dodgy," says Earl.

"Sorry you've lost me here," says Damo, interrupting the exchange.

"What Boof here is saying, Damo, is that he hid it in a cigar tube up his arse."

Damo, who is in the process of reaching for the document, recoils, snatching his hand away in horror. "Jesus, I'm not handling that. Put it away, it's a bloody health hazard."

"It was in a cigar tube mate. Don't know what your problem is." explains Boof, slightly offended.

Irritated that the conversation is wandering off topic, Earl is keen to get the discussion back on track. Particularly, when he has several concerns that need to be resolved before committing to the proposal.

"Okay then. How do we know which warehouse to go to? There must be quite a few at the airport," asks Earl.

"It's all covered. Smithy told me. It was moved from the original warehouse to separate it from the main consignment. He described the location and, to make sure I had the right one, Smithy told me the name of the manager. It'll be a piece of cake. We go in, ask for the manager, and, if it's the right man, it's plain sailing."

"Is the manager in on this as well?" asks Damo.

"Nope. Now that Smithy is no longer with us, God rest his soul," Boof makes the sign of the cross over his chest, "we are the only ones involved. When we turn up at the warehouse, all that the staff will be worried about is whether we have the right paperwork. We're just delivery men collecting a crate and have the paperwork to prove it."

Twenty questions later, Damo and Earl are satisfied that all bases are covered and their business is concluded. As they leave, the server smiles at Damo and says, "Thank you for coming to 'A man and his monkey café'. Hope to see you again soon." When they step into the street Earl asks, "Is that a man or a woman?"

"No idea," replies Damo, smoothing his side parting, "but, either way, I reckon I got the come on."

* * *

Twenty-four hours later they return to 'A Man and his Monkey Café', but this time they meet in the carpark at the rear. When they see Boof approaching, carrying a black canvas bag in hand, Damo and Earl climb out of the cab of their lorry. Patting the door on the driver's side, Earl asks, "Whaddya think, is this gonna be large enough?

Examining the vehicle, Boof replies, "Looks good, Earl. Should be more than big enough to do the job?"

Having followed Boof's instructions, they are wearing shorts and a tee shirt so they can slip on the overalls easily. Reaching into the bag Boof pulls out the packages, inspects them, and throws one to Damo and another to Earl.

"There you go. Slip those on. It's the Top Gun overalls."

They tear the polythene packaging and examine

the overalls before putting them on over their clothes. Chuckling, they stand and inspect each other.

"You've put on a tiny bit of pork, Damo," says Earl, pointing to his friend's mid-section.

"Could've done with a size up," complains Damo.

"You asked for an XL," says Boof. "It's an XL."

"Must be a small XL," replies Damo.

Sniggering, Earl says, "It's Top Gun, not Top Gut, mate. Should've got an XXL or to be safe an XXXL."

"Piss off," replies Damo sulkily.

"Anway lads, best we get off," suggests Boof, whose own costume hangs off him as if his body has shrunk inside it.

On the way to the airport Boof lays out the plan which involves leaving him to do everything. He will do the talking, show the paperwork, and ensure the staff at the facility are kept sweet and suspect nothing. There is little conversation on the rest of the journey, each contemplating what may lie ahead.

Finding the warehouse takes much longer than they envisaged. Several times they drive expectantly into an area, convinced it is the correct location, only to discover it is not where they need to be. When a baggage handler, who greets them at one building, tells them he knows where their warehouse is, their hopes and mood rocket skywards. With the apparent confidence of a man who knows what he is talking about, he gives them specific directions which turn out to be a dead end. Irritation and frustration charge the atmosphere in the cab of the van, and Damo and Earl get increasingly impatient. Rapidly approaching the point where Earl wants to grab Boof by the throat and shake him, Damo shouts out hopefully and points to a large building in the distance.

"Hey, Boof, is that it? It's got that flag you're looking for on the roof. That's the United Nations one, isn't it?"

"Can't see where you're looking. A flag, you say. Is it light blue? Map of the world on it surrounded by leaves."

"Yeah, look through the gap of those buildings, yer must be able to see it."

After pulling over, Earl says, "Let's take a breather. You two get out, Damo can point to where he is looking and you, Boof, can tell him if it's the right flag."

With Earl staying in the lorry, impatiently tapping on the steering wheel, Damo and Boof peer through a fence at the roadside. Damo's impatience is also getting tested, and he gets increasingly annoyed with Boof who cannot see the building. Then, Boof smiles as he finally sets eyes on the flag.

From the fist pumping and back slapping, Earl surmises, back in the cab of the lorry, that they have found the right place. They run over, jump back in and Earl sets off, barely allowing Damo time to close the passenger door. Working their way to the facility through a network of small roads, they eventually arrive at their destination. All three scramble out of the lorry and walk to the main entrance. They are greeted by a scruffy-looking individual.

"G'day, what can I do for you?" asks Brenton.

"Morning mate. We're here to collect a crate," replies Boof, handing over his blue copy of the manifest.

It takes an uncomfortably long time for Brenton to comprehend what is written on the paper, which raises doubts and concerns in the minds of the three men.

"Everything okay, mate?" asks Boof.

Furrowing his brow and then scratching his chin, Brenton continues to examine the paper and occasionally glances up at them.

"Yeah, no. Sorry mate, I'm not sure what to do with this. Yeah! Come with me. I'll take you to my boss and he can sort it out."

They file behind Brenton, exchanging quizzical glances as he leads them through the warehouse. Crossing the main loading area, they head to the far corner until Brenton steps aside and gestures for them to enter an office. Inside they see a large imposing beast of a man squeezed behind a small desk. Handing over the paper to his boss, Brenton steps back awaiting a decision. His boss reads it with barely a glance at the three men. With increasing concern, Boof addresses the man at the desk.

"Is there a problem?" asks Boof.

Looking directly into Boof's eyes, the boss replies. "Are you from the same lot who came yesterday? I told them, and am now going to tell you, that we do not have a record of this crate. So, I don't appreciate being hassled like this. Therefore, I am going to tell you what I told your mate yesterday. Namely to bugger off."

"Bluey?"

The man behind the desk screws his eyes up and focuses on Damo. "Do I know you?"

"It's Damo. From Randwick footy club."

"No way, is that you Damo? Jeez, sorry mate, didn't recognize you in the uniform. You look like a character from Top Gun. It's been a fair old while since I've seen you mate. Looks as though you've put a bit of weight round the middle," jokes Bluey Edwards.

Pushing past Boof, Damo approaches Bluey and shakes his hand and then turns back to Boof and Earl. "These two dodgy looking characters are my workmates."

"Sorry mate. If I'd realised that it was you, I wouldn't have given you the 'kiss off'. I had to send this rude little dickhead off, yesterday, with his tail between his legs.

Rude bastard and tried to threaten me. Can yer believe it? Threaten me! He was after the same thing as you lot."

"Obviously, he didn't know who he was dealing with. The Eastern Suburbs smiling assassin," says Damo, giving a good-natured chuckle.

"Ha. That was many years ago mate. Getting old, but not too old to deal with entitled, skinny little shits like that."

"So why did you send him packing?"

Well, I could see he was a wrong 'un and didn't like his attitude. And it's not as though he had any paperwork for it. Unlike you guys," replies Bluey, waving the blue sheet of paper.

"Excellent, so can we get what we came for then?" asks Damo, "and then we can get out of your hair."

When Bluey's smile fades to a frown, Boof, Earl and Damo know that they have a problem. They get the whole story, start to finish, and their hopes sink further with each sentence uttered. Although Bluey is recounting the events firsthand, he is unaware that the three men in front of him know far more about the crate and how it ended up in the warehouse, than Bluey did himself. Damo feels a tinge of guilt, listening to Bluey's story and having to feign surprise. When Bluey tells them the crate turned up, from nowhere, without any paperwork, they all give a sympathetic, supportive shake of the head. As his tale progresses they murmur with empathy in appreciation of the warehouseman's dilemma. Recounting his meeting with Kemal, he tells them with relish that he sent him packing with his tail between his legs. Once the story finishes, they all mutter 'good on yer.'

Their sympathy and understanding takes a nosedive when Bluey reveals a further piece of information, which is like a stab in the heart. He has been too efficient for his own, and their own, good. He tells them that he called the American embassy, and they sent a military aircraft, which was already on its way to Africa. No blue manifest copy, like the one Damo and his mates had, was needed. A large Hurricane with US Air Force insignia was all the credentials they had to provide to take charge of the crate.

What confuses Bluey is why Damo and his mates had been sent to get the crate, when it had already been collected almost a week ago. Seeing Damo and Earl freeze in front of the proverbial headlights, Boof's thinking is much quicker off the mark.

It was Bluey's turn to nod sympathetically throughout Boof's long and drawn-out explanation of poor communication, inept management, wasted taxpayer resources and mindless bureaucracy. Those poor African kids deserved better. With Boof's last comment, Bluey tuts sympathetically. This proves to be the light at the end of a tunnel that leads the three of them to the dark continent.

"Yeah, I know Bluey, it's stuff like this that makes our job worthwhile. Kids getting books and an education in these third world countries," says Damo, laying it on a bit thick for Earl's liking.

Eyes narrowing with compassion, Bluey says, "I know mate, but in this case it all worked out for the best. Didn't it? I spoke to a yank who rang me back the other day to thank me. She told me that the books had been delivered safely to the Ugandan kids. Funny thing is, she said loads of books have been sent before and not opened. The children never get 'em. They're untouched for years. She said it's the way these Africans think. If they get a gift, they feel they have a responsibility to look after it. So, they just store them somewhere safe.

"Bloody Africans eh!" tuts Boof, sympathetically.

The straws of hope are there, and Boof intervenes to grasp them. Although the books have long since gone, he believes there is a good chance the cash has not been discovered.

"I know all that first-hand Bluey, I went there as a volunteer when I was younger," lies Boof, who had never been out of Australia, let alone to Africa. "I worked in Kenya and Uganda when I was over there. Yer don't happen to know where the books ended up, do you?"

"Yer was a volunteer in Africa? Good on yer mate. Look, I can't remember the name of the place off hand but, as it happens, I might be able to tell you, if you give me a minute. That American Sheila told me that they aren't sending any more books but are now building a school instead. Hang on, no, it isn't a school, it's a college for training teachers. Anyway, the place where the books went is where that project is. She mentions it in her email. Just hang on."

For what seems like an eternity to the three men, Bluey taps the keyboard ponderously with his large, sausage like, fingers. Whilst he types, he talks, which slows his typing still further. Explaining that his son is a bricky, who is interested in volunteering abroad, Bluey tells them that the American woman sent him an email about their project so he could pass it on to his son. He explains that they are desperate for skilled, experienced tradespeople.

"That's amazing Bluey, you've got a great kid there and what a coincidence. It's the sort of thing I was thinking of doing again. Any chance I can have the details on the email, once you find it?" asks Boof.

Bluey nods and sluggishly presses keys until he finally, and proudly, announces he has found it. Scanning it to make sure it was the right email, he then presses more keys which prompts his printer, resting on a small filing cabinet next to him, into life. Snatching the paper from the machine, he passes it to Damo, who is nearest. He then starts to read the email on the screen and explains its content.

"Damo's got a full hard copy of the email which has the American Sheila's contact details as well as some information on the project. It's volunteer work but they'll pay for travel and provide food and a place to sleep when you are over there. There's an email and number to contact them if you're interested."

While Bluey is talking, Damo scans the hard copy in his hand and gives Boof and Earl the thumbs up. The three exchange smiles which transform to a more serious expression when Bluey adds a final bit of information.

"As yer can see from the email, the crate you came to collect was dropped near a town called Kabale. No idea where that is, but she says it ended up in a small village in the Rubirizi District in Western Uganda. My son is thinking about going out there. He's only just finished his apprenticeship, but I reckon they would snap up experienced blokes like yourselves. If yer'all up for it, then all I can say is good on yer, and good luck."

"Thanks Bluey, you've been a bloody star," says Damo with the other two in the background nodding in agreement. "Anyway, we've taken up enough of your time, so we'll be on our way."

"No worries lads. Nice to meet you Boof, and you Earl. Just sorry you've had a wasted journey. Hope you won't get any trouble from your bosses, turning up empty handed. Bloody pen pushers, they need to take a good look at themselves. But at least the books ended up where they're needed. Y'know, for those poor kids."

Leaving the airport, they decide to drive to Earl's two bed unit to regroup and plan their next move. Assuming there is even going to be a next move. Between the three of them, only two have ever left the country but even

Earl and Damo have doubts. Africa may be a bit too different and a bit more challenging than Bali, America, and New Zealand.

Sitting in the living room, each with a can of Victoria Bitter in hand, they work round the options. They soon distil them down to two. Drop the whole idea or do a spot of volunteering in regional Uganda. Opening the conversation, Boof tries to explore the thinking of the other two, without first offering a view of his own.

Damo's response is lukewarm. It seems too risky. How could they find the exact location of the crate? How could they get the money out of the country undetected? What if the money had been discovered? What if it was still hidden, but they got caught taking it? What if they ended up in an Ugandan prison?

With a similar degree of reticence, Boof reflects that he has spent more time in jail than outside Sydney. He tells them he has never been to South Australia, let alone South Africa or bloody Uganda, wherever that is.

Of the three, Earl, eventually, makes the first bold move. He tells them he is getting too old for FIFO work, let alone facing the risk of getting hospitalised by some Meth charged lunatic trying to take his head off at the door of the club. All things considered, he suggests it may be worth an investment of their time to come away with one or two million each.

Damo remains more reticent. They have no idea if the money is still there, especially once the locals get their hands on the books. Boof, who is slowly coming round to Earl's thinking, reminds them that books have been dropped for several years and apparently many crates have never been opened. Not only that, but the Ugandans also have a habit of keeping them packed, safe and secure. To his way of thinking, if they got out there relatively quickly, the chances of the money remaining undiscovered were high.

Driven by the fear of missing out, when the other two seem to be edging toward going, Damo declares he is in. If they both were in, that is. And once the main naysayer became a yes-sayer, the die is cast. Earl agrees to apply for the volunteer program whilst Damo offers to help Boof, who is the only one of the three without a passport. Damo has a mate in the Passport Office who can assist and help Boof's application fly through the fast-track process.

With Earl's experience of working on construction sites in the bush, the USAID funded program administrator practically snatches his hand off once the application is submitted. He has applied as a team of three. Boof's and Damo's limited experience in the building industry is crafted into something more substantial, making the application highly attractive to the project administrator. What the administrator does not share with the applicants is that the proximity to Rwanda, and the on-going civil war, gives the region a degree of instability which tended to discourage other prospective volunteers. As fate would have it, both sides have been economical with the truth.

A DISAPPOINTED SURFER
AND AN ARREST

RECLINING ON EARL'S battered leather sofa, Damo is holding a can of beer. With an amused grin, he watches his friend sort through a large pile of clothes in the middle of the living room floor, heaped next to an empty suitcase. Both had arranged cover with their employers for their expected time away. Both were equally as hopeful that their current employers would be their past employers by the time they returned to Australian soil. Struggling to concentrate and focus on deciding what he needs for his journey, Earl finds Damo's incessant commentary irritating and unhelpful.

"I take it you're sat here annoying me because you're all sorted, and you've packed?" snipes Earl.

"Not yet mate, just wanted to pop by and see what you're packing and get some advice and ideas."

"Really?"

"Yes mate. First thing I noticed from that pile you are sifting through, is that you don't seem to be packing much in the way of boardies."

"So."

"Well mate, it's hot out there and I thought we'd be up for a swim on occasion. Maybe even have a surf. I'm thinking of taking my old surfboard. Don't want to risk losing my good one. Whaddya think?"

Kneeling next to the clothes pile, Earl frowns with annoyance, puts his hands on his hips and stares up.

Oblivious to the attention, Damo is busy draining the last dregs of his beer. Shaking the can to indicate he is ready for another one, Damo catches Earl's eye.

"What's wrong?" asks Damo.

"*What's wrong,*" echoes Earl. "You're asking me what's wrong?"

"Yeah, what's wrong? Why're you looking at me like that?"

"Because, you idiot, we're not going on a bloody holiday. We're supposed to be working, and once we find what we're going for, we need to leave, sharpish. Not stay for an extended holiday."

"Just 'cause we're working, doesn't mean we can't have a bit of relaxation at the end of the day. A few beers. A swim and a bit of a surf."

"Really, you wanna surf, do you?"

"Yeah, why not?"

"Have you looked at a map of Africa?"

"Naw, why?"

"Because, you idiot, Uganda is a land locked country, there's nowhere to surf. Nearest water to us is Lake Victoria."

"Oh well," says Damo cheerfully, "least we can pack the boardies for a swim."

"Mate, aside from the fact the Lake's gonna be over a hundred kilometres away from where we are heading, you ain't gonna be going for an early evening dip in it. There's Hippos living there."

"Who's worried about a few, fat cuddly hippos?" asks Damo.

"Mate, it's not like the Disney film with the dancing ones. Hippos are the most dangerous animals living there. They kill more humans than any other animal. And if they don't get you, the crocodiles will."

"What, an even bigger killer than Tigers?"

"Africa doesn't have Tigers, but yeah?"

Damo sits worriedly scratching his eyebrow, trying to process this new and unwelcome information. Resuming his clothes sorting, Earl adds, "That's if the snail doesn't get you." He is now beginning to enjoy the increasing discomfort of his irritating mate.

"What snail?" asks Damo, trying to picture a giant snail, large and fast enough to threaten him.

"Snails that swim in the Lake," replies Earl, purposely being obtuse.

"You're just making this shit up now. You're having a laugh."

"God's truth. Deadly snails which carry a parasite called bilharzia. It can kill you."

"You're joking?"

"No mate, I'm not joking. So I wouldn't be packing lots of boardies and certainly wouldn't be packing your surfboard. You need to start using your noggin mate. Do yer research like me. We're going to a strange place, somewhere that's not like any place we've ever been. Not only that, but we'll also be out in the bush, not in some big city."

"Okay mate, I've got it. Message received and understood."

"Good. So why don't you bugger off and do your own packing with all this useful knowledge in your possession. Yer gonna need construction clobber and a pair of work boots."

When the front door closes, leaving him alone once more, Earl mutters to himself. "Bloody idiot, needs to take a good look at himself."

* * *

It came as no great surprise to Kemal that Hakan is displeased with his news. After enduring ten long minutes of relentless venting and expletives in his uncle's office, he awaits further instructions. Hakan finally calms down to simmering anger.

"A crate of books cannot disappear into thin air," says Hakan, exasperated.

"No Uncle, but the managers in both warehouses claim they know nothing of the whereabouts of the crate."

"Did you search the warehouse yourself?"

"They took me round to the area where the crates were stored before they were flown to Africa."

"So, you did not search the whole warehouse?"

"No uncle, not the second one but I did the search everywhere in the first one, where the crate was supposed to be. The manager at the second warehouse refused my request, and I did not want to draw too much attention. But he is certain the crate is not there. Jacko assumes it's been taken with the others."

"Before I make the call to our Kenyan friends with some half-assed story, I need certainty that the crate has left Australia. When I have that certainty, we're going to have to come up with some credible story, probably claiming that the crate was sent as usual. Maybe, try to shift the blame onto them. I'm not giving up the cash that easily."

"What do you want me to do?"

"I said I need certainty. That means searching all the warehouses, top to bottom."

"But uncle, they would not allow it. If I try to force them, they will get the police involved."

"In that case you'll need to search it without their permission and without their knowledge. Use your brain. Don't come back until you can tell me you have covered every inch."

"Yes uncle."

"Until you can say with absolute certainty that the crate is no longer there. Understand?"

"Yes uncle."

* * *

The latest occupant of Earl's sofa is Boof, who has also called in for advice on what to pack having never travelled abroad. Rapidly reaching the conclusion that he was going to have his hands full babysitting a couple of idiots throughout the trip, his doubts about the likely success of their venture begins to grow.

"Mate don't look at me like that. I've never been abroad before," pleads Boof.

"Well at least you haven't asked me whether or not to bring a surfboard," replies Earl.

"Eh! Whaddya mean?"

"Never mind," says Earl. "It'll be hot, and you're going to need to buy workwear."

"Why?"

"Because, dickhead, you're supposed to be part of a construction team. Even if you don't know the difference between a lintel and a lentil, you at least need to look the part."

"Can you lend me some?"

"No mate, I can't. What I've got won't fit you. You look as though you wouldn't tip sixty kilos on the scales after a full meal. Just get some boots and overalls, Treat it as an investment."

"Anything else?" asks Boof.

"Yeah, you need to buy one of those khaki safari suits, like you see in the old films. It's standard wear for white people in Africa."

"Really?" asks Boof.

"No, you idiot."

"But you are going to need a load of vaccinations, so get yerself down to the doctors."

"Are you joking? I hate needles," whines Boof.

"No mate, I'm not joking."

"What for? What do I need vaccinations for?"

"Scarlet fever, yellow fever, blue with pink spots fever. Mate, I'm not a doctor. Just go and find out."

Rapidly losing the will to live, Earl wonders whether it would be better to leave Boof behind and hints at the option. Motivated by a mixture of greed and suspicion Boof discounts the idea, even though the thought of avoiding flying, injections, foreign food and restless natives is appealing. Armed with the address of the supplier of trade attire, Boof sets off to 'Totally Workwear'.

* * *

Serenaded by cicadas singing in the hot night summer air, the airport security team conducts a cursory drive-by of the storage and holding facilities in the northern sector of Sydney airport. They fail to notice that the padlock has been jimmied off the main door of the warehouse managed by Bluey Edwards. The door itself is closed and, from the outside, the metal building appears to be in total darkness.

Inside, a beam of torchlight tracks slowly along the west wall, illuminating boxes and crates along the way. It has been a long and fruitless night for Kemal. Covered in sweat Kemal curses, the warehouse has only cooled slightly after the relentless sun of the summer day superheated the metal walls and roof. The ambient heat radiating into the facility is now unchecked by air-conditioning and fans which lay dormant, having been switched off once the working day ended.

Twice, Kemal thinks he has found the elusive crate. Twice he is disappointed and having checked and rechecked the whole facility, he reluctantly comes to the realisation that wherever the crate is, it is not in the warehouse. Turning to make his way towards the front door, his mind is occupied with thoughts of a cold shower and colder beer until he hears shuffling. Eyes widen with alarm when he finds himself face to face with a large shadowy figure.

Kemal's world turns to darkness.

Light from the mobile phone of his assailant illuminates the prone shadow of Kemal, laid unconscious on the floor. Pressing triple zero with large pudgy fingers, the caller is eventually put through to the police.

"Yeah, hello. G'day. This is Mick Edwards; I am calling to report a break-in at my warehouse at the airport."

A monotone, matter of fact voice on the other end of the line systematically draws a series of pertinent facts regarding the circumstances. The police officer then, as an afterthought, checks in on Bluey's welfare.

"Yeah, No. I'm good. I caught him prowling around. Looks like he was looking for something specific and, when he turned round, I chinned him. He's out fer the count now."

After listening to instructions from the policeman on the other end of the phone, Bluey responds.

"Yeah, no worries. He's still unconscious but breathing. I've used plastic ties that I had in my office drawer to keep him secure.

Unfortunately for Kemal, Bluey had left his mobile phone on his office desk. When he returned to collect it, he found the broken padlock on the ground. Sensing trouble, he crept stealthily though into the humid darkness of the warehouse. Almost immediately, he spotted a beam of torchlight sweeping across crates on the south wall. No one was going to turn over Bluey's warehouse. With a set jaw, he took matters into his own hands.

* * *

Once he is given the 'all clear' by the medical officer at the station, Kemal is released on bail after being charged with trespassing. Much to Bluey's disappointment, the police sergeant decides that no other charges, such as theft, are likely to stick. Other than a broken padlock, there is not even a realistic chance of laying charges of vandalism or willful damage to property. When Bluey expresses himself more vocally and directs his frustration at the police, the sergeant's mood darkens. Feeling that this minor non-event threatens to absorb a disproportionate amount of police time when more serious matters are pressing, the sergeant decides to put Bluey in his place.

"All things considered sir, you can count yourself lucky," he advises.

"Lucky!" exclaims Bluey, incredulously.

Keeping a deadpan expression, the sergeant confirms his statement. "Yes lucky, Mister Edwards."

"And how exactly do you work that one out mate?" Bluey's pale skin has turned puce with anger. A colour that clashes with his ginger hair.

"My advice is to calm yourself, sir," says the sergeant, behind an impassive expression.

Controlling his anger as best he can, Bluey asks for clarification, adopting as reasonable a tone as he can muster. "I'd just like to know how you figure that I'm the lucky one, when that little shit has walked away scot-free?"

"Not scot-free, sir, he is charged with trespassing. We

cannot really tie anything like theft to him. In fact, sir, from what I can tell, shortly after he allegedly broke into the premises, you admit to assaulting him. It's not as though he threatened you physically. According to your own account he turned around and you punched him. And that is why I am telling you that I think you are lucky." Seeing Bluey nod expectantly for more information, the sergeant adds, "The young gentleman could have a case against you for actual bodily harm."

"But he broke in."

"Yes sir, I accept that is what you allege. But knocking a person unconscious for trespassing, with no indication he was physically threatening you, can be deemed by the courts as excessive and unnecessary force. Added to that, there is no sign that he caused any damage to property in the warehouse."

"Crikey! Are you serious? Yeah, bloody oath I smacked him one and in the same situation I'd give him a crack again."

"I wouldn't advise that sir. Firstly, as I said, he could bring charges for assault. But you may want to bear in mind, also, that this young man does appear to have close connections with some serious people."

"What, like politicians?"

"No sir, with the underworld. Criminals. Particularly nasty ones at that."

TURKISH DELIGHT

SITTING BEHIND HIS office desk, Hakan shakes his head and looks across at the sorry figure slumped in the chair in front of him. Sheepishly staring at the floor as if engrossed in the intricate patterns on the Persian rug, Kemal does his best to avoid eye contact. It has been a particularly challenging few days and he has had the unfamiliar and uncomfortable experience of crossing swords with people who were willing to stand up to him. Worse still, he had come off second best on both occasions. For Kemal it is unchartered territory, normally operating unopposed and secure behind the shield of his uncle's reputation.

With recent events, Kemal's ego has taken a battering, but his uncle's office provides no sympathetic refuge.

"Perhaps nephew, I need to send you to Yusuf, to brush up on your boxing skills."

Kemal, knowing better than to respond, nervously strokes his shiny jet-black hair and runs his hand down his ponytail.

"Or perhaps you need to choose your fights more carefully. Perhaps you shouldn't bite off more than you can chew."

"It was a coward's attack, uncle," moans Kemal, desperate to save face. "It wasn't my fault, he crept up behind and hit me as I turned."

"Are you familiar with the Turkish phrase 'Armut, agacin dibine duser,' young Kemal?"

"Yes uncle, it means 'a pear drops to the bottom of its own tree'."

"It does. Here, the Australians talk about apples or being a chip off the old block. I think you have a lot of work to do to honour the legacy of your late father. You need to learn to control your temper. Use the sword only when a sword is needed. Sometimes words are mightier. Use your intelligence. Be smarter Kemal. Be smarter. Choose your battles. Don't leave yourself vulnerable. If you are angry, don't let your enemy see you are angry. Strike when they least expect it. Strike when you're smiling."

"Yes, uncle."

"Now the lecture is over, I must decide how I am going to deal with the Kenyans and the Ugandans." Pausing briefly in thought, Hakan asks, "You are certain that the crate is no longer in the warehouse?"

"Yes uncle."

"I am equally as certain that those who work for us at the airport have not taken the money. They wouldn't dare."

"What about Ahmet, uncle?"

"Kemal, what have I told you? Use your intelligence. Ahmet has been with us through thick and thin for over thirty years. He is practically family. His strength lies in muscle, but don't be fooled, he isn't stupid and he is loyal. He isn't capable of such disloyalty."

"Then I can't think who would be responsible? What do we tell the Africans?"

"We tell them nothing, Kemal. It's possible the crate was found and taken with the main consignment. So let us, for a moment, run with that thought."

"What do you mean, uncle?"

"When the Africans get restless and demand their money, we act innocent. We tell them that, as usual, the crate with the money was transported. Maybe, we tell them that they should look closer to home. Investigate those in the airport at their end. I wouldn't trust any African. They are a race without honour. They don't even trust each other."

"What if they don't believe us, uncle?"

"We hold firm. At least at first. We've run everything smoothly for over ten years. They always supply, we always pay. It would make no sense for us to risk cheating them and destroying our arrangements over one transaction. They will see that. I hope."

Hakan does not share his less optimistic thoughts with his nephew. Inwardly, he doubts that they will swallow his story or that it will end well.

* * *

Leaving with the impression that his uncle trusted he had done a thorough job at the airport, Kemal feels a sense of relief. He has renewed belief that his uncle has faith in him, blissfully unaware that this is not actually the case. Hakan despises the arrogant youth but indulges and protects him from a sense of duty to his departed brother, who was killed five years ago in a gangland shooting. On the other hand, he trusts Ahmet unconditionally and dispatches him to the airport to try to uncover what has happened to the crate.

Ahmet wastes neither time nor effort. Having satisfied himself that the crate is nowhere to be found at Jacko's warehouse, he heads straight to the second one. This time Jacko is told it is best that he does not come in case things get out of hand and his own position becomes compromised.

Filling in for Bluey, who has taken three days leave to attend his daughter's wedding in Perth, Brenton is left in charge. By the end of this day, he wishes Bluey's daughter had done what she had threatened to do throughout her stormy engagement – cancel the wedding. After a quiet morning devoted to ordering others to do the hard graft, Brenton sits behind Bluey's desk tucking into a meat pie whilst basking in his temporarily elevated authority. Pausing between mouthfuls, he senses a subtle change in the light within the office. Looking up from his pie he first sees a shadow which transforms into the imposing figure of Ahmet blocking all the light that normally filters through the office doorway.

Fresh in Brenton's mind is a film, Lego Movie 2. To give his overworked sister a break, he took his young niece to see it the previous weekend. Standing in the doorway is a man who looks more like a Lego Man than the movie characters themselves. It is not so much the Turk's height, he is barely six feet, it is more the shape and dimensions of his build. Incredibly thick legs supporting a body like a concrete block, with a cuboid head placed on square shoulders. There is no discernible neck. Even Ahmet's haircut is box shaped. A straight low hairline across the expanse of his forehead halted abruptly by straight cut vertical lines, making his hairstyle resemble a shiny black helmet. A menacing, threatening stare exudes from the mahogany brown eyes of the Turk, whose linear thick eyebrows offer a single twitch. Not a nervous tick, but something far more intimidating.

Through the black suit and shirt, Brenton can see that his visitor's impressive width is not body fat, but solid muscle. Whilst Brenton is not aware that Ahmet has an Olympic silver medal in powerlifting, it does cross his mind that if this man is employed in the warehouse, the forklift truck would quickly become redundant.

In an instant, Brenton finds himself prone on the

floor underneath Ahmet, who is sitting astride him firing questions.

Dissatisfied with Brenton's answers, Ahmet resorts to a less subtle technique of interrogation. It is not the crushing weight that most concerns Brenton, but the imagined outcome if Ahmet tightens his grip. As Brenton's tongue loosens, so does Ahmet's grasp of his victim's testicles.

It is as much psychological as physical relief, which causes Brenton to exhale and let out a sharp gasp, when Ahmet lifts his bulky frame to a standing position. Unsure what to do, Brenton remains on his back looking up at his nemesis, who is nonchalantly straightening his jacket after the brief physical encounter.

Grabbing him roughly by the collar, Ahmet hauls Brenton to his feet with one hand. Once he is satisfied he has been told everything, he releases his grip on the warehouseman's shirt. He orders Brenton to take him on a tour around the facility, to prove beyond all doubt that the crate is no longer present. As expected, the search is unsuccessful leaving Ahmet pondering and Brenton fearful of what is being pondered.

Desperate to expedite the departure of his unwelcome visitor, Brenton has a light bulb moment. Urging Ahmet to follow, he takes him to Bluey's office. With nervous enthusiasm, he shows Ahmet the transit log, which records the date the crate was collected. Running his thick index finger underneath the entry in the log, like an infant learning to read for the first time, Ahmet pauses in thought before he pulls out his mobile and takes a photograph of the page. After firing more questions at Brenton, the Turk finally grunts, turns, and walks out of the warehouse and Brenton's life. There is no polite 'goodbye' offered, which is perfectly okay as far as Brenton is concerned.

Occupying most of the two-seater sofa in Hakan's office, Ahmet briefs his boss on the events and findings at the warehouse.

"So boss, I'm certain the crate is no longer at the airport. I searched both warehouses thoroughly and I can assure you the man I questioned was very co-operative."

Hakan's smile reveals that he did not doubt it.

"Also, boss, I think this pretty much settles it," says Ahmet. Once he has pressed and swiped the screen of his mobile a few times, he hands it over. Whilst Hakan is reading the image on the screen, Ahmet explains, "it's a record of the movement of items. You can see the line which records the crate and confirms that it was dispatched to Uganda a few days ago on a military aircraft."

Squinting at the image, Hakan says, "I can see that, but all it says is Uganda. The other items in the photo give more precise locations." Pointing up and down the image on the screen, Hakan lists some examples, "This one says Nairobi, Kenya, this one says Mombasa, Kenya and this one says Lusaka, Zambia. Why was it not specified for Uganda? Did it go to Kampala?"

"I'm not sure, boss, the warehouseman didn't know. But he claimed they were told the books were sent to a school. They could have gone to Kampala first, but he admitted he didn't know that for a fact. That is why they just wrote 'Uganda'. He said it's possible that it was taken directly to a school because it was collected by a military, not a commercial, aircraft."

"And he had no idea which school and where?"

"No boss, I'm certain he didn't."

"You have done well Ahmet. At least we have a story to tell, along with proof that the crate was dispatched. Maybe our African partners can track it down."

BANANAS AND GOAT

WHEN EARL RECEIVES formal confirmation of their appointment from his USAID contact, he rings Boof and Damo to let them know that a briefing has been arranged. They are invited to attend a session at the offices of the U.S. Consulate General in North Sydney. All three are beginning to get excited at the prospect of their adventure, but they play it cool with each other. Despite travelling separately from different directions, they all arrive at the offices at the same time with five minutes to spare. Once again Earl repeats his firm instruction that he should do the talking. He need not have worried; the briefing proves to be a relaxed affair.

A friendly official leads them through the Consulate office suite, past three small offices on their left and an open plan area on their right. At the end of the central corridor, they are ushered into the conference room, offered a drink, and sit down at a large table facing a gigantic screen on the wall. Explaining that the Program Manager based in Kabale would shortly join them, the official turns to leave but is halted by Damo's comment.

"Jeez, it's good of him to come all this way just to brief us. Very impressive," says Damo.

With a smile the official replies, "I think you are mistaken sir, the Program Manager, Mister Seymour Johnson, will be joining you by Teams."

"What, he's bringing his team as well?" asks Earl.

"No, sir. He will join you using Microsoft Teams. If you look over there, he will login in shortly," replies the official pointing to the screen on the wall.

"Wow, modern technology," says Boof.

"Indeed," replies the official, who then leaves them alone in the room.

Bored from staring at the blank screen for a couple of minutes, Damo turns to Earl and is about to speak when it comes to life, revealing the tanned smiling face of Seymour Johnson. He is younger than they expect, in his early thirties, with shoulder-length blond hair. Damo whispers that the American would not look out of place on a Beach Boys album cover.

"Yo! gentlemen, great to meet you. I've had a good read of your application and can't wait to get yawl over here, it'll be cool. I'm Seymour, perhaps you can tell me who is who, amongst you." The American sits back smirking at his own little rhyme.

Each introduces himself and Seymour commences his briefing, firstly explaining that construction is about to start once the administrative processes are completed. Earl asks Seymour what he means by administrative processes. The American tells him that it is about getting the permits and permissions from Government officials and local chieftains. With the business end of the discussion finally over after a further fifteen minutes of dry discussion, Seymour turns to more personal matters.

"So, gentlemen, what do you do when you are not constructing buildings? You Aussies love to surf, I hear. Me too, I'm from Texas but live in Santa Barbara, California."

"Yep, we do," confirms Earl.

"Well, I know you are due to fly in a couple of days, so get as much in as you can. No surfing here and it's the one thing I miss."

"Will do," says Damo.

"Just to give you a feel for what to expect, let me explain a few things," says Seymour. "We won't be putting you up in the Hilton I'm afraid, at least not when you're in Kabale. Mind you, you'll get a couple of nights in the Sheraton in Kampala before we take you to your new home. You'll be picked up by one of my team and then you've got a bit of a road trip ahead of you. So, make the most of the facilities at the Sheraton, it's a nice hotel. Now I must warn you that accommodation in Kabale will be a little more basic. In fact, you'll be sharing a room. It's a sort of mini dorm with four beds and communal washing facilities. All your meals will be provided by two women from the village, who are good cooks. Hope you like goat and matoke."

"What's matoke?" asks Damo, whose diet consists primarily of hot chips, pies, steak and sausages.

"It's plantain,"

"Sorry?"

"Plantain Damo, it's a sort of banana they cook," explains Seymour.

"What, they put bananas and goat on the same plate?" replies Damo, getting increasingly alarmed. "I've never had goat, and the only banana I ever ate came on top of a Pav."

"Pav?"

"Yeah, a Pavlova. It's a national Aussie dish," clarifies Damo.

"Don't know what a Pav is, but I love your Aussie sense of humour," replies Seymour, failing to appreciate Damo's genuine concern at the prospect of bananas and goat. "There'll also be chicken, pork and fish, so you'll get a bit of variety."

"What about snaggers?" asks Damo, with increasing desperation.

"Snaggers?" asks Seymour.

"He means sausages," interrupts Earl, who is rapidly growing tired of discussing Damo's limited dietary requirements.

"They don't do sausages much out in the bush. Most meals are one pot, like a stew. Sorry Damo," apologises Seymour.

"What about bars?" asks Earl.

"Not too much in the way of nightlife either, as you'll appreciate, and the bars are not like you'll get in Sydney."

"But there are bars?" asks Earl.

"Yep, the village bar is open most days of the week," assures Seymour. Seeking to make the situation sound more positive, he adds, "And you'll get a daily allowance. Ten thousand Uganda shillings."

"Ten thousand, is that for the whole stay?" asks Boof, whose ears prick up once he hears the sizable figure.

Laughing, Seymour responds. "Love your Aussie humour. No, Boof, it's ten thousand a day of course."

Having talked for an hour, the briefing ends when the official from the consulate enters and provides each with a plastic folder.

Watching this happen from his office in Kabale, Seymour formally brings the meeting to a close. "So, gentleman, I can see you now have your packs. They should include lots of information on the program, the region you will be staying in and its customs. Lots of 'do's' and 'don'ts' for you to consider. You should also find your travel itinerary, tickets, and anything else you need for your journey. Can't wait to meet you all face to face in a few days. Goodbye gentleman."

"Yep, we'll see more of you Seymour," jokes Damo.

"Ha! Ha! I geddit. See more of Seymour. Love that Aussie humour," are the American's parting words before the screen goes blank.

Having offered to answer any final questions, of which there were none, the official escorts the three men out of the building. Once outside, they briefly discuss the meeting and agree to reconvene that evening at five o'clock in the Dog.

At the twilight hour between the end of the afternoon and the start of the evening the bar is almost empty, imbued with a typical mid-week vibe. A few customers are scattered around the bar, sipping their beers with the awkwardness of the lonely solo drinker. To add to the sombre atmosphere, the jukebox apologetically pumps out Sinead O'Connor's doleful voice, singing 'Nothing Compares to You'.

In contrast to the rest of the pub, the table in the corner is occupied by three animated companions, all upbeat and keen to discuss their upcoming adventure. Reading through the checklist of essential items that he extracted from his briefing pack, Earl looks expectantly at Damo and Boof. With each item they nod to indicate they have it covered. A few items fail to make Boof's tick list, earning a reproachful look from Earl.

"No need to worry, mate," says Boof defensively.

"You won't be saying that when you get malaria 'cause you haven't brought along yer tablets. Or the mossy repellent. Or all the other stuff you still haven't got." chides Earl.

"It's no big deal, mate, I can pop down to the shops when I'm there. It's not as though we're gonna be short of cash. Are we? We're getting ten grand a day. We'll be rolling in money."

"Mate, we are talking about Ugandan shillings, not dollars. Do you know how much ten grand is worth?"

"I'm not stupid mate. There used to be twenty shillings to a pound back in the day over here. I paid attention at school when they did history. Y'know, pre-decimalisation. According to the calculator on my phone, ten thousand shilling at twenty to the pound is around five hundred quid. Which is around a thousand dollars." Boof sits back and smugly swigs his beer, confident he has outsmarted Earl.

"Stupid doesn't cover it, you idiot."

"Whaddya mean?" asks Boof, with doubt starting to eat away at his erstwhile confidence.

"Read the briefing pack, look at your notes. Look up the exchange rate, mate. Ten thousand Ugandan shillings is worth about five dollars on a good day. Yer gonna get about five dollars a day. Which, if you ask me, still means they're overpaying for a dickhead like you."

Deflated but not willing to show his disappointment nor that he is beaten, Boof responds. "Whatever mate, anyway five dollars will buy a lot more in Africa than it will here. I can still get what I need when I'm there."

"Mate, we're gonna be in remote southwest Uganda, deep in the bush. Read the information pack you were given. It'll be a lot worse than a remote country town here. And it ain't Sydney. There're not any bleeding shopping malls where we're going. Their high street will amount to about six shacks. Two of them will have a couple of tables and chairs outside which will be their version of our cafes and pubs. Another one will sell local ciggies and other items you might get from a Deli. Another might sell meat with a hundred flies buzzing round it. Another might sell fruit or vegetables. So good luck with all of that."

"But …"

"No 'buts' mate, yer gonna have to take all you need on the list with you. My advice is that you piss off out to the shops tomorrow and get all the things that are on the list. Geddit?"

"Yes mate," replies Boof, sulkily.

Over twelve thousand kilometres away, Boof, Damo and Earl were blissfully unaware that they were the subject of a conversation. Enjoying an evening cocktail in the bar of the Sheraton hotel in Kampala accompanied by his right-hand man, Chief Masika has just finished a meeting with officials from the American embassy.

"Well, it appears that the project is finally happening. A college for training teachers will be valuable for the region," says Masika.

"Indeed, Chief. Let's hope the three mzungus that they are sending are as qualified as we are told."

"They appear to be. I've not had any dealings with Australians. In fact, I've never been to Australia. They're a bit different from the English. Strange accent. Strange names. In all my years as a student studying in England, I've never come across people with names like these three. I mixed with Theodores, Harrys and Ruperts. You wouldn't find a Damo or Boof in Magdelene College, I can tell you. Not only that, but the only Earl in the college was Frederick. A member of the British aristocracy. You know, like Earl Spencer, the brother of dear old Lady Di."

"Yes, I know of Lady Di, Chief," replies Eze, taking a sip from his cocktail. "I assume this Earl is not a titled Earl, if you know what I mean."

"Quite right. Apparently, it's just his name. I suspect these Australians will be a hugely different breed from my peers at Cambridge. I just hope they know what they are doing. They're all ancestors of the criminal class, you know."

"If those at the embassy are to be believed, they are qualified to assist in the construction of the college.

It seems that they've worked in remote areas in their own country. It sounds promising, Chief."

"Maybe Eze. Though I must admit, I find it hard to believe anything that escapes from the mouth of Ambassador Bagley. He's a diplomat, trained to lie."

"And to smile whilst he is doing it," replies Eze, and adds with a smirk, "well at least he compensated you for the goat. It was a very generous price."

Laughing, Masika responds, "It will be peanuts to him, he will have drawn it from petty cash at the embassy. Hopefully he'll now stop dropping books on our goats."

"And our villagers," jokes Eze.

Both men are still chuckling, when a waitress approaches them. "Your table is ready sir, if you would like to follow me."

Walking side by side behind the waitress, the two men continue to chuckle. Masika asks her if she knows what the special is tonight. She turns and smiles. Her answer of 'goat' prompts renewed laughter from the two men, causing her to frown, wondering what is so amusing about having goat on the menu.

A JET SETTER IS BORN

STARING WIDE EYED at the bank of screens showing foreign and exotic destinations, Boof is finding his first ever visit to an airport overwhelming. People walking in all directions, beeping electric vehicles carrying older infirm passengers through the terminal and a multitude of desks with queues of people with suitcases checking in to their flights. To Boof, it was total chaos. Without a clue what to do, he stays glued to Earl and Damo. He follows them to the queue that leads to their check-in desk and waits behind them as they edge their way closer to the front.

Earl, then Damo, go to the desk, place their suitcase on the conveyor belt and provide the clerk with their passports. Having seen the check-in process twice, Boof approaches the desk more confidently. When the clerk hands back his passport with two cards, Boof asks what they are for.

"These are your boarding passes, sir."

"Excuse me, why do I need two?"

"One is for the flight to Dubai and the second is for the flight to Kampala," explains the clerk.

"Oh! I see," replies Boof, who picks up his backpack and walks to his two friends who are waiting to one side.

Staring at the boarding passes, Boof looks confused.

"Everything okay mate?" asks Earl.

"Not sure," replies Boof

"Those are boarding passes. You'll need to keep them and show them as we work our way through security and eventually when we board the plane."

"Security, what security?"

"They'll scan your hand luggage. Y'know, yer backpack. You'll get searched. They used to give you a pat down but now they have this big scanning device. Just stand on the marked space and hold your arms out and it scans you," explains Earl.

Concerned, Damo interrupts. "Hang on mate, you've nothing dodgy in your backpack have you?"

"No mate," replies Boof, slightly offended at the suggestion. "Just a few bits and pieces that you told me to take and a couple of cans of VB."

"Mate, you can't take liquids on board, you'll need to get rid of them," says Damo.

"What's wrong with taking a couple of frothies on the flight?"

"It's the rule," replies Damo exasperated.

"Well, I'm not wasting them," announces Boof, petulantly. He removes the cans, pulls open the tabs and sinks each, one after the other. Belching, he walks over to a nearby bin to dispose of the empty cans. Earl and Damo look at each other and shake their heads.

"There, satisfied," snaps Boof.

"Actually, no," replies Damo.

"What's wrong," asks Earl.

"Well, what's his name?" asks Damo, pointing to Boof.

"What's with the stupid questions? You know his name, it's Boof," says Earl, irritably.

"Exactly. And why is he called Boof?"

The point Damo is making becomes clear to Earl, who turns to Boof.

"What?" asks Boof, concerned at Earl's expression.

"Mate, we are about to go through security, and you'll get scanned. Have you got a cigar tube up your arse?"

Affronted, Boof replies, "No mate, I haven't got a sodding cigar tube up my arse."

"Anything else?" asks Earl.

"No mate, give me a break."

"You sure?"

"Yes … I … am … sure,' says Boof, emphasising each word.

"Not that I don't trust you, but you can go through on your own. We'll go first and you wait for a couple of minutes," says Earl.

"For fuck's sake," replies Boof.

"Stop whinging and just make sure you don't have anything that you shouldn't have in your bag, or your arse for that matter."

"I don't, mate."

And so, it proved. They find a bar and sit with a drink watching, through the large glass windows, planes arrive and depart from the gates near them. Mesmerised, Boof sips his beer and stares at each aircraft trundling to and from their assigned gate. Damo spends most of his time watching videos on his phone and Earl sits quietly, formulating their plan once they land on African soil.

Despite evidence to the contrary, having watched several aircraft take off, Boof is struggling to understand the mystery of aircraft and flight. In disbelief, he ponders how machines this large and heavy can take off the ground. And once they are airborne, why do they not fall from the air? He turns to Damo.

"How the hell can those things get off the ground and then stay in the air? They must weigh tons," says Boof.

"Air pressure, mate," responds Damo, as he absentmindedly swipes across his screen.

"What?"

"Air pressure. I saw a documentary about the history of flight."

"Full of surprises, aren't you," chips in Earl. "I've got Boof here, who is a student of philosophy and you're a specialist on aero bleeding dynamics."

Eyes still glued to his screen, Damo says, "Yep, air pressure. The wings are designed to make air move faster above the wing than below it. When the air moves faster, the air pressure decreases above the wing and is less than the pressure on the bottom of the wing. This causes it to lift."

"If that's the case," replies Boof, "how come they don't keep going up and up into space?"

Cutting off Damo, whose mouth is shaping to provide Boof with an answer, Earl holds up his hand.

"Let's not worry about all of that and focus on what we're going to Africa for."

By the time Earl takes them through the itinerary and his proposed plan, the sign at their Gate changes from 'Open' to 'Boarding'. Twenty minutes later they are settled into their seats occupying a row of three at the side of the aircraft. Boof is by the window next to Earl in the middle, with Damo on the aisle seat. Boof's nervousness increases as the cabin crew prepare the plane for take-off and the last few stragglers take their seats. Muttering to himself about air pressure, Boof fidgets and knocks over Earl's bottle of water. An attractive female air steward leans across to tell Boof to fasten his safety belt. This timely intervention rescues Boof from Earl's anger.

Throughout the safety briefing and take-off, Boof does not move an inch nor mutter a word. Fear paralysed him. Once airborne, the pilot announces that the safety belt sign is switched off, but Earl ignores the advice to keep it fastened, and presses the button to release the buckle. Having slightly relaxed, Boof releases his own buckle and stares out of the window.

"Do you know what makes me laugh?" asks Damo, seeking to lighten the mood. "Those bloody safety briefings. There's no point in adopting the brace position if you are heading into the side of a sodding mountain. It ain't gonna be much help," he says in a cheery matter of fact tone. "And what about the thing under your seat, what good is that if the plane crashes. I mean, a bloody life jacket with a whistle. Are you kidding me?"

Looking nervously across from the window, Boof asks," Whaddya mean?"

"Well mate if the plane hits the water the whole craft will disintegrate. Everyone would get crushed. I reckon a parachute under yer seat would be of more use. Whaddya think Earl?"

"I think you need to shut the fuck up, Damo. Boof, here, is already shitting his pants."

Squeezing past them, Boof goes to the toilet, ashen faced. In the cramped confines of the toilet, Boof tries to compose himself by splashing water over his face. He presses the button marked 'flush.' The toilet responds with a loud sucking sound, causing him to let out a strangled scream of fright and recoil from the metal bowl. "Jesus Christ," he exclaims.

During Boof's toilet visit, Earl makes Damo swap seats with him, to provide a barrier from Boof. He tells Damo that if Boof does not control his nerves he will have to kill him and they would be sharing the money two ways, not three. Returning to his seat, Boof squeezes past Earl and Damo, not noticing they have swapped places.

Once Boof is settled, Damo taps him on the shoulder. "You okay, Boof? You look as white as a sheet."

"Why didn't you tell me about the toilets? I thought I was gonna get sucked out into the sky at ten thousand feet."

"Just settle you two. We've a long flight ahead and it'll be over twenty hours until we land at Entebbe," says Earl.

"I saw a film about that," says Damo, cheerfully. Still trying to lighten the mood. "Called Raid on Entebbe. Based on a true story about a plane hijacked at that airport. Palestinian and German terrorists demanding the release of prisoners in return for freeing the hostages on the plane. Only a couple of hostages were killed, and the Israeli special forces shot all the terrorists."

Giving Damo a sideways glance of reproach, Earl shakes his head. It was already too late to change the subject.

"Hang on," says Boof, whose voice was beginning to quiver in panic, "you're telling me we're flying to an airport with a history of terrorists and hijacking?"

"Just settle down Boof and watch a film for God's sake. It was thirty or forty years ago. Nothing has happened there since," says Earl.

"Yeah mate, but terrorists and Israeli special forces in a bloody shootout. That's worrying."

"I tell you what, the Israelis are worse than the terrorists, they don't take any prisoners. Literally," adds Damo.

"No Damo. I'll tell you what. Shut up, watch a film and, you Boof, do the same. You're both doing my head in." Angrily, Earl adjusts his seat, puts on his headphones, and starts to press selections on his screen.

All three settle into a film. On the menu Earl sees one of the new releases is a documentary on the disappearance of the Malaysia Airlines flight 370. Leaning over and checking what Boof is watching, Earl is relieved to find it is a comedy. An hour in they are approached by the steward who offers them lunch. Without the option of sausages, steaks or hot chips, Damo declines and Earl takes the Thai green chicken curry which he pushes aside after two mouthfuls. Boof, on the other hand, ploughs through an unpleasant grey congealed mess which purports to be beef stroganoff and rice.

"I take it you're hungry," says Earl, sarcastically.

"Great tucker," responds Boof, chewing the last remnant of his meal. He points to Earl's tray. "Aren't you eating that?"

Passing over the curry, Earl says, "I guess if you've just had a few months of prison slop, a can of dog food would taste good."

Well at least it's taken his mind off the flight, thinks Earl.

"How much longer to go?" asks Boof, finishing off Earl's curry and then a small fluorescent sponge that purports to be dessert.

"A fair way to Dubai yet mate, then we change. About three films worth, so knock yerself out and enjoy. Otherwise, try to get some kip," replies Earl.

"I was thinking about that. Isn't Dubai in the middle east? Y'know, more terrorists. Where that ISIS lot are?"

Removing his headphones, Damo joins the conversation. "No mate, Dubai is the United Arab Emirates. There's no ISIS there. That would be more like Syria. Which is different."

Once Boof puts his headphones back on, Earl and Damo exchange glances and the remainder of the flight is uneventful until the pilot announces that they have started their descent. This proves to be another stressful milestone for Boof, being his first ever landing. Knuckles white, he grips the arms of his seat and squeezes his eyes tight shut. A little whimper escapes from him when the tyres hit the tarmac with a judder and the reverse thrusters of the engines roar into life to slow down the plane.

Following Earl and Damo off the plane, like a frightened puppy trailing after its mother, Boof's nerves begin to settle. Wide-eyed, he tries to take in the scene around him as he follows Earl through the airport. Thousands of people of different nationalities, an array of skin tones and dress, mill around the airport. Women adorned in elegant black flowing Abayas, covering their whole body except their faces, hands, and feet. Men walking beside them, in their white robes, Kanduras. European businessmen and women in suits rushing through the airport, purposefully. Excited young children in tee shirts and shorts, buzzing around the feet of their parents going on their long-haul vacations. Other holidaymakers looking stressed, trying to find their way through the vast airport, with bored teenagers, glued to their mobile phones, trailing behind. Three large Ghanaian women pass by them, wearing head-dresses and robes of vibrant oranges, greens, blues and browns. Boof stares open mouthed.

"Stop drooling, Boof, and close your mouth or you'll get us arrested," says Earl.

"This place is massive," replies Boof. "And all these shops. Where the hell are we? Where do we go now?"

"We've got a couple of hours before our connection, so let's just find a place to get a drink, and relax," replies Earl.

Pointing to the large screen which lists all the arrivals and departures, Damo says," Look there, we're going to be at Gate thirty-four.

"It'll be down that way," Earl adds, pointing to a sign that indicates Gates Twenty-two to Forty are down a large corridor to their right. "There's a bar over there. Let's go and get a beer and a bite to eat. I couldn't stomach that shite on the plane. There's a hamburger place next door Damo, you can get something there."

"Well, I'm stuffed to bursting," replies Boof, "but could murder a beer."

Four hours later, Boof is enthusiastically tucking into another meal, thirty-five thousand feet above sea level. He now has the air of a seasoned traveller and a connoisseur of airline cuisine. Damo looks across at him with a vague expression of disgust as he examines the contents of Boof's tray. It appears to Damo that what Boof is chewing had possibly spent its previous life at the bottom of the ocean, but he had no idea of what it was. Whatever it was, Boof loved it. When he finishes his dessert, some sort of yellow jelly-like substance with canned whipped cream on top, he turns to Earl.

"Delicious, how much longer until we get there."

Checking the remaining flight time indicated on his screen, Earl replies, "Time enough for at least one more film, maybe two."

"Excellent," says Boof, relaxed and replete.

Leaning over to Damo, Earl whispers, "Check out Mister fucking International Jet Setter over there."

Damo looks across at Boof, who is now laughing at whatever he is watching on the screen. When Boof notices Damo staring at him, he gives him the thumbs up.

Nearing the end of the flight, the pilot announces that shortly they will be descending and Boof looks out of the window to see Africa for the first time. Screwing up his eyes, he stares intently at the ground.

"Hey Earl, check this out. The airport looks a shithole. There're old planes that look like they haven't moved for years. The buildings are wrecked. I don't like the look of this place."

Leaning over Boof, Earl stares out, and though he shares Boof's concerns, elects to remain silent. Damo, who is on the aisle seat, cannot see but gives Earl a questioning look. Earl just gives a shrug. About to voice further concerns, Boof is silenced by an announcement from the pilot.

"For those passengers aware of the history of Entebbe, and for first time visitors to Kampala, I would encourage those near the windows on the left to look down. What you can now see is the old airport at Entebbe. This was the scene of the famous hi-jacking and rescuing of hostages. There now just remains old disused aircraft and buildings, but do not worry, this is not our destination. We are now cruising towards Entebbe International Airport. The old one you can see here is used by the military."

"See Boof, nothing to worry about," says Earl, as if he knew all along.

"Flight attendants, prepare the cabin for landing, please," announces the captain.

LOCUSTS AND PHILOSOPHERS

SKIPPING OFF THE last step of the aircraft and onto the African soil for the first time in their life, three things strike them. Two are familiar. The punishing heat and the red brown soil, both reminding them immediately of the outback in Australia. The third, unfamiliar thing, is the smell. The smell of Africa. Distinctive, different.

The odour of the continent often becomes imprinted into the memories of those who visit from foreign lands and remains a constant connection to their time in Africa. And so, it would for Earl, Boof and Damo. A musty smell pervades the air, borne from the more primitive environment that besets a continent less dominated by the stench of mankind's polluting industry. A continent where the erosion of nature by man is far less prevalent. A land where the primal forces of hunters and the hunted are more pervasive. More immediate. With it, comes a greater proximity of life to death. A land where, for most, life is far more fragile. Within a month the fragility of life would be reality for two Australians visiting Uganda for the first time.

Passengers walk in single file across the tarmac, engulfed by the punishing heat assaulting them after leaving the sanctuary of their air-conditioned plane. Squinting towards their destination, Boof stares at the terminal, shimmering in the heat waves rising from the ground. Turning and then shouting back to his friends, he says, "Sure looks in better shape than the old airport."

Nodding in acknowledgement, Earl points beyond Boof, urging him to concentrate on where he is walking after he almost bowls over a shuffling octogenarian in front of him.

Once in the cooler sanctuary of the terminal, they follow the passengers from Business Class who were given priority to disembark from the aircraft. Compared to the larger, busier airport terminal they had travelled through in Dubai, the arrival procedure is refreshingly quick and simple. In a surprisingly short amount of time, they drag their cases through customs and into the arrivals hall. Damo and Earl pick up their walking pace to catch up to Boof, who has forged ahead, now the very picture of a seasoned traveller. Whilst Earl is searching for Taxi signs, a small, athletic looking Ugandan man in his forties catches his eye. Holding a small placard that reads, 'Mister Earl, Mister Damo and Mister Boof', the man waves hopefully at Earl who waves back in acknowledgement. A large welcoming smile revealing a glowing set of white teeth lights up the expression of the man sent to collect them.

Responding with his own smile, Earl's less impressive dental work impacted by years of nightclub scuffles lacks the cheeriness of the Ugandan. Shaking hands, Earl introduces himself, then Boof and Damo. The Ugandan points to the exit.

"Welcome to Uganda and our wonderful city of Kampala, gentlemen. My name is Mukasa, and it is my pleasure to drive you to your hotel. Please come with me. Would you like me to get a porter to carry your bags to the car?"

"No thanks mate, we can manage," replies Earl.

Having parked in a prime position, which to Earl's

surprise is immediately outside the main sliding doors of the airport, Mukasa points his key fob at the vehicle and the rear hatch of the white Toyota Hilux pops up. They load their suitcases and Mukasa then slams the door shut. Earl climbs into the front passenger seat and the other two jump into the rear.

"Great parking spot you got there Mukasa," says Earl, making conversation as they drive off.

"Yes, Mister Earl. This is a government vehicle, so we are allowed to park where we choose."

"Useful."

"Yes very, Mister Earl. I am instructed to take you to the Sheraton Hotel where you will be staying for two nights before we drive down to Kabale. I am to be your assigned driver for the duration of your stay."

"Well, nice to meet you," calls Damo from the rear.

"Thank you, Mister Damo. And, welcome once again Mister Boof. If I may say so, these are unusual names you have. Are they typically Australian? Forgive me, but you are the first Australians I have ever met. We usually have American and British people working on our programs."

Damo responds. "To be honest, I haven't come across many Earls myself, but my name is short for Damien. Which is more common."

"And you, Mister Boof. Is your name also common? What does it mean?"

"It's just a nickname," replies Boof, ignoring the smirks from the other two.

"I thought Nick was a name," says Mukasa, a little confused.

"No mate, a nickname is just one that's been made up by friends … usually." After giving a pointed glare to Damo, whose smirk threatens to transform into a belly laugh, Boof adds, "Most Aussies have a nickname, but, usually, it involves shortening their actual name or adding on a 'y' or an 'o' or an 'a'."

"Oh, I see. What would an Australian call me, because my name already ends in an 'a'."

"Not sure, mate," replies Boof, "possibly Mukko or Kassy."

"You Australians are very amusing," replies Mukasa, laughing.

Placed majestically on a hill, the Sheraton Hotel comes into view. Driving to the entrance, passing manicured lawns and palm trees, Mukasa parks and unloads their cases which are immediately snatched up by waiting porters. Bidding them farewell, he gestures to them to walk to the reception desk. Seeing their concern at the porters disappearing off with the suitcases, he assures them everything is fine and tells them he will meet them tomorrow after breakfast. Both welcoming and efficient, the receptionist checks them in and gives Earl an envelope. He opens it and reads a short, handwritten note.

"What's going on?" asks Damo.

"It's from Chief Masika. He says welcome and invites us to meet him in reception at six for a sundowner. He must be the head man at Kabale. I guess."

"I'm always up for a free drink. That gives us a couple of hours to have a shower and a quick nap. I'm knackered," says Damo.

"Me too," says Boof.

They take a lift to the sixth floor and, before entering their rooms, agree to meet back downstairs in reception at the allotted time.

Refreshed, they meet two hours later and await their host, unsure of what to expect. Checking his phone, Earl sees that six o'clock has passed and searches the hotel lobby for a likely candidate that might be a Chieftain. Seeing the three men looking lost, the receptionist calls over to them.

"Excuse me gentlemen, are you Mister Earl, Mister Damo and Mister Boof?"

"Yes," answers Damo.

"I believe you're here to meet Chief Masika. He asked me to take you to him when you arrive. He's in La Terrasse Garden Lounge. Please let me take you through." She walks round the desk and gestures for them to follow her.

The lounge area has four cabanas, each housing two sofas made from dark wood with cream cushions and a matching chair. A broad smile from the man in the chair welcomes them. With a quiet grunt he lifts his bulk to stand as they approach him. Once upright he straightens his white linen jacket and offers his hand, which Earl shakes first, followed by Damo and Boof. Extending his large palms outwards, he invites the three to take a seat. The receptionist waits patiently whilst the drinks are decided upon and ordered. All three ask for a beer and accept the Chief's suggestion of trying a local lager.

"That will be three Nile Golds for these gentlemen and a gin and tonic for me."

"Yes, Chief Masika, would you like Waragi Gin?"

"I think not my dear, I'm not a fan of Ugandan gin. Perhaps a Hendricks would be good, with a slice of grapefruit, not lemon."

"Certainly, shall I bring some evening snacks?"

"That would be lovely, what's in season?"

"This week we are serving chocolate covered nsenene."

"Delicious, please bring a couple of bowls with the drinks."

"Certainly sir."

Soon after they conclude their initial small talk and introductions, the waitress arrives with the drinks and places the glasses down from her tray onto the table, followed by two bowls of small dark brown snacks. Masika reaches and grabs one popping it into his mouth, chews, swallows, and immediately takes a second.

"Delicious," he announces, "do help yourselves, I love them."

Cautiously, the three men reach over and take one. Boof chews, swallows, and grabs two more, which he dispatches in the time it takes Earl and Damo to finish their first one. They are less enthusiastic than Boof and both quickly wash it down with their beer. Masika looks over to Boof and gives him a wide smile. "I can see, Mister Boof, that you are a huge fan of the nsenene. Have you had them before?"

"No mate, but they're yummo. Sort of nutty and chocolatey."

"I agree, but they are not always to the taste of the Western palate."

"Naw mate, they're a beauty," replies Boof, helping himself to two more.

"Good, Mister Boof, you are practically Ugandan already," says Masika, his belly shakes when he laughs.

"Cheers," replies Boof, taking another one from the bowl.

"I love nsenene, Mister Boof."

"What are they exactly?" asks Damo, looking at the bowl suspiciously.

"Oh! I assumed you knew," replied Masika, "they are what you might call grasshoppers or locusts."

Having made a rare detour from his core diet of sausages, steak and hot chips, Damo lapses into mild shock and starts to turn pale. After excusing himself, he makes a beeline back inside to the reception area in search of the nearest toilet. Although Earl feels slightly queasy, he manages to control the feeling by sinking the rest of his beer. Unperturbed Boof grabs a few more. This causes Earl to avert his gaze as his friend pops them into his mouth and crunches loudly.

"I can see, Mister Boof, that you seem to be a man of sophistication. Willing to explore our culture and try local dishes."

"Yer a bit posh yerself," replies Boof, "you sound more like a POM to me, rather than African."

"POM?"

"Yeah, sorry Chief, it's what we call the English."

"Yes, I see what you mean. It is probably due to my time in England. My parents sent me there for my education. My years at Eton and Magdalene College, in Cambridge, were responsible for my accent. Did you read at University, Mister Boof?"

"Read?"

"Yes, you know, study a subject."

"No mate, I don't really do much reading. Just the occasional footy record."

"Pardon me, I don't understand. What's a footy record?"

"Yeah, sorry mate. It's like a little magazine that they sell at the footy games."

"Oh! I see. We call them matchday programs in Uganda," explains the Chief. "So, you didn't attend University then?"

"Yeah. Not really. But I did a short course recently at a local institution, it was on philosophy."

"Really, how wonderful. A fantastic subject, I studied the classics you know, so dipped my toe into philosophy as well. Who did you study?"

Pausing to finish chewing the locusts, Boof empties his beer bottle to help them down. This prompts Masika to flick his fingers to indicate to the waitress that all the drinks need replenishing. Eventually, Boof can answer.

"Yes, sorry mate, those last two were a bit chewy. Yeah, we learnt about Immanuel Kant."

"Really how interesting, I'm afraid in the classics we only touched on the ancient philosophers of Greece and Rome. Cicero, Aurelius, Plato, Aristotle and the like. I was always a bit disappointed we did not get to study the thoughts of the great modern thinkers."

"Don't think Kant is that modern, is he? I think the Governor said he lived two hundred years ago."

"Indeed," replies Masika, not wishing to contradict his guest on the definition of modern in philosophical terms.

To Earl's relief, the discussion is interrupted by Damo's return, whose complexion has returned to a healthier colour. When the waitress arrives with fresh drinks, Earl uses the interruption as an opportunity to get off the subject of philosophy.

"So Chief Masika, I understand we are going to be working in your hometown."

"Indeed you are, Mister Earl, I am very much looking forward to getting this project underway. A teacher training college is just what we need to ensure our children get the education they deserve. I am afraid the standard of teaching is poor. It's impossible to attract good teachers to such a remote region, so if we can train people locally or even attract student teachers from nearby regions, I believe this will make a real difference."

"I certainly hope so, Chief Masika." Seizing the opportunity to ask the question he was straining to ask, Earl leans forward. "I understand that, before this project, the American Government provided you with textbooks. Do they still do this?"

"Good God no, Mister Earl. They commissioned a

report which revealed that dropping books was not the answer to our problem. In fact, local elders kept them in stores that they built specially, and many of the book crates were never opened. The consultants attribute this to our Ugandan culture. When we get gifts, it is respectful to take care of them. Hence, although the elders were well intentioned, they were stored safely but unused."

"You sound a little sceptical about the value of dropping books at all," said Damo.

"No, Mister Damo, not entirely. There is some truth to your observation but, without good teachers, books have less value anyway. Also, the Americans had the unfortunate tendency to parachute them in on crates and this, in some cases, proved to be disastrous."

"How so?" asked Earl.

"People were injured by the crates and in a few cases fatalities occurred."

"No, really, fatalities? Are you serious?" asks Damo.

"Yes. Believe it or not, despite a report by their own consultants recommending no more books, they recently dropped some more. The last one killed one of my goats."

"No way, that's appalling," says Earl, trying to muster up a sympathetic tone once he learnt that the fatality the Chief referred to earlier was a goat and not a human.

"So you say that they dropped one recently Chief," says Damo, nonchalantly, trying to pin down whether it was the crate that they were looking for.

"Yes, very recently. It wasn't expected and came out of the blue, if you pardon my little joke."

"So, what did you do with the books, did you send them back?" asks Earl.

"No Mister Earl, of course not. They're still in the village. The latest crate is with the other ones, unopened in a shed near my home. But you must excuse me, I need to use the restroom."

They watch the Chief haul his considerable weight out of the chair and walk with a rolling gait towards the reception area. Once he is out of sight, they exchange glances and begin to fist pump the air.

"I think we may have a result," says Earl, with a smile wide enough to reveal the gap in his teeth.

"Reckon yer right," says Damo.

"Me too," adds Boof, polishing off the last of the locusts.

Elated, they chatter excitedly, all the while keeping an eye on the reception area awaiting the return of Masika. Followed by a waitress holding a tray of three more Nile Golds, Masika approaches them and explains that he must leave.

"I look forward to catching up with you in Kabale in a week or so gentlemen. It was marvellous to meet you and we'll have a drink at my home when I return from my business in Kampala." Looking at Boof, Masika adds, "I also look forward to chatting further with you Mister Boof. Next time, you can tell me about your thoughts on Immanual Kant. I get very little opportunity nowadays to discuss philosophy with a fellow student. There isn't exactly a surfeit of philosophy academics in Kabale."

"No worries," replies Boof, wondering who 'Sir Feet' was. Undeterred, he holds up his glass and toasts the Chief, "And thanks for the frothies."

"Frothies? Is that an Australian name for beer?" asks Masika.

"Bloody oath," replies Boof.

"Very well then gentlemen, I bid you goodbye."

They watch the Chief walk, with his laboured gait, out of the hotel and into the rear of a black limousine.

Chuckling, they clink their glasses in celebration.

"Looks like you have a new best mate Boof," jokes Damo.

"Yeah," adds Earl, sardonically, "shared interests in Ugandan cuisine and philosophy."

"What can I say, some of us 'ave sophistication, some don't," replies Boof, smugly.

"Well mate, you're gonna have to brush up on Immanuel Carnt," says Earl.

"It's Kant."

"Whatever. Either way the Chief's going to want a big discussion, so I suggest you start preparing. He said he was going to invite us over."

"Already have," says Boof, smugly.

"What, are you serious?" asks Earl.

"Yep, a mate of mine called Genius, used to sing a Monty Python song all the time."

"You're not making any sense. Who is Genius and what song are you talking about?" asks Earl.

"Genius was one of that group of us who were given the lecture by the Governor at Long Bay. He's a clever bloke. He got done for fraud."

"Well, he can't be that clever can he, if he got caught," says Damo.

"Ignore Damo, just explain what you are rattling on about," says Earl, irritably.

"The lecture by the Governor was for a group of us who were about to be released. Y'know, the recidivism thing he was into. Genius was in the group; he was due out around the same time as me."

"Mate, just get to the point."

"After our lecture Genius would sing a song all the time. It used to get on my nerves. He called it Bruce's philosopher song. Supposed to have been sung by a load of Aussie lecturers, all called Bruce. They're from Woolloomooloo University in Sydney."

"There's no such place. Least I've never heard of it," says Damo.

"Not sure mate, probably part of the joke," says Boof.

Rolling his eyes upwards, Earl says, "Joke? Yeah mate, just get to the point."

"Kant is mentioned in the Monty Python song. Apparently, he was a bit too fond of the grog. The first line goes, Immanuel Kant was a real piss-ant who was very rarely stable."

"And you think this amazing piece of wisdom will carry you through an intellectual discussion with the Chief?" asks Damo, sarcastically.

"It's interesting and relevant, isn't it?" retorts Boof.

"Mate, I don't think that will cut it with Chief Masika. He told us he was a bloody Cambridge graduate for God's sake," says Damo, incredulous at Boof's line of thinking.

"Mate, so were the Monty Pythons' lot," replies Boof, and takes a victorious, argument winning, swig of his beer.

12

TORTURE, TILAPIA AND TONGUE
(OF A GIRAFFE)

AT BREAKFAST, THE conversation is sluggish. A cursory exchange of pleasantries bidding each other 'good morning' lapses into near silence, save the mechanical crunching of toast. Intermittent yawns and nods of thanks to the waitress each time she refills their coffee cups continue through breakfast until Damo finally offers a comment. Stretching his arms wide, and giving another yawn, he says, "Geez, I'm knackered. It took me ages to get to sleep and when I finally passed out, I was awake again an hour later."

"Me too. I feel weird. Sort of zoned out," says Boof.

"It's jet lag, you won't have had it before," suggests Earl.

"Does it last until you get back?"

"What, back to Australia? Naw mate. You should be okay in a few days."

"What about you, are you jet lagged?"

Shaking his head, Earl says, "No mate, I don't feel too bad. Just woke up in the middle of the night and couldn't believe how quiet and dark it was. Too dark."

"Isn't that a good thing if you need to sleep?" asks Boof.

Laughing, Damo says, "No, not for our mate Earl. Didn't you know he's afraid of the dark?"

"No, really, are you serious?" asks Boof.

"A hundred percent. Earl's a big, well not so big, tough man. But he doesn't like the dark," chuckles Damo.

"Is that right Earl? You scared of ghosts?" asks Boof, grinning.

Glaring, Earl replies, "I suggest you drop it, or you'll be picking up yer teeth off the floor."

In a sarcastic camp tone, Damo says, "OOOOh, Mister Earl is getting all butch and tough."

Holding out his palms to placate his friend, Boof says, "Hey mate, take it easy, we're just taking the piss."

"Well take it elsewhere. You too Damo."

Having killed the conversation, Earl turns his attention back to the food on his plate. Damo and Boof exchange knowing looks, trying to hold in their mirth. Glancing side to side at his companions, Earl is about to explode when a visitor to the breakfast table saves the day. They look up from their plates to see the smiling face of Mukasa.

"Good morning gentlemen, I hope you all slept well?"

"Not great," replies Damo, "jet lag and too dark."

Boof bursts into a fit of giggles which receives an angry scowl from Earl and a confused expression from Mukasa, who chooses to move the conversation on.

"Sorry to hear that, but that's to be expected. You've all travelled from the other side of the world." Mukasa surveys the fatigued expressions around the table. "Never mind, I hope the lovely Ugandan sun will freshen you up and enliven your spirits. I'm here, at your service, and happy to assist you to enjoy your one full day in Kampala. I'd like you to see the city before we travel south tomorrow."

"Sounds great but we've never been here. We've no idea what to do or where to go," says Boof.

"Not to worry Mister Boof, I assumed that this may be the case. I've given it some thought and have prepared an itinerary for you." Looking at Earl's sour expression, he adds, "That is, if I've your permission and if you're happy for me to be your guide."

Smiling, Damo replies, "Sounds great, let's do it."

Nursing their vacant jet lag feeling, they sit quietly in Mukasa's Hilux, barely taking in the scenery as they pass through the avenues and streets of Kampala. Sensing their indifferent mood, Mukasa is happy to do all the talking and assumes the role of tour guide pointing out places of interest. His first planned stop is Old Kampala Hill, which is dotted with several colonial era buildings, some refurbished and some the worse for wear.

Mukasa narrates a potted history of the city as he drives up the hill which is mostly met with silence until he finally gets a response from his guests. A couple of ironic snorts come from the back of the car when he tells them that the hill originally housed the headquarters of the Imperial British East Africa Company. Not understanding the phrase 'bloody POMs', Mukasa continues his narrative. More derisory snorts of 'bloody POMs,' come from the rear when he explains that the colonial rulers used the hill as a hunting ground for local deer called impala. "This is how the city got its name, Kampala. It translates to 'Hill of Impala.'" Mukasa's historical revelation does not have the impact he hoped for and is met with thinly disguised yawns.

Undeterred by the failure of the visiting Australians to demonstrate any enthusiasm for the Kampala's past, Mukasa pushes on with his tour taking them to the National Museum and the majestic Bahai Temple constructed from white marble with a breathtaking aquamarine dome. A more encouraging spark of interest comes from Damo when they visit the Central Mosque and he learns that it was constructed as a gift from Colonel Gaddafi to the Ugandan people.

This prompts Damo to fire a series of questions all at once. "I thought he's Libyan, isn't that in the Middle east? Wonder why he was interested in an African country? Anyway, wasn't he a dictator? Mad as a cut snake?"

Pleased that he has finally generated some enthusiasm, Mukasa considers his answer, and replies. "Some say that Mister Damo, but he was also a devout Muslim, and there are many of that faith in Uganda." Respectfully, Mukasa chooses not to correct Damo's errant geography.

Having squeezed the last dregs of enthusiasm for the Mosque from his guests, Mukasa shifts the vehicle into gear and drives on. Eventually, one of the locations on Mukasa's itinerary stirs the curiosity of Earl. They approach a cream building with a low sweeping frontage. At its centre is a clock tower and a large brassy dome.

"This is Kabaka's Palace," announces Mukasa, "but it is a Palace no longer. Thanks to one of our most shameful leaders. Colonel Idi Amin."

Previously slumped in his seat fading with jet lag, Earl sits up straight to rouse himself. "I saw a film about him on the plane. I checked it out 'cause the description of the film mentioned Uganda although the title was the King of Scotland."

"Yes, indeed Mister Earl. He declared himself the last King of Scotland amongst many other titles."

"Sounds a bit of a nutjob," offers Boof.

"So, what happened to this place? You said it isn't 'now' a Palace? What's it nowadays?" asks Earl.

"Milton Obote, the Prime Minister, ordered Amin to attack the Palace and the King was forced to flee. Then, eventually, Obote was overthrown by Idi Amin in a coup d'etat."

"A what?" asks Boof.

"It's French. It means an overthrow of rule by the military. Idi Amin turned the place into an army barracks. It became a place of evil."

"What do you mean? How was it evil?" asks Earl, with increasing interest.

Taking a deep breath followed by an audible sigh, Mukasa explains. "Amin ordered the construction of an underground prison and torture chamber. There is a dark concrete tunnel underneath, with many damp cells, which were surrounded by electrified water to prevent escape. It was a dark time in our history, Mister Earl."

"Sounds to me that your country has had a lot of dark times. Not to mention bad leaders," says Damo.

"That, Mister Damo, is what you would call an understatement."

Conscious of the need to lighten the mood and have a break from impromptu history lessons, Mukasa takes a short drive to the shore of Lake Victoria. With a welcome opportunity to stretch their legs, they amble along the shoreline, surveying the vast expanse of water. Mukasa tells them that Lake Victoria is the world's largest tropical lake.

Having handed each man a beer from a cold box in the back of the Hilux, Mukasa invites them to sit and take in the scenery whilst he approaches a vendor, who is grilling fish on a primitive barbeque. Small stones surround hot coals, and a slightly rusted metal grill is balanced on top. Words are exchanged and the vendor offers a price whilst looking over Mukasa's shoulders at the white faces of Boof, Earl and Damo. This prompts a short lived, but enthusiastic, bartering skirmish between the two Ugandans. Mukasa, uncharacteristically animated because he is outraged at the initial offer, feigns walking away. Grabbing Mukasa's sleeve, the vendor pulls him back. With a downwardly re-adjusted price agreed, four fish are placed side by side on the grill and basted with oil, infused with herbs and spices. Minutes later Mukasa brings the food over. Each piece of fish rests on brown paper and is accompanied by a slice of white bread.

"You had a bit of a blue there, Mukasa. Can I give you some money?" asks Damo.

"No thank you. Lunch is on the Project. A blue? If you mean an argument, well yes. He was trying to charge me mzungu prices for the fish."

"Mzungu prices?"

"Yes, five times what locals pay but I sorted it out. I am afraid you'll have to eat the Ugandan way, using your hands," laughs Mukasa.

Warily the Boof and Earl pull off a piece of the fish and put it into their mouths. Their frowns transform into smiles.

"Very tasty Mukasa," says Boof, "what is it?"

"My favourite fish," replies Mukasa, "Tilapia, but it is becoming rare due to the predators such as Nile Perch."

"We've got some awesome fish in Oz, but this is pretty good," says Earl.

Damo looks at it doubtfully. Noticing he has not touched his fish, Mukasa asks, "Is everything okay, Mister Damo?"

"Don't worry about him. All he eats is snaggers and chips. Here give it to me," says Earl, taking the fish from Damo.

"What are snaggers, Mister Earl?"

"Sausages, Mukasa. We'll have to teach you basic Oz," laughs Earl.

Turning to Damo, Mukasa says, "Well, don't worry Mister Damo. There are plenty of places in Kampala that make excellent beef sausages."

Sitting side by side, they take in the panorama of the vast Lake and the frenetic activity of the traders and fishermen on the shoreline whilst sipping on a second bottle of Nile Gold. Seeing Boof's head lilt to the side, as he nearly dozes off in the warm sun, Mukasa rouses them.

"I think you gentlemen are fatigued. I have planned one more little adventure but if you've had enough, I can take you back to your hotel."

"Naw, mate. We're all a bit jet lagged. If we fall asleep now, we'll be awake all night," says Earl, elbowing Boof in the ribs. "Come on Boof, best we stay awake."

Reluctantly Boof and Damo drag themselves to their feet and trudge behind Earl and Mukasa who are chatting, a few yards ahead of them, as they make their way to the Hilux. A short drive later they arrive at a large compound that is fenced off. A wooden circular building with a thatched conical roof stands in the distance. After a discussion through his car window with a man in a small wooden ticket booth, Mukasa enters the compound and parks the vehicle near the building. Climbing out of the car he gestures for them to follow him, and they stroll towards the strange structure. They climb the wide stairs that lead up to a balcony that runs the whole circumference of the building.

At the top of the stairs, they are given a container full of food pellets which the staff member explains are to feed the giraffes. Seeing the men look inquisitively at the bowls of food they are holding, Mukasa explains that the pellets are made from corn, wheat, molasses and grass. Once they have walked around the balcony to the other side of the building, they get a clear view of the giraffes. Awe struck at the sight of the majestic animals in such proximity, they gape in wonderment. One giraffe spots the bowls of feed they are holding and glides over to them, its elongated neck swaying elegantly as it approaches. Given the height of the balcony, the inquisitive giraffe only needs to bend its head slightly to reach under the roof and over the rail. All three laugh with joy at their face-to-face encounter with the statuesque beast.

Urged on by Mukasa, Damo holds out a small pile of pellets on a flat outstretched hand, which are effortlessly swept away by the large rough tongue of the giraffe. Damo laughs with delight and tells the others to have a go. With an encouraging nod, Mukasa tells Boof and Earl to offer some feed, but advises caution and vigilance, given the size of the animals.

Turning away from the giraffe to speak to Mukasa, Damo says, "Mate, there's nothing to worry about, it's as gentle as a lamb."

With widening eyes, Mukasa shouts a warning, but it is too late. Swinging its enormous head, the giraffe hits Damo from behind, knocking him off his feet and sending his food bowl skittering across the balcony floor, scattering its contents before it comes to a halt. Without a pause, the giraffe uses its large tongue to sweep up all the spilled pellets in one smooth movement, leaving Damo lying prone on the wooden floor. Damo hears a chorus of chuckles and looks up to see a small group of camera laden Japanese tourists, one of whom is recording the scene for posterity. Boof and Earl are bent double with laughter in contrast to Mukasa's concerned expression.

"I was about to warn you that they like to swing their heads," says Mukasa, redundantly. This creates renewed laughter from Boof and Earl.

A message notification tone on his mobile prompts Mukasa to check his phone. He frowns as he reads the message. "If you will excuse me gentlemen, I'm afraid we have to leave as I have a matter to attend to."

"Is everything okay, Mukasa?"

"Yes, fine, Mister Earl. It's just a request from my colleague. I must pick up another visitor from the airport because his vehicle has broken down. Anyway, it's probably a good time to return now, because my message also says that Mister Bruce and Mister Sexton have invited you for drinks in your hotel. If we leave now, you'll have plenty of time to rest and shower before your meeting."

"Sorry mate, who're Bruce and Sexton?" asks Earl, suspiciously.

"They are both very important men. Mister Sexton is the American Ambassador and Mister Bruce is a senior official from the Australian embassy. I assume they want to meet you because you have volunteered for the project and want to express their thanks."

Waving at Mukasa as he drives away from the hotel entrance, the three men wait until they see him disappear out of sight before they walk into the reception area. The receptionist hands Earl a note along with his room key. After reading the message, he tells Boof and Damo that it is from Mister Bruce Paterson, inviting them to join him and the American Ambassador in La Terrasse for nibbles and cocktails at five thirty.

"We're moving in high circles nowadays,' jokes Damo.

Pointing at Boof, Earl says, "Well, our old mate here is used to it, spending lots of time at His Majesty's pleasure."

"Bloody hilarious, you two are," snarls Boof.

"Now, now," replies Damo, "you'll need to watch your language in front of the Ambassador."

Looking at the large clock behind the reception desk, Earl says, "We've got a couple of hours. I suggest a short kip and shower and we'll meet back in reception. And Boof."

"Yeah?"

"A short kip. No more than half an hour, or you won't sleep tonight," advises Earl. "And Boof."

"Yeah?"

"Make sure you spruce yerself up. We're meeting the Ambassador and need to make an impression."

"Why?"

"Because, you idiot, we don't want to arouse any suspicion. You need to look respectable, not like some ex-inmate of Long Bay."

"Whaddya mean?"

"Like some dodgy sod who'd pick yer pockets with one hand, whilst shaking yer hand with the other. Just make sure you're tidy and presentable."

"Whatever, Earl," replies Boof, sulkily walking off.

When Boof is out of earshot, Damo whispers, "Mate, you could put an Armani suit on him and he'd still look like he's homeless."

"And as for you, mate, yer gonna need to pull yer head in. I don't want any of your smartarse comments. Understand?"

"Fully mate, fully," replies Damo, as they make their way to the lifts.

13

THE NATIVES ARE RESTLESS

IT CAME AS no great surprise to Hakan, that his African partners had not taken the news of the missing crate well. Even less of a surprise was that enquiries with various Kenyan operatives in the chain of command drew a blank. Resolution of a problem of this magnitude was above all their pay grades. Reluctantly, he accepts a scheduled Microsoft Teams meeting with the man at the top of the food chain, the Chairman of the Mungiki, Eric Muchai.

Operating from Mathere, Nairobi's second largest slum, the Mungiki was originally formed as a politically motivated militia, established to protect the land of Kikuyu farmers who were in dispute with a competing tribe, the Maasai. They modelled themselves on the Mau Mau, who were feared resistance fighters that challenged colonial rule. Severe unemployment, poverty and economic decline fostered an inevitable growth in crime, and this shaped the direction of the Mungiki's future from protectors to gangsters.

Accustomed to the use of violence, Mungiki activities mutated from small-time extortion of the impoverished inhabitants in the slums, into far more sophisticated criminal activity. Gradually, the Mungiki became highly organised. So much so, that they were labelled by authorities as the Kenyan Cosa Nostra, the African Mafia. Legions of jobless, disaffected youth with no alternative future, provided a fertile recruiting ground for foot soldiers, giving the Mungiki its fearsome reputation and power base.

Hakan prided himself on fearing no-one, whichever side of the law they sat, but he had the wisdom to treat the likes of Eric Muchai and his Mungiki with care and respect. More so, given the long and fruitful business relationship they enjoyed together. Rarely did Hakan enter a conversation without knowing the outcome. Even rarer were the occasions when the expected outcome was unfavourable. Dialling into the meeting, a thought had fleetingly crossed his mind that this may prove to be one of those rare occasions.

A stern expression fills Hakan's screen as Muchai brushes the palm of one of his spade-like hands over his tightly cropped, greying black curls. Attempting to keep the exchange as light as possible, bearing in mind the circumstances of their impending discussion, Hakan waves and gives a cheery greeting.

"Good evening, Eric, it's been a long time since we have spoken."

"Karibu, Hakan. However, it is not evening here, it is lunchtime," replies Muchai with a stern expression.

"Of course, the time difference, I forgot."

"I am sure neither of us wishes to dwell on the pleasantries. I understand we have a problem. Or rather, you have a problem," says Muchai, in a challenging tone.

Rankled, Hakan holds back his anger and responds diplomatically despite the provocation. "With the greatest respect, you were right the first time. We … have a problem to resolve."

"An interesting perspective Hakan. From what I am told we have provided you with the merchandise as usual, but this time you have not provided us with the payment. I fail to see how it is my problem and not yours."

"I am not sure what you have been told by your people Eric, but the payment has been dispatched. Your men have been furnished with a copy of the shipment note."

"I have seen a photograph of the document you're talking about. Even if it's genuine, it's not helpful. It simply records 'Uganda' as the destination."

"I know, Eric, but that is normal, isn't it? All the crates are destined for Uganda, but they all go through Nairobi airport, where your men find it a new home."

"There is no record of this crate going through Nairobi airport, therefore I assume it never did. So, it is clear to me that the payment has not been made. Has it?"

"I give you my word the payment was in that crate, as it has been many times before. If it has gone missing in Nairobi, then you may want to question your people. We all know that record keeping isn't a strong point in the airport. You may have people who are dipping their fingers into your pie."

Looking intently at the screen to gauge the Kenyan's reaction, Hakan inwardly winces as he sees a pair of eyes steeped in intense anger. Stroking his facial scar, Muchai leans towards the screen and points directly at Hakan.

"You may need to choose your words carefully my Turkish friend. If you think that I am so weak that any of my men would dare to swindle me, then you're gravely underestimating who you are dealing with."

"Please accept my apologies for the clumsy way I expressed myself Eric. We've had many years of profitable business together and I hope many more. Surely, you don't think I would jeopardise our relationship with such a glowing future ahead of us."

"We can go in circles for hours with this talk and, at the end of it, will be the same conclusion. I need my money and I haven't got it." Muchai leans back, stroking his facial scar once more.

"If we are certain that the crate didn't go through Nairobi, could it possibly have gone directly to Uganda?" asks Hakan.

"It may be possible, but where?"

"Possibly to Entebbe airport. Kampala is the most likely destination," suggests Hakan.

"You may have a point, but how does this help us?"

"I was going to suggest that, maybe, you could send your men to investigate."

"Why don't you send your men?" asks Muchai, petulantly.

"I'm happy to, Eric, but time is of the essence, and Nairobi is just over an hour away from Kampala. Not only that, but I'm also sure you have far better contacts."

"Maybe so, but why should I try to sort out your mess?"

"Please Eric, with all due respect, the records show the crate was dispatched. We can blame and accuse each other, but we've millions of reasons in that crate to work together to sort it out."

Leaning forward once more, Muchai's face fills the screen. "And what exactly are you doing to sort out this mess whilst I send my own men?"

Straining to maintain his conciliatory tone, whilst inwardly wanting to smash the Kenyans face into the surface of his desk, Hakan responds. "I'll make further inquiries here. I'll see if we can get a more precise location of its destination. I know the main consignment of books is dropped somewhere in the southwest of Uganda. Perhaps this one went to the same area. If that's the case I will send my people over. As a gesture of sincerity and trust, I'll send my best man and my nephew, if necessary."

Satisfied, Muchai leans back into his seat. "Agreed.

Let's hope that we find it and wasting an airfare on your nephew, and his babysitter, is not necessary."

"Then we have a plan. Call me once your men have done their work. I'll let you know if we have any further information from here."

With a grunt of acknowledgement, Muchai ends the call abruptly. In frustration, Hakan shouts a series of expletives across the empty office. Reaching over to the decanter on the corner of his desk, he pours a large measure of whisky and sinks it in one gulp. After pouring a second, he takes a sip and hearing a knock on the door, puts the glass down.

"Yes."

"It's Ahmet."

"Come in."

Squeezing his bulk through the doorway, Ahmet looks at his boss to assess his mood and realises that the meeting may not have gone perfectly. Years of service to Hakan have trained Ahmet well. He knows when a respectful silence trumps the desire to ask questions and shoehorns himself into the chair in front of Hakan's desk. Surprisingly, this raises a slight smile taking the edge off Hakans scowl.

"I'm going to have to get something bigger, Ahmet. Either the chair has shrunk, or you've got larger over the years."

"None of us are getting any younger, boss," replies Ahmet.

"Ever been to Africa?" asks Hakan.

"No boss."

"Well, you may be going soon. And you'll be taking Kemal with you."

Hakan studies Ahmet's expression but fails to get a read on what he is thinking. Smirking, he adds, "I always thought you'd make a good poker player, Ahmet."

This elicits a wry smile from the enforcer, who then

listens intently as his boss describes the discussion with Muchai. Hakan outlines the proposed plan, assessing the reaction of his enforcer whilst he does so. Once more, Hakan cannot not discern what Ahmet is thinking. It is just as well. Behind the neutral expression, Ahmet's thoughts are rising and plummeting like a small fishing boat in a storm. He has a bad feeling about this and has no desire to go to Kenya, Uganda or anywhere in Africa. Even less, to accompany a loose cannon like Kemal.

Alone in his office, once more, Hakan's own feelings are not dissimilar.

Two hours later, Hakan repeats the conversation and the plan with Kemal. This time the discussion concentrates on how his nephew would need to conduct himself and the consequences if he failed to follow instructions.

"But uncle, why do I have to go to a shithole like Africa?"

A red mist rises, but outwardly Hakan's temper remains even. "Have you ever been to Africa?" asks Hakan, already knowing the answer.

"No."

"Then how can you have an opinion? This is precisely the attitude that I've just told you will ensure things end badly. You'll be coming home in a box if you speak to the Mungiki in that manner."

"Yes, sorry uncle. What I meant was, why send me and not one of the others to go with Ahmet?"

"I hope for our sake, particularly yours, that such a trip is not necessary. The reason I'm sending you, if it turns out to be necessary, is because you're my nephew. Sending a family member will demonstrate trust and that we have been honest."

"I don't understand."

Waving his nephew away dismissively, Hakan snaps out

an order with his patience exhausted. "I'll leave it for you to work out. Now get out of my sight before you displease me further."

Barely three days had passed when Hakan tapped a button on his keyboard to reveal the face of Muchai on his laptop screen. Although Hakan has a clear line, there is difficulty from the Kenyan end with the sound. A younger man's face appears in front of the screen with a nervous expression. He busily clicks buttons on Muchai's keyboard, until the irritated voice of Muchai booms through Hakan's speakers. The younger man is getting a brow beaten and visibly breathes a gasp of relief when he resolves the problem. Wincing, Hakan turns down the volume and speaks.

"It's good now, Eric. I can hear you?"

"Useless idiots, I'm surrounded by useless idiots," shouts Muchai, unaware the issue was more a user error on his part, than a technical glitch. The younger man knew better than to appraise Muchai of this fact.

"I sympathise, Eric, but I can hear you clearly now."

Not a great start, thinks Hakan, as he looks at the irate expression of the Kenyan. Given the sensitivity of their discussion, he was hoping for a calmer mood.

Waving away his assistant, Muchai focuses on the screen. Without any formalities, the Kenyan gets straight to business.

"I've done as agreed and we now need to discuss the next steps."

"Happy to, Eric." Inwardly, Hakan was not the least bit happy. Next steps clearly indicated that the money had not been found.

Muchai leans closer to the screen and launches into the sequence of events since they last spoke. Hakan sits in respectful silence, allowing the Kenyan to tell the full story.

Although desperate to learn the outcome, he nods and murmurs politely in affirmation as Muchai's story slowly unfolds.

Having sent two of his best foot soldiers to Uganda, it seems as though their trip, whilst not entirely successful, was not wasted. What Muchai's story does reveal is his cunning and political acumen, which Hakan notes and is a timely reminder of who he is dealing with.

During the visit, Muchai's men touched base with his Ugandan equivalent. Under Muchai's instruction, they were careful not to reveal much detail and were circumspect with the Ugandan's questions. They made general enquiries as to where lost crates might end up if they were not intercepted in Nairobi. No specific crates nor timescales were mentioned. Nor was what was hidden inside them. No Ugandans were to be trusted, was their boss's instruction. Though suspicious, the Ugandans were helpful, especially when a reciprocal favour was put on the table. Unsurprisingly, Muchai chose not to reveal the nature of the favour to Hakan.

Enquiries with Ugandan airport officials, all on their partner's payroll, revealed that crates of this nature had been sent, over the years, to six sub-regions. Kyenjojo and Kasese in the West, Rubirizi and Kabale in the Southwest and Moroto and Kaabong in the Northeast. When the Ugandans tried to probe for more detail, such as when the crates went missing, Muchai's men were non-committal. Nevertheless, after a carefully crafted discussion, their enquiries revealed that earlier drops were in the Northeast and more recent ones in the West and South-West. Both of Muchai's operatives remained deadpan when the Ugandan's revealed that the most recent drops, only a few weeks ago, were in Rubirizi. They were sharp enough to deflect attention away from Rubirizi, feigning dis-interest, by enquiring about earlier drops made to Kasese.

With an air of self-satisfied triumph, Muchai concludes. "There you have it Hakan. I then instructed my men to make a trip to Kasese, ask a few questions, nose around and then return home."

"Very clever Eric," says Hakan.

Unmoved by the flattery, Muchai continues his briefing. "This will keep them off the trail. There is no doubt in my mind that the Ugandans will have monitored the movements of my men. They are not stupid. Hopefully, seeing my men return home, they will conclude our business is finished. They will not know what we were looking for, but they will have seen that our interest lies in Kasese, not Rubirizi."

"I realise that Muchai. As I say, you've been very clever," says Hakan.

"Good. Then I expect that it is now also clear to you that I cannot send my men back to Rubirizi. It will raise suspicion and give the game away. You will also appreciate that it is now time to send your man and your nephew. They're not known by the Ugandans and will look much more like tourists than my Mungiki soldiers."

Already a step ahead, Hakan knew where the conversation was heading. Trying to formulate a response which would give him an escape clause, he had run out of time. Not only that, what Muchai said made a lot of sense. Two Australian tourists would be much less likely to draw unwanted attention. His only recourse is to agree. It is an objective business decision.

"As ever, Eric, what you say makes perfect sense. Leave it with me."

Once the screen goes blank, Hakan slams his fist on the desk. It was all getting very untidy.

14

SLEEP

WATCHING THE WAITRESS carefully place a drink in front of him, Sexton Bagley thanks her and picks up the glass. Dressed casually in a light blue Pierre Cardin polo shirt and white chino shorts, he awaits his guests in La Terrasse. First to arrive is Bruce Paterson, who catches the waitress on his way in and orders a gin and tonic.

"Brucey, how are things?"

"Good," replies Paterson, taking a seat opposite. "I saw you'd just got a drink so took the liberty of ordering one myself. I could do with one."

"So, I saw. Has it been a hard day?" asks Bagley, shuffling in his seat and adjusting his shirt, which had slightly ridden up over his paunch.

Grinning, Paterson replies, "Looks like the good life here is beginning to show. Perhaps, a bit more time in the gym and a bit less in the bar."

"Cheeky bastard, perhaps you should join me," replies Bagley, pointing to the strained lower buttons on Paterson's linen shirt.

"Fair comment," laughs Paterson. Seeing the waitress place a drink down in front of him, he thanks her.

"Tell me Bruce, have you spoken to your three fellow Australians yet?"

"Not at all, I know very little about them."

"Oh! You're telling me you don't know much. Business as usual at the Australian embassy then," jokes Bagley.

Picking at an errant thread on his shirt, Paterson asks, "Killed any locals with your book drops recently?"

"Touche, mon antipodean. As a matter of fact, no. We're too busy building training facilities nowadays, not dropping books."

"In that case you'd better be careful where you drop the bricks," chuckles Paterson.

Reaching into his pocket, Bagley extracts a slim wallet, and then pulls out a note. "That reminds me. Here is the hundred dollars I owe you for the Chief's dead goat. I take it American currency is acceptable."

"It certainly is. Just glad you didn't pay me in Uganda Shillings, my trouser pockets couldn't cope, it would be around four hundred thousand at the current rates. Anyway, I expect my fellow countrymen will be arriving any minute. Hope they've settled in. The quicker this thing gets built, the better."

Whilst the two men continue to chat and banter, another three are gathering in the reception area. Earl asks the others how they are feeling and hears that both had managed a short nap to see them through the evening. Recognising them from earlier in the day, the receptionist walks from behind her desk to let them know that their hosts are already seated in La Terrasse. She leads them into the open-air bar and to their table. Bagley and Paterson rise to greet their guests. Following a flurry of handshakes, Bagley gestures for them to take a seat whilst signalling the waitress, who glides in and takes their order. By the time the introductions are complete the waitress returns with three ice cold Nile Golds, placing a bottle in front of each man before giving Bagley and Sexton their second Gin and Tonics. She asks if they require anything else and Bagley orders an assortment of table snacks and canapes.

"Does all that sound acceptable, gentlemen?"

They all nod, except for Boof, who gets a quizzical look from Bagley.

"Don't be shy, Boof. If there is something you want, just say so. It's all on us."

Turning to the waitress, Boof asks, "Excuse me Miss, do you happen to have any of those nonsenses?"

"Pardon me?" replies the waitress, frowning as she tries to understand the request.

Amidst the confused expressions, Paterson is the first to respond.

"I think you mean Nsenene, don't you? The locusts?"

"That's them," confirms Boof, "bloody good tucker."

"Well, well, well. It hasn't taken you long to absorb the culture, good on you Boof," says Bagley. He asks the waitress to bring a bowl, before turning to address everyone at the table. "So gentlemen, on behalf of the American government, I would like, formally, to welcome you to Uganda. I believe this is a first time for all of you, including our Nsenene connoisseur," he says, pointing to Boof.

They all murmur their acknowledgement and Bagley turns to Boof. "Tell me, does Boof mean something?"

Looking across the table sheepishly, Boof hesitates, then replies, "Er, not really Mister Bagley,"

"Or is it short for something?" persists Bagley.

"Naw, not really mate, it's just a sort of nickname."

Damo's smirk goes unnoticed.

Moving the conversation on, Bagley addresses Earl. "I can see you and the others have already developed a taste for the local beer."

"Yep," replies Earl, holding up the bottle, as if he needs to confirm it. "It's not too bad actually."

"Like Australian beer?"

"Yeah, I suppose so," replies Earl.

"And tell me Earl, how do you think you'll go with the project? I understand you're the one in the team with the most experience of construction projects in remote areas."

"True," says Earl, "I've worked in some remote parts of Oz. It can be challenging, with the heat and dust. I don't think that'll be a problem though. It's more about if you've got reasonable tools and materials. And a good willing labour force, obviously."

"Sounds like you're the man for the job here."

"Hope so."

"What prompted the idea of building a teacher training school?" asks Damo, trying hard to show some interest. Jetlag was creeping over him, like a heavy blanket.

"Our American friends here kept killing goats," chuckled Paterson.

"Sorry?"

"They kept dropping crates of school textbooks near villages in remote areas. Unfortunately, they kept landing on goats."

"Oh! ignore this idiot," says Bagley, "he must always have his little jokes."

Earl could have kissed Paterson. He had an opening. "So, when did you last drop books?"

"Right up until a couple of weeks ago. Co-incidentally, the last crate was dropped near the village where you're going to be working. Strange really, no one seemed to know about it. It came out of the blue, literally. Cost me a few dollars I can tell you, killed the local Chief's prize goat."

"Shame," replies Earl, barely able to contain a smile. Glancing over to Damo, he gets a surreptitious thumbs up.

"Nice locusts," says Boof oblivious to the conversation, being too focused on the food in front of him.

"So, what happened to the books?" asks Earl, with as much nonchalance as he can muster.

"Still there as far as we know," says Paterson, "probably unopened like all the others."

"Really? Is that so?" says Earl.

"Anyway, never mind the books, I want you gentlemen to do me a favour," says Bagley.

"Okay, just name it," replies Earl.

"Just take your time to build good relationships with the Chief, do a decent job and all that. And be sure to keep referencing the American government. We are, after all, putting a significant amount of funding into the area. Dead goats or not, you'd think they'd show a bit more gratitude," Bagley adds, huffily.

"Any more of these locusts?" asks Boof, holding up the empty bowl.

Paterson gestures to the waitress, who returns with a fresh bowl, which she places in front of Boof. Watching with a slightly repulsed, but curious, fascination, Bagley is mesmerised as Boof makes short work of the contents of the bowl. Damo, who has gone quiet, jerks when his head lolls to one side. Jet lag combined with the long day and the beer, starts to hit him.

"I can see Damo, that the flight and time zone change has taken its toll. I'm sure you gentlemen will all be keen to get some shut eye before your long trip tomorrow. I believe you've already met Mukasa who'll be looking after you. He's one of my best drivers," says Bagley.

"I won't lie, Mister Bagley," says Earl, "I think we're all ready for bed."

"Then let us bid you goodnight. Thank you again for agreeing to come over here at short notice."

"Yep, the same from me," says Paterson. Pointing upwards to the heavens, he adds, "It's good of you to do this. I know you've all volunteered, but at least it'll get you some credit with the main man above."

Alone in the hotel lift the three men discuss the evening.

"Sounds hopeful about the books," says Damo.

"Whaddya mean?" asks Boof.

"Yer missed it. Too busy stuffing your face with insects," replies Earl.

"Not much gets past you, does it Boof?" says Damo. "Earl here played a blinder. It seems certain that the books with the money were dropped near the town where we are going to be working. It's exactly what the Chief told us. In a couple of weeks, we'll be on a beach in Bali."

"Yeah," adds Earl, "it's a bloody relief that we aren't going on a wild goose chase through the farking jungle."

With the ping of the lift bell, announcing that their floor had been reached, the three men go to their rooms and sleep the sleep of the just and virtuous.

* * *

Over twelve thousand kilometres away, Ahmet had not slept at all, whether it be just, virtuous, or otherwise. Prone on an apartment bed, Kemal snores, almost comatose, after a bad-tempered drug and alcohol fueled night. Earlier that evening, Ahmet had been called back into Hakan's office where he found Kemal sulkily brooding in the corner. It was immediately obvious to Ahmet that he was about to receive the news he did not want to hear. With the slightest hint of regret, Hakan explained that the Uganda trip is on, and Kemal would be accompanying him.

When the two left Hakan's office, Kemal announced he was going to his uncle's club. After three hours of bingeing on amphetamine and alcohol, his frustration and fears were converted into displaced anger directed at an unsuspecting youth who was out with his friends celebrating his eighteenth birthday. Kemal, looking for a fight and spotting the youth as an easy target, asked him what he was looking at.

Buoyed by his own Dutch courage, borne out of beer and the safety net of his friends behind him, the youth chose to return Kemal's attitude with interest. Seconds later the youth was laid out with Kemal on his chest, punching and screaming. His friends stood still, frozen in shock, but fortunately, the beating was cut short. Ahmet dragged the out-of-control Kemal away from his bloodied victim and into the back office. Thirty minutes passed before Kemal was calm enough to be escorted out of the back of the club by Ahmet.

Enduring the mindless ranting and empty threats coming from Kemal, who sat in the backseat of his car, Ahmet wanted to teach his boss's nephew a lesson of his own. But he held his peace and parked in one of the visitors' spaces in front of a block of high-end apartments. It housed one of Hakan's penthouses, which Kemal and other family members were allowed to use if out in the city. Thankful for the small mercy that his passenger had not vomited in his new car, Ahmet dragged Kemal through the entrance and into the lift, where Kemal did vomit. Once he corralled Kemal into the penthouse, Ahmet threw him onto the bed in the master bedroom. He expected a torrent of abuse but was greeted with a loud snort, before the young gangster passed out. For a moment Ahmet was concerned that Kemal had stopped breathing and he looked anxiously down at the prone, still body. It was a mixture of relief and disappointment for Ahmet when saw Kemal stir slightly. Kemal's mumbling quickly developed into loud reverberating snores.

Out of duty to his boss, Ahmet sat out a considerable part of the night in the apartment watching an early morning vintage horror film. Periodically he would check on Kemal to ensure he did not choke on his own vomit. The hours passed slowly.

Dawn broke and the sun rose over the Sydney harbour bridge, bathing Ahmet in sunlight as he walked to his car. Kemal had woken, the worst for wear, but in no mortal danger, other than from the wrath of his uncle.

It was Ahmet's hope that, once he had reported Kemal's latest escapade, Hakan would rethink the idea of sending his nephew on such a delicate mission. A job fraught with danger did not need to be made more perilous by having to babysit a hot-headed idiot. Unfortunately, it transpired that Hakan would not be swayed. A promise had been made to the Kenyans and, as a matter of honour and trust, a family member would be sent. To renege on this promise would make an already delicate situation worse.

Leaving Hakan's office, Ahmet reflected that events of the previous night may have conspired to cement rather than weaken his boss's resolve. There was a lot to be said for removing Kemal from Sydney for a while. He was beginning to develop a growing habit of upsetting people who did not need to be upset, let alone random kids on a night out.

* * *

Relaxing in the garden of his Kampala retreat, Chief Masika lounges in a large bamboo chair accompanied by his right-hand man, Eze. They both sip an expensive Scottish whisky imported directly from Orkney. Savouring the smooth, honeyed finish of the twenty-year single malt, Masika basks in the early evening sun.

Turning to Eze, he says, "I hope you appreciate this, it's the finest whisky I have."

"Yes Chief, it is indeed a fine drink."

"I take it everything is in place ready for our visitors when they arrive."

"Yes Chief, a proper welcome has been arranged for them in Kabale. Their accommodation is ready, and our men are keen to get started and work with the mzungus once they arrive."

"What about all the books, are they stored safely?"

"Yes Chief, the ones we received recently have been put in the shed near the others."

"Good, Eze. The Australian mzungus seemed to be interested in the books, they were asking about them when we met at the hotel. I did wonder if they'd been asked by the Americans to check that we still have them. I want to be sure all are present and safely stored. We don't want to jeopardise our funding, nor this project. It is too important for our future."

"Don't worry Chief, everything is in hand. You can sleep easily."

15

IT'S NOT THE COLOUR OF MONEY ... IT'S THE WEIGHT OF IT

ARRIVING AT BREAKFAST together, Damo and Earl search the dining area for a spare table until their eyes rest on Boof, working his way through a plate of food piled high. Shovelling a forkful into his mouth, Boof spots them and waves them over.

"Jesus Boof, the amount of food you pack away is astounding," jokes Damo, as he takes a seat.

"Mate, after a long time sampling prison food, I've a lot of catching up to do," replies Boof, stabbing his fork into a slice of cold meat.

Looking at his watch Earl says, "Come on Damo, we'd better get a move on, Mukasa will be here soon."

They tour the buffet laden with fruit, cold meats, cereals and bread and each return with a hearty breakfast. Chatting as they eat, they discuss the trip and agree a plan, which is to settle in for a few days to assess the lie of the land and get the trust of the locals. It was clear from the conversation with Masika that the books are safely stored and untouched. They all agree that they have plenty of time to pick the best moment to make their move without rousing suspicion.

"There's a problem that's been worrying me," says Earl, in a half whisper, scanning the neighbouring tables to ensure no one was in earshot.

"Go on," says Damo, adopting the same soft tone.

"How much does, say, a million dollars weigh?"

"No idea, why?" asks Damo, giving Earl a quizzical look.

"Because, you muppet, if we manage to get to it, how are we gonna get it back to Kampala? Or out of the country, for that matter."

"Hadn't thought of that," replies Damo.

"It depends," says Boof, who, having cleared all the plates in front of him, is staring at his mobile phone.

"On what?" asks Earl.

"On the size of the notes."

"What?"

Remaining glued to the screen on his phone, Boof says, "On the denomination, y'know, fifty, one hundred, five-hundred-dollar bills."

"What are you looking at," asks Damo, "and for the record there aren't any five-hundred-dollar notes."

"I've got it here, a money weight calculator. It's amazing what yer can get on the internet," answers Boof, triumphantly.

"Yer kidding me," says Earl.

"Nope, just key in the total amount into the calculator along with the denomination of the notes and it gives you the answer. I just put in a million dollars in one-hundred Australian dollar notes and it comes to ten kilos." With his new discovery, Boof is on a mission. "Now I have to say we're buggered if it's in dollar coins, 'cause a million weighs over eight thousand kilos."

"Well, it isn't gonna be in one-dollar coins, is it," says Damo, before filling his mouth with cereal.

"Naw, yeah, I know. I'm just saying," protests Boof, affronted and aggrieved at the constant criticism. It is unfair, especially when he is the one who found the calculator.

Scratching his pale, freckled forehead, Earl says, "Look, we don't know how much it is, but if it's in hundreds, which I suppose is most likely, then we could easily carry a couple of million each without too much bother."

Having found a new toy, Boof was not ready to let go. "Even better if there was such a thing as a five-hundred-dollar note. A million would only weigh a couple of kilos."

"Yeah, okay Boof, I think we've got the idea now."

It fell on deaf ears, Boof was too engrossed in the calculator. "Yeah. If it's fifty dollars it'll be more of a problem, that's about twenty kilos per million. Now if it's twenty-dollar bills then we are up to fifty kilos per million. It'll be too bloody heavy."

Contemplating reaching across the table to grab Boof by the neck and slap him, Earl is stopped in his tracks by a voice behind him.

"Morning gentlemen, so what will be too heavy Mister Boof?" asks Mukasa, with a beaming white smile.

"Aw, nothing important," says Boof, seeing Earl's expression darken.

Hoping Mukasa had not heard any earlier parts of the conversation, Earl thinks on his feet. "We were just wondering if our luggage allowance would be too heavy when we return to Oz. In case we want to buy souvenirs. Like one of those carved stools that we saw from that trader on the Lake yesterday."

"Oh, I see Mister Earl. For a minute I thought you were concerned about the luggage you came with. The receptionist told me you'd left it near her desk, so I took the liberty of loading it all into the Hilux. I hope that's okay. You've all travelled quite light from what I can see."

"Great, thanks Mukasa, much appreciated," replies Earl.

"That's no problem, Mister Earl. Please finish your

breakfast and I'll wait for you in the car, outside. We've a long journey ahead of us, almost four hundred kilometres."

"No worries, we won't be long," says Earl, and watches Mukasa leave and pass through the restaurant door, out of sight. He immediately turns to Boof. "You need to keep your mouth shut mate."

"Sorry Earl, do you think he heard?"

"Naw," says Damo, "I saw him come in. You two had your back to him. I was about to tell you, but it was too late. I think it's okay. I mean, Boof was just spouting out a load of numbers for the last minute or so and barely made any sense to us, let alone some poor sod coming in at the tail end of the conversation."

"Well, Boof has just about cleared the fucking buffet table, so we may as well head off," says Earl, standing up and shooting an angry glance. Damo winks at Boof, who shrugs back in return, as Earl marches off to the exit.

Outside the main entrance of the hotel, Mukasa waits in the Hilux. He waves over to the three men who squint and shield their eyes as they leave the cool shade of the front canopy branded with the hotel's name and into the direct sunlight. Watching his passengers as they climb into the car, Mukasa tells them the journey is likely to take five to six hours, but they can stop off a few times on the way.

Before he starts the engine, he gives each a wad of money consisting of four tightly wrapped bundles held together with a network of large elastic bands. Wide eyed, Boof asks if they are getting all their money for the trip up front. With a chuckle, Mukasa tells him it is his allowance for the day. Boof holds up one of the four bundles he has been given, each the size of a half kilo packet of sugar. Mukasa explains that each bundle has ten thousand shillings. Flicking the crisscrossed elastic bands holding each bundle secure, Damo complains that every time they want to buy anything, it will take five minutes to unpack and extract the right number of notes. Once more Mukasa chuckles and explains that nobody ever unwraps the bundles. They are handed over intact as payment, with each bundle being barely worth four Australian dollars. Damo whispers to Boof, sarcastically asking him how much a million shillings weighs. He gets no response.

Very quickly, they are out of the confines of Kampala and on the main route to the southwest. When they eventually come across a placard indicating they are approaching Mpigi, after driving for an hour, Earl expresses surprise at the lack of road signs. Mukasa assures him he knows the way but agrees the country could do with a few more to help tourists.

An hour later, another sign appears by the roadside indicating that they have reached Masaka. Driving through slowly, Mukasa gives them an impromptu potted history lesson after Boof lets out a cry of surprise when he spots a burnt-out army tank on the township boundary. Mukasa explains that the town was of strategic importance during the Uganda-Tanzania war, where Ugandan troops were garrisoned. Following a fierce battle, the town fell to Tanzanian forces. Glancing in his rear-view mirror, Mukasa sees a look of concern cross Boof's face, so he assures him that it is all ancient history.

Progressing further into rural Uganda, the condition of the road begins to deteriorate as they drive deeper into the southwest region. Gradually, the proportion of road surface devoid of tarmac increases until they are driving predominately on dirt. Tightly gripping their seats and door handles, they juggle around in the Hilux as Mukasa navigates the vehicle through the dirt and, now more abundant, potholes. Some are so large that Mukasa occasionally must weave off the main road and onto the verge to avoid them.

Red, clayish murram, used to fill the potholes, is tossed into the air by the wheels of the Hilux. Behind them a cloud of dust billows as they negotiate the dirt roads. Frequently, Mukasa slows to almost a halt when sections of road narrow through erosion and there is only enough room for one vehicle to pass. Trucks from the Hima cement works of Kasese frequently bully the Hilux off the road, as they speed towards Kampala in the opposite direction. Other truck drivers carrying rice, salt, maize and casavas are less aggressive and, on occasion, politely give way.

In between chatting and banter, the men fall into periods of silence and stare out of the windows, marvelling at the lushness and variety of the landscape. Rocky outcrops in the distance can be seen across vast grasslands and sweeping valleys. Open savannah forests and acacia woodlands occasionally give way to greener tropical forests. Moisture from Lake Victoria provides water to the southern area of the country promoting the growth of rich vegetation. Verdant large-leaved trees, dripping with green plantains, appear in cultivated rows, in areas where Ugandan farmers have harnessed nature. Having worked in isolated areas of Australia, the green abundance of the land in regional Uganda surprises Earl, who expected a more familiar red, dusty, barren environment.

Making their way further south, they pass through several towns and smaller settlements. Silent for most of the journey, Boof comments on the number of funeral businesses when he sees yet another wooden shack sitting behind a variety of crosses, coffins, and simple headstones. With a weak smile that portrays a mixture of sadness and acceptance, Mukasa simply replies that death comes easily in Uganda. In their brief time in the country, the three friends begin to get a feel for the historic and violent strife that the Ugandans have endured. Yet despite this, they are warm, happy and generous people who are keen to welcome outsiders.

An hour after they leave the outskirts of Mbarara, they notice Mukasa turn off the main highway into Ntungamo and look at each other in surprise.

"What's going on Mukasa, are we here?"

"No Mister Earl, but I am afraid we are going to have to stay here for the night. The old girl is overheating," he says, patting the dashboard. "I don't want to risk going further and leave us stranded in the middle of nowhere."

Damo looks at Earl, the irony of the phrase not lost on them considering, in their view, they had entered the middle of nowhere a couple of hundred kilometres ago.

"Don't worry Mister Earl. It's not the Sheraton, but my cousin, Akello, has a small place where we can stay for the night."

Driving through Ntungamo town centre, which comprises one street with a few assorted businesses, including two funeral directors, Mukasa bears right. A further hundred metres down the road leads them to cousin Akello's hotel. All eight parking spaces at the front are free and Mukasa pulls up to the main entrance.

Sceptically, Earl eyes the building, which comprises of a small office surrounded by eight white chalets, all of which are raised slightly off the ground. Stone stairs, bordered by yellow railings, provide access to each chalet. Appearing at the open office door, a bald, bearded man dressed head to toe in white, walks out to greet them holding his arms in an open gesture. He hugs Mukasa who then extracts himself to turn and make the introductions. Akello invites them to follow him into the office. With Akello behind his desk, they all take one of the seats lined along the wall opposite.

Brandishing a broad smile, Akello says, "Please, please, let me welcome you to the Ntungamo International Resort. It is my desire to make your short stay comfortable, so please avail yourselves of our facilities."

Seeing Damo take a deep breath, which usually heralds a witty rejoinder, Earl gives him a sharp nudge in the ribs. Replying, before Damo has a chance to speak, Earl thanks Akello. However, Boof has more important matters that need clarification.

"Is there a restaurant in the hotel, I'm starving?" asks Boof.

Apologetically, Akello replies as he hands each their room key, "I'm terribly sorry, the Ntungamo Bistro is temporarily under refurbishment but there is a bar and restaurant on the High Street."

"Yes, it will provide you with a good meal," adds Mukasa, "and Auntie Dembe is an excellent cook." Beaming with pride, Mukasa says, "Why don't you all settle into your rooms, rest and freshen up and we can meet in an hour." They all nod in agreement and Akello takes them one by one to their chalets.

Unlocking the door to his room and placing the bag down next to the bed, Earl appraises what the rooms at the Ntungamo International Resort have to offer. Furnishings consist of a single bed with a mosquito net hanging above it, a small side table and a four-drawer wooden chest. Adjacent to the bedroom is another small area, without a door, which houses the bathing facilities. A metal bath, slightly rusted around the tap fittings and a wobbly washstand complete what Akello described as the facilities.

Rested and freshened, the four men sit at the best table in Dembe's Diner. With a choice of two options, selecting from the menu did not present too much of a challenge and they all opt for Dembe's special. Having taken their orders, Auntie Dembe disappears into the kitchen leaving the three Australians to enjoy their Nile Golds whilst Mukasa sips from a glass of locally made lemonade.

"It's very nice here Mukasa, is this where you're from?" asks Boof, trying to sound genuine and enthused.

"No Mister Boof, I was brought up in Kabale. But I have family here."

"So, we noticed," says Earl, who had quickly concluded that the unplanned stopover was more about bringing a bit of business to his relatives than resting an overheated vehicle.

"Ah! Dinner is served," replies Mukasa, keen to change the subject.

Placing bowls in front of them Auntie Dembe tells them to 'enjoy' and disappears back into the kitchen. They are left to examine their bowl of indeterminate meat swimming in a dark brown gravy against a yellow mound of mashed plantain, speckled with black pepper. Without hesitation Boof tucks in, whilst Damo just stares at the contents of his bowl. Hesitantly, he moves it around before finally scooping up a bit with his spoon.

"Goat and plantain. What do you think?" asks Mukasa.

"Bloody good tucker," says Boof.

"It's actually not bad, tastes like lamb," says Earl.

"I've had worse," says Damo, trying to chew off a piece of stubborn gristle.

Standing outside Dembe's diner, after their meal, Damo examines what the high street has to offer and concludes, like the others, that the answer is 'not a lot.' Agreeing on an early night, they all head to their rooms. Other than having to eject an unwelcome guest or two from their baths and wash stands, they all settle in to sleep, in what they now hope is a cockroach free boudoir.

At breakfast they meet in the Continental Sunrise Lounge which, contrary to the impression that its grandiose title suggests, is a small room with six tables shoehorned into it. With a bit of effort, they gain entry to the lounge by easing the glass sliding door which had initially given some stubborn resistance due to dust and dirt in the runners. A small window with a view onto the main road gives slight relief to the garish yellow painted walls that surround them. Akello insists that if they woke earlier, they would have seen the sun rise through the window, hence the name of the lounge. Sadly, as they would be leaving after breakfast, that once in a lifetime opportunity had eluded them. All four nod politely when Akello expresses his hope that they will see it next time. Everyone had a fairly good idea that there was close to a zero chance of the likelihood of a 'next time'.

Munching on the dry bread with the taste and texture of sawdust held together with slightly soggy flour, they sit in silence. Keen to lift their spirits, Mukasa attempts to make light conversation.

"It is a beautiful day, my Australian friends. I trust you all slept peacefully."

"Not really," replies Earl.

"Aside from the mosquitos, I'm sure I heard gunshots," adds Boof.

"Yer did? So did I," says Damo, "what's going on?"

"It's normal, just a few rebels from the DRC, who are probably poaching."

"What's the DRC?"

"Sorry, Mister Damo, I forget this is your first time in Uganda. DRC is the Democratic Republic of Congo. We occasionally get a few bandits here and there. Our defence force usually captures them or at least scares them off. It's the first gunshot I've heard in almost three months."

"Jeez," exclaims Boof.

"Oh! Well, that's okay then," adds Damo, sarcastically.

"Please do not concern yourselves, there's nothing to worry about, they will not come to any larger settlements like here or in Kabale. They know better than to attack white people because of the consequences. It will be the death penalty. Our President wants people to visit our country, to bring wealth. He has made the consequences of harming tourists clear."

Leaning forward over the table, Earl looks directly into the eyes of Mukasa. "Mate, I know yer playing it down, but people in Australia don't wander around with guns shooting at people. After a mass shooting in Tassie a few years ago, we have strong gun control. It's not easy for us to take it easy, if you see what I mean."

"What is Tassie?" asks Mukasa.

"It's Tasmania mate," clarifies Damo. "A bloke shot over fifty people in a place called Port Arthur. A lot of them died."

"I am most sorry to hear that, Mister Damo. So sad. But I assure you, attacks on tourists are rare. Exceedingly rare. Such things happen everywhere in the world, even in your home country. There are crazy people everywhere."

"He's got a point Damo," says Boof finishing off the fruit platter, "what about the bloke who held those people hostage in Sydney."

"What? You mean the Lindt café siege? But he was just a nutter," protests Damo.

"My point exactly, Mister Damo. There are crazy people everywhere. In your city you can go for a cup of coffee and get shot, even killed," says Mukasa, believing he had proved his point.

"He's got a point," says Boof, finishing off a small plate of meat which looked like beef but probably was not.

16

SWITZERLAND BUT NO WILLIAM TELL

HAVING BEEN WAVED off enthusiastically by Akello and Auntie Dembe, they settle in for a journey which they all assume will take at least half the day, given the insistence of Mukasa that they had to rest overnight in Ntungamo. Their assumption is wrong, and the trip is straightforward and relatively short. With the passing of each kilometre, the surrounding countryside becomes greener, lusher and leafier. Flourishing vegetation oozes a moist freshness that surprises the three friends, who are more accustomed to the harsher remote bushland of their home country. Scattered along the highway, roadside traders sit in the shade, selling their wares, waving and entreating them to stop. Mukasa speeds past them, unmoved. Winding down the window Earl sniffs the air, which is cleaner and thinner than in the countryside they travelled through the previous day. Seeing his passenger wind down his window and take deep breaths, Mukasa speaks for the first time in this last leg of their journey.

"I see, Mister Earl, you are enjoying the air in this part of Uganda."

"Yeah Mukasa. I can't explain it, but it seems fresher. I was expecting it to be hotter and dryer as we got further into the bush."

"Yes, Mister Earl, the air is fresher because Kabale is at a higher altitude. You will notice for the first few weeks that if you exercise or work energetically, you may get breathless until you acclimatise."

"I wasn't expecting this."

Laughing, Mukasa addresses Earl and turns round to catch the eyes of Damo and Boof in the back. "It's the same with all you mzungus. You all think Africa is just humid, hot jungles and scorched savannas. On the contrary, you are now entering what we call the Switzerland of Africa. Kabale is the heart of south-west Uganda. It's hilly and cooler here because we're over six thousand feet above sea level. My homeland is a truly beautiful place," he says with pride, pointing to the landscape and mountains surrounding them.

"So, are you lot any good with the crossbow?" asks Damo.

"Sorry, I don't understand," replies Mukasa.

"William Tell, he's a hero from Switzerland, an expert with a crossbow. When I was a kid we used to see him on telly. I saw Tarzan as well," replies Damo.

Perplexed, Mukasa desperately searches for an appropriate response, but Earl changes the subject after shooting Damo a quizzical glance.

"Ignore him Mukasa, sometimes the way his mind works is a mystery to the rest of humanity. We were told Kabale is a small place, but the way you describe it, it sounds quite big," says Earl.

"Small? No, that's not true. Kabale has grown, it is a town. There are many bars, restaurants, and places to see."

"Excellent. But we were told where we're going is small. Just a village, barely a shop, let alone bars and restaurants."

"I am not saying it is like Kampala, Mister Earl, but we do not consider it small. Maybe they were talking about Chief Masika's village, Kikungiri, which is outside Kabale.

That is where you will be based. And yes, there you'll not find too much but enough for your day-to-day needs."

"So why is the project located there and not in Kabale?" asks Damo.

"The Chief has influence; he's much respected. Besides, it's not that far from the University. Afterall, you are building a place of learning. Kikungiri may be a village, but we're not savages living in the jungle and scrabbling in the dirt wearing loincloths," laughs Mukasa.

"Never thought that you were," lies Damo, desperately trawling his childhood memories to recall what villages looked like in episodes of Tarzan.

With the conversation lapsing into a comfortable silence, Mukasa soon reaches the outskirts of Kabale. Conscious of kicking up dust from the main road which leads into the town, Mukasa slows his vehicle to avoid showering the occasional pedestrian with dirt. Buildings appear more frequently, until the road turns from red dust to greyish asphalt which glistens with recent rain. Reaching the main thoroughfare, they now see a steady stream of buildings on either side of the road.

The high street has predominantly brown or cream single-storey buildings. Many are in desperate need of maintenance to restore them to their original glory. Food stores sit alongside vendors of electronic goods, money exchanges, restaurants, and tailors. Men on small motorbikes lazily weave in and out of the cars parked on either side of the street and skillfully avoid oncoming traffic despite not bothering to use their indicators. Mukasa remains unfazed and brakes intermittently to avoid a collision. The steady stream of single level retailers is occasionally broken by a derelict shop or a two-tier structure, one of which is a hotel and another the municipal headquarters. Behind all the buildings, a line of trees towers above the roof line on both sides of the thoroughfare. Beyond the trees, green rolling majestic hills surround and embrace the town, like the arm of a protective mother.

Although Kabale is busy compared to most of the towns they have passed through, the centre is far from bustling. Men, mainly dressed in jeans and tee-shirts, go about their business ambling along the paths that run either side of the high street. Women, less in number, wear flowing robes and headscarves.

Leaving the town centre, Mukasa weaves through the surrounding suburbs. Roads turn back from asphalt to red dirt, with pools of muddy brown water the only telltale sign of recent rainfall. Men pedal through the streets on their bicycles, avoiding the puddles. Mukasa's Hilux is now the only car in sight. The frontages of buildings and shops are painted in more garish colours. An array of yellows, reds, blues, oranges and greens seek to entice passersby, seemingly to mask the more dilapidated state of the buildings.

Leaving the town by the western road, Mukasa slows the vehicle and points to his right. Beyond a low cream wall, they can see a group of well-maintained low-rise buildings. A square arched gateway with Kabale University emblazoned across the top, provides access to the campus. Mukasa slows the car so Boof, Earl and Damo can get a good look at the university campus. Once he is satisfied that his passengers have seen enough, he speeds up. Leaving the outskirts they pass what they have now come to expect as a typical landmark of all towns. Kabale offers two remnants of the armed conflict and civil strife that haunts the country. Next to a burnt-out tank, the twisted body of a military jeep lies forlornly on its side. With an expression of sad resignation, Mukasa raises his eyebrows in acknowledgement of what they have just seen.

No comment nor explanation is necessary. They are now familiar with the dark history of the country that lies hidden beneath the natural beauty of the land.

Now arriving at Kikungiri, their first impression is underwhelming. By comparison, Kabale is a teeming metropolis. Parking the vehicle in the main village square, Mukasa invites them to take a closer look. They jump out of the car and circle it to stretch their legs whilst surveying their new home. Pointing to a group of buildings, two built from wood and three more from brown compressed earth blocks, Mukasa describes the facilities offered within the village centre. Each time Mukasa describes a building he refers to it as 'somewhere'. A couple of minutes later they all know the full extent of what Kikungiri has to offer. In Mukasa's words, 'somewhere' to get something to eat, 'somewhere' to get a beer, 'somewhere' to get provisions, 'somewhere' to get meat and 'somewhere' to hold meetings. Conscious that his guests are clearly disappointed, a mildly embarrassed Mukasa could not bring himself to grace the facilities with nouns such as restaurant, bar, supermarket, butcher and council offices.

"Welcome to Kikungiri," says a disembodied voice with an American accent, which wrestles them from their nonplussed stupor. They all turn around and see a handsome, bronzed, blue-eyed figure. Brushing back his shoulder length blond hair, he beams a smile packed with perfect, capped teeth. Damo immediately recognizes the project manager, who they met on screen back in Sydney.

"G'day Seymour. I'm Damo and this is Earl and Boof."

Following an exchange of handshakes, Seymour ushers them into the building that Mukasa had described as 'somewhere to hold meetings'. Passing a young smiling woman sitting behind the reception desk, they enter an open plan area with a large table and, at Seymour's invitation, take a seat. Pointing to the only other room in the small building, a private office to the rear, Seymour explains that this is where Chief Masika normally conducts his business but reminds them that he is still out of town.

"Once again, welcome gentlemen. I'll give you a quick briefing then show you to your quarters. As I explained at our virtual meeting, there is a cabin with four beds for you."

"Cheers mate," replies Earl, slightly peeved. "I thought you'd told us that we would be in Kabale. Looks like there's a bit more going on there."

"Did I? I think I recall saying that your accommodation is not exactly the Sheraton in Kampala. As for the location, I guess I think of Kikungiri as part of Kabale. It's practically a suburb and not too far to travel if you get a bit of cabin fever staying in the village. Remember, you've got Mukasa here and he is always at your disposal."

Embarrassed at Earl's abruptness, Damo tries to lighten the tone, "No worries, mate, it all looks good.".

Examining Earl's expression, which had slightly softened, Seymour responds warily. "Okay then. The good news is that you start with a bit of R and R after your trip. The local workers will not be back until Monday, so you have the weekend to settle yourselves in."

"Sounds good," says Boof. "Could do with a beer and I'm starving."

"What else is there to do?" asks Damo.

"Funny you should ask, Damo. I can see from your CV that you are a bit of a sports star," says Seymour, who then points to Mukasa. "Mukasa, here, runs the local team, Kikungiri Rovers. They have a game tomorrow and are a player short."

Excited to hear this news, Mukasa grasps the opportunity. "Yes, Mister Damo, I understand you play football in Australia. Would you be willing to play?" He stares at Damo with a hopeful expression on his face.

"Yeah mate, I play a bit of footy for Randwick. Would be happy to help but I ain't got my boots though, just trainers."

"Perfect," replies Mukasa with a broad grin, "no-one here has boots anyway. The pitch is quite hard, so trainers will be perfect. We can give you some spare kit."

"An amazing start then," announces Seymour. "Let me show you to your quarters and then we'll get you something to eat. Our cook, Namono, has prepared a meal for you. The other guys love her, she's a star in the kitchen. She's done her specialty, Matoke and Goat."

Once settled into their cabin, which consists of four beds with a bathing area and toilet attached, the three men make their way to the dining hut where Mukasa is waiting patiently. He gestures for them to sit and then signals to Namono, who is looking through the hatch between the kitchen and dining area.

With a shy smile, she places the bowls of food in front of them, muttering 'please enjoy'. Without hesitation, Boof snatches up his spoon and starts to shovel the food into his mouth. Earl elbows him in the side and he stops eating until Mukasa finishes reciting grace. Damo unenthusiastically pushes around the food before trying it, but, to his surprise, finds it pleasant. Boof looks up and encourages his friend.

"Come on mate, it's good tucker. Tastes like lamb. Yer like lamb, don't yer?"

"It's okay," offers Damo, begrudgingly.

Addressing Mukasa, who is watching Damo with interest, Earl says, "Don't worry about him Mukasa, he's a fussy bastard. It's very nice." Also spotting Namono looking nervously through the kitchen hatch, Earl shouts over to her, "It's very tasty, we love it."

With an excited clap of her hands, Namona disappears from the hatch back into the kitchen. When the bowls are all emptied, Mukasa re-ignites the football conversation.

"I want to thank you once more, Mister Damo, for bringing your football skills to our team."

"No worries mate. What position do you want me to play? I normally play wing or centre."

"That would be good, Mister Damo, centre-forward is ideal."

"Centre forward? Hang on, who kind of footy do you play?" asks Damo.

"We play Football Mister Damo, of course," replies Mukasa, grinning, "you Australians are always having a joke."

About to clarify that the football he plays is Rugby Union, not soccer, Damo is interrupted by Earl. "Don't worry Mukasa, Damo will be fine. He's a natural sportsman." He then turns to Damo with a pointed expression. "You'll be okay, won't you Damo?"

"Excellent," says Mukasa. "But you please must forgive me. I am exhausted from all the driving, so if you will excuse me I want to get an early night. Namona will bring you some beer. Please enjoy."

Once they are left alone, Damo snaps at Earl. "Mate, what the hell are you doing, I can't play soccer, it's a shit game."

"Mate, to this lot over here it's the only game, the world game. They love it. What the hell did you think they meant by football?"

"Mate, I thought they meant Rugby Football. He said he'd seen my CV. It says Rugby not Soccer."

"Mate, I suspect it says Randwick RFC. He's a yank, they don't do much Rugby, so he probably assumed the FC meant Football Club. Football, as in soccer."

"Yer reckon. Do yer think I should tell 'em?"

"Mate, this is a chance to get them all on our side. Blend in. You're quite fast and …"

Cutting off Earl, Damo says, "Not so much now. Used to be."

"Alright" agrees Earl, eyeing Damo's slight paunch. "Yer not quite as fast as you used to be, but hopefully yer can kick straight. So, suck it up and don't let us down. Look mate, it'll only be a casual game between a couple of villages. The standard will be low anyway."

"But I don't know what to do?"

"Mate, you're a centre-forward, from what I've seen you just hang around their goal, like a full forward in Aussie footy and kick it when it comes your way."

"Or head it," adds Boof, trying to be helpful and get involved in the conversation.

"Head it, y'know, what they call 'a falcon' in footy," says Earl.

"Yeah mate, I know what bloody 'heading it' and a 'falcon' means. I'm not an idiot."

"No comment," replies Earl.

"And when you get near the penalty box, just fall over and you'll get a penalty. It's not a proper game, that's what they all do. They dive around," advises Boof, who had now got the bit between his teeth.

"And what makes you the bloody expert?" asks Damo.

"Played it in prison," replies Boof. "They started with footy, Aussie Rules footy, not this game, but it gave far too much licence and opportunity for the lags to knock the shit out of each other. Y'know, settle some scores. Players would get carried off minutes into any game that was played.

Anyway, the Governor eventually banned it and replaced it with soccer."

"So did you play much?"

"For about three minutes, I got hacked down by Plugger Sheehan and had to be carried off."

Looking at each other, Damo and Earl decide one of them had to ask the obvious question.

"Why did this Plugger bloke hack you down?" asks Damo.

"Because I lost his drugs. He asked me to keep them for him. Got the tip that his cell was gonna be searched."

"So how did you lose his drugs?" asks Earl, re-joining the discussion.

"You know, the usual place where I hide stuff Earl. Unfortunately, the screws were given the tip by somebody, and I was given an enema by the guards."

"Out popped Plugger's drugs, along with another item of mine."

"Which was?" asks Damo.

"A compact mobile phone." With a sorrowful expression, Boof adds, "It wasn't a good night, I can tell you."

Both Earl and Damo decided they had heard enough. Making their way to their cabin, Earl turns to Damo and says, "Mate, if you do good tomorrow, then we'll all be local heroes. It'll take the pressure off us; we'll be accepted, and we can get what we came for and bugger off."

"No worries, I'll give it my best shot."

17

IT'S MESSY, BUT HE'S NO LIONEL

REFRESHED FROM A solid eight-hour sleep, Damo finds himself standing next to Mukasa in front of ten players sitting on the ground. He looks over their heads as Mukasa prepares to talk. Behind the group, the Kikungiri home pitch presents a sad picture. The red dirt, dotted with random patches of grass, is marked with lines which are barely visible. This will be the arena on which Kikungiri Rovers do battle for the glory of the village.

Their opposition, the Lutobo Lions, travel forty kilometres to get to the game. Warming up in their red strip, they look as though they mean business. They take shots at goal to provide their keeper with a warmup, as part of their pre-match routine. A hard driven shot flashes past his outstretched arm and crashes against the post, causing the whole goal to shake precariously. But it holds firm. Damo winces, they look very good.

Mukasa, focusing on his team talk, raises his voice, which snatches Damo's attention away from the Lions warm up, back to the pre-match briefing. Squeezed into the green shirt and shorts of the usual centre forward, who is injured, Damo stands in front of his new teammates. All of them applaud vigorously when Mukasa introduces the eleventh-hour replacement. Behind Damo, sits Earl and Boof, who snigger when Damo waves, taking the plaudits handed out by Mukasa.

Whispering in Boof's ear, Earl says, "I think this lot are in for a big disappointment."

Boof chuckles and Damo continues to wave until the applause dies down, then sits on the ground with them. With a struggle, he pulls on his black socks and trainers.

"Well, other than the slightly bulging gut, which is giving the stitching of that shirt a run for its money, he sort of looks the part," says Boof.

Not responding, Earl watches the Rovers jog on to the dirt to warm up in the opposite goal. A handful of spectators are scattered around the pitch, some of them point at Damo, who is the only white person on the field. A sharp blow of the whistle brings the two captains to the middle to join the referee, who tosses a coin. Rovers have the kickoff.

Following Mukasa's instructions, Damo passes the ball back and makes a beeline for the edge of the Lion's penalty area. He is immediately joined by a Lions central defender who towers above him. "Good luck mzungu," whispers the defender in a menacing tone.

Still following his coach's instructions, Damo moves from side to side across the edge of the penalty area. He is shadowed by the defender. In the initial minutes, the Lions dominate possession, and the game is played in the Rovers half, away from Damo who patiently waits up the other end of the field. He can feel the defender's hot breath on his neck. They stand together, alone in the Lions half, whilst Damo's teammates repel wave after wave of attack from the Lions.

Out of nowhere, the ball is hoisted high into the air by a Rovers defender, and it descends towards Damo. It is an act of desperation by the team captain, who tries to relieve the constant pressure by punting the ball as high and far away from their goal as possible. Seeing the ball drop towards him, Damo runs to meet it but, before he reaches the ball, the defender clips his ankle. He tumbles down onto the hard dirt, grunting as he scuffs his knees. Having drawn blood, the defender chuckles to himself. The whistle blows and Rovers are awarded a free kick six yards outside the penalty area, slightly right of the middle. The broad, evil smile revealing the defender's yellow teeth, mocks Damo. Showing false remorse, for the benefit of the referee, the Lutobo player offers Damo a hand and pulls him up off the ground. Seeing the defender's gesture, the referee rethinks his initial plan to issue a yellow card.

Mukasa shouts encouragement, "Well played, Mister Damo."

The crowd, which is surreptitiously growing in number, chants "Barlay, Barlay." Smiling, Bale, the Rovers star midfielder, picks up the ball and places it carefully where the referee determines the kick should be taken. Lutobo forms a wall and shuffles from side to side in response to instructions from their keeper, who moves back and forth across his goal line. When the referee is satisfied that the wall is settled and ten yards away, he whistles for the kick to be taken. After a short stuttering run up, Bale expertly curls the ball around the wall with his left foot. Damo and his team hold their breath. A loud thud can be heard as the ball hits wood, the crossbar judders, but the ball floats harmlessly out of play. The result, a Lutobo goal kick.

With Lutobo dominating, the game continues to be mostly played in the Rover's half. Damo does not get possession, but a few short runs are surprisingly taxing for his body and his heart begins to pound. Ignoring the increasing discomfort, he runs for the ball when it is booted forward once more. This time he is determined to get it and as it comes down towards him, he leaps, catches the ball, turns, and runs. Much to Damo's surprise, none of the Lutobo defenders react and his run is brought to a halt by the piercing sound of the referee's whistle.

"It's football, not rugby," shouts Earl.

Sheepishly he looks over to the team captain. Trying to hide his irritation, the captain says, "Use your feet Mister Damo, not your hands."

Through blurred vision Damo mutters an apology before, overcome by dizziness, he collapses to the ground. Mukasa rushes onto the pitch closely followed by Earl. Handing Damo water, who remains prone, Mukasa asks what is wrong. Gasping, Damo explains that he is struggling to breathe. Mukasa tells him to lie still and remain calm. Once he has recovered sufficiently, Damo is helped to his feet and escorted to the side-line by Mukasa. The Rovers defend valiantly with ten men for the remaining few minutes and, to the relief of all, the whistle blows for half-time. The score is still goalless.

Leaving his team to rest and take in water, Mukasa tends to Damo.

"Are you alright Mister Damo?"

"Yeah mate. Cheers. Much better now. Don't know what came over me."

Seeing the concern on Earl and Boof's faces, Mukasa tries to set their minds at rest.

"Don't worry Mister Damo, I know what the problem is. In Kabale we're at a high altitude. I assume this is a new experience for you. Your body needs time to adjust and you have only been in the region a couple of days."

"Shit," says Damo. "I feel bad that I've let you down."

"Not at all Mister Damo, I'm the one at fault. I should have foreseen this and not asked you to play."

"So, is he gonna be okay?" asks Earl.

"He'll be fine, Mister Earl. He just needs to be aware of the altitude and its effect on him. In fact, you all need to be."

"Mate, it's a bit of a weight off my mind," replies Earl. "I been wondering why I felt breathless. Even just climbing stairs is harder. Didn't think of that."

"Me too," says Boof.

The whistle blows calling the players back to the pitch. Damo suggests they put the substitute on, but Mukasa reminds him that they have no other players available, so the team will have to play the second half with a player short. After a brief argument, Damo ignores Mukasa's instruction and starts to jog on to the pitch. Pulling him back, Mukasa gives him advice and suggests a compromise before he returns to the pitch. Damo is asked to hold his position and gently jog around the opponents goal area to take up the attention of the central defender. At least this will keep one of their players occupied and remove the advantage of an extra man.

"Run sparingly, Mister Damo," is Mukasa's final instruction before the whistle blows for the second half.

For the first fifteen minutes Damo follows the instructions to the letter. Lutobo's domination persists, and they miss several chances leaving the score at nil-nil. In almost identical circumstances to the first half, the ball is hoisted up field, high into the air, in a desperate attempt to relieve the incessant pressure of Lutobo. Damo runs towards the ball and the excited crowd reacts with an expectant cheer.

Without warning a resounding roar engulfs the pitch causing Earl to look around. What started out as a mere handful of supporters has swelled in number and the pitch is surrounded by villagers. Word had spread at halftime, and they have all come to see the mzungu. No mzungu has ever played in Kikungiri, let alone for Kikungiri. Earl and Boof are so engrossed in the game that they had not noticed the gradual swelling of numbers in the crowd.

"MZUNGU, MZUNGU, MUZUNGU," chant the villagers.

Spurred on by the loud vocal support of the crowd, Damo gets a rush of adrenaline and leaps to meet the ball, instinctively raising his hands to catch it.

Fearfully, Mukasa shouts, "NO HANDS, NO HANDS, MISTER DAMO."

Reflexively, Damo responds by dropping his arms to his side. The ball hits him full in the face before dropping to his feet. Eyes watering, he looks down, sees the blurred outline of the ball, and tries to control it whilst turning towards Lutobo's goal.

His legs are swept from under him when his nemesis, the Lutobo central defender, slides in from behind. Hitting the ground with an audible thump, Damo cries out in pain and lies prone on the edge of the penalty area. Blowing on his whistle furiously, the referee sprints towards the prostrate Damo, examines where he is lying and points to the penalty spot. With a histrionic flash of a yellow card, the defender is booked. Thunderous cheers from the crowd are followed by sympathetic applause for Damo who is hauled to his feet by the team captain.

More cheering of "mzungu" accompanies Damo as he limps off the pitch for the second time in the game, assisted by Mukasa. Sheepishly Damo lifts his arm to acknowledge the crowd, who cheer and applaud enthusiastically, whilst Earl and Boof stare in disbelief. Numbers on the sideline have now swelled from a handful of villagers to over two hundred. Rhythmic chanting engulfs the pitch once more, it is louder than ever. "MZUNGU, MZUNGU, MZUNGU."

Like the conductor of an orchestra, Mukasa turns in a

circle to face each section of the crowd and gestures for silence. Eventually the noise peters out to a nervous hush as Bale carefully places the ball on the penalty spot. He takes three steps back whilst the goalkeeper bounces up and down on the line, waving his arms vigorously, attempting to distract the star midfielder. Three short stuttering steps and Bale curls the ball to the keepers right. The keeper has guessed correctly and dives athletically getting his fingertips to the ball.

An audible gasp from the supporters.

But Bale had aimed his shot well. Despite the heroic effort of the goalkeeper, he only manages to divert the shot onto the inside of the post. With the keeper prone on the dirt, the ball does not enter the goal but rolls agonisingly behind him along the goal line. It comes to a halt in the middle of the goal. Seeing that the ball has not crossed the line, the goalkeeper desperately scrambles to his feet and dives to complete the save. Mukasa, Earl, Damo, Boof and the whole of Kikungiri village are transfixed on the ball which lies stationary on the line. No-one sees Bale nonchalantly jogging up to tap it in, as the keeper slides, too late, past his feet.

One nil to the Rovers.

The outpouring of excitement and joy, evident in the roar of the crowd, almost brings a tear to Earl's eye. But not quite. Lions players surround the referee in protest. They argue that it is illegal to kick the ball twice when taking a penalty. Waving them away, the referee screams back at them. The goalkeeper touched the ball when making the save; therefore, the penalty taker is allowed a second touch. The goal stands.

With the heady mix of emotion and altitude, Damo is no longer able to stand and sits on the grass watching hordes of villagers run onto the pitch to celebrate. It takes five minutes for the referee and players to persuade them to leave and allow the match to continue. Blowing his whistle once more, the referee restarts the game. Taking deep breaths, Damo slowly recovers and Mukasa crouches beside him.

"Well played Mister Damo. " says Mukasa, oblivious to the sceptical frowns on the faces of Earl and Boof who are standing behind him.

"No worries, but I'm sorry, I can't go back on. I'm done," replies Damo, apologetically.

Examining his watch, Mukasa then concentrates on the game, commenting that there is still twenty minutes left to play. He tells Damo that he has instructed the team to park the bus. Hearing that comment, Boof offers to do that for them and asks for the keys. With a loud guffaw, Mukasa thanks Boof and explains that 'parking the bus' is a football term, meaning that the whole team pack the defence.

Wave after wave of attacks from the Lions are met with a stiff determined resistance from the ten men of the Rovers, who are buoyed by the support of the crowd.

No further goals are scored, and the end of the game is drawing near.

"How much longer?" asks Earl.

"About two minutes," replies Mukasa, examining his watch.

Seconds later, a Lions attacker is clumsily tackled outside the penalty area and the referee blows for a foul.

"This is bad," mutters Mukasa, "their number ten is exceptionally good at free kicks. He's a legend in these parts. They give him the nickname, Lionel Messi."

"Messi? You mean the Argentinian soccer player?" asks Damo.

"Indeed, Mister Damo," replies Mukasa, who is now staring intently at Lutobo's star player as he places the ball. On the pitch there is a flurry of activity. Patiently waiting for the Rovers to set up a wall to the satisfaction of their goalkeeper, the referee then measures out ten paces to indicate where the wall must stand. Damo's teammates take three paces back to comply with the official's instruction. Hushed silence blankets the pitch. In the distance a goat, in the adjoining field, bleats.

"Jeez, those goats not only taste like sheep but sound like them," says Boof, who has not grasped the significance of the moment.

"Just shut the fuck up Boof," snaps Earl.

Blowing his whistle once more, the referee waves his hand, allowing play to recommence. The Lutobo player nods in acknowledgement, takes four quick steps and strikes the ball. At the same moment, the defenders all jump simultaneously to increase the height of the wall. Initially the trajectory of the ball looks goal bound heading for the far top corner of the goal. But the Lutobo player puts his hands to his head in despair when it glances off the top of the head of the tallest defender in the wall. The pitch is swamped by a cacophonous wave of sound from the crowd, who cheer when they see the ball balloon over the bar.

Hushed once more the anxious crowd waits for the corner to be taken. The ball flies across the face of the goal as defenders and attackers all leap, attempting to make contact. It is calmly plucked out of the air by the Rovers keeper. Immediately the referee blows for the final time and the crowd erupts. Villagers run onto the pitch and surround the players who are hugging each other with pure joy. Spotting a tear escape from Mukasa's watery eyes, Earl moves next to him and puts an arm round his shoulders.

Boof jumps to one side to avoid the swarm of players. They run directly towards Damo who is still sitting on the ground in stunned silence. Damo disappears under a pile of green shirts. Shouting angrily, Mukasa orders them to get off and, to his relief, Damo re-appears with a broad grin on his face.

Once things quieten down, Earl turns to Mukasa.

"That was good mate, but it was all a bit over the top for a friendly little game, wasn't it? You'd think they'd won a Grand Final."

"It was no Grand Final, Mister Earl, but it was the first time in the club's history that we have reached the semi-final of the Cup. This is a day to remember. The elders will talk about it for generations whether they win or lose the next game."

"What? I thought it was just a friendly local game between two villages."

"Not so Mister Earl. It was an official fixture for the UIFA Cup."

"What's that?"

"It stands for the Uganda Intercity Football and Athletics Cup. It is our national amateur competition."

"You're not serious? Bugger me, it's a good job Damo didn't know. He'd have crapped himself."

Laughing, Mukasa walks away to congratulate the players and join in the celebrations. Earl walks over towards Damo but one of the supporters runs in front of him to hug the hero of the hour. Nonplussed, Damo offers a handshake, but the supporter brushes past his outstretched hand and gives him another hug. When they separate, Earl explains the enormity and importance of the game to Damo, whilst the supporter watches on, nodding in agreement.

Tearful but with an earnest expression, the supporter

then speaks. "I am filled with immense joy. It's a great day for the village and we are privileged to have Mukasa as our coach."

"Yep, he seems to know his stuff," replies Earl.

"He's a legend here. Everybody in the village prayed to God in thanks when he agreed to become coach of Kikungiri Rovers. We were honoured. We're blessed."

"Honoured? Blessed?" asks Earl.

"Yes. Perhaps you do not know, but Mukasa himself was a talented player. In his youth he played for Busoga United in our Premier league. He even played two games for the mighty Cranes."

"Cranes?"

"Yes, Cranes. The Ugandan national bird. It's the name of our national team. It is because of him that our star player, Bale, came to play for us when he finished his own professional career. Please accept my gratitude. I will now leave you alone, but I wanted to thank you," says the supporter, patting Damo on the shoulder.

Once the crowd has dispersed, Mukasa gathers the players together, who sit on the ground in a semi-circle whilst he remains standing to address them. Before he speaks, he invites Damo, Boof and Earl to join them.

Beaming with joy, Mukasa starts his post-match speech. "You all played like Lions against the Lutobo Lions. I am so proud of you all."

Waving away polite applause, he continues. "You defended with courage, and it was your indomitable spirit that won the day against a team who were the favourites to win the Cup. Truly amazing."

More applause. "I also want to thank Mister Damo here," says Mukasa, pointing to the blushing Australian. "It was because of his skill that we won the penalty, which decided the result." More applause aimed at Damo, who gets several pats on the back from those near him. "So, now my team, go back to your families and I will see you all at training on Wednesday. But before you go, I have one more announcement. I have just spoken to Chief Masika, who called to enquire about the result. He asked me to tell you that he is proud of you all. What is more, he accepted my recommendation that Mister Damo is to be made a lifetime member of Kikungiri Rovers."

A final cheer goes up and the players line up in front of Damo. Each player gives Damo a hug, before they make their way home, victorious.

A FIESTY LITTLE WINE

WORK ON CONSTRUCTION of the training college starts in earnest the following Monday morning. Seymour introduces them to all the men in the team, from the supervising architect to the hod carrier. To Earl's relief, the technical aspects are being managed by the architect and the plans are clear and straightforward, revealing a simplistic build design. His own role is to be little more than a supervising foreman. Boof, who has not built anything beyond a Lego house when he was at kindergarten, takes on the role of Earl's assistant and general gopher.

Although Damo's skillset is more substantial than Boof's, his output on day one is far less because the construction team, and half the village, insist on meeting the newly crowned local hero. A steady stream of admirers approach Damo replaying highlights of the match in extended conversations. Most finish by taking a selfie with him. Having acquired the title of 'Lion Slayer', Damo wallows in the villagers' adoration. Outwardly, Earl feigns annoyance at Damo's failure to knuckle down to some hard work, but he is secretly pleased with how things have gone. Not only have they quickly got the trust of the villagers after the heroics on the football field, but they have adopted Damo as one of their own.

Able to bathe in reflected glory, Earl and Boof are also warmly accepted into the fold by the villagers. They are practically part of the furniture after just one weekend.

Pondering the events of the last few days, Earl concludes that this unexpected development will make their task easier. It will be a matter of keeping their heads down for a while. Avoiding close attention, they can covertly learn where the books are stored and plan how to get at them unobserved, without raising suspicion.

One major worry that was nagging within Earl's mind before they arrived in Kikungiri, was the presence of Seymour. His experience of Project Managers on site in Australia's outback is that they are, by nature, all-knowing and controlling, with eyes like a hawk. Not the attributes he wants around the place when they are trying to sneak off and extract several million dollars from a crate of books. It soon became clear that he need not have worried. All his initial fears dissolved the day before when they attended Seymour's impromptu briefing.

The previous day, they received word from Mukasa that Seymour would like to see them in his cabin. When they approached the American's home they found him outside on a small porch, beer in hand, reclining in a hammock. It was hung precariously between two wooden posts that did not look as though they could take the weight of a small child, let alone a ninety-kilogram muscle toned Texan.

Without bothering to get up, he told them to grab a beer, pointing lackadaisically to the chill box by the door. Lazily swinging in the hammock, he invited them to make themselves comfortable. There was only a small, two-seater cane couch on the porch, which Damo and Earl took, whilst Boof sat on the steps.

If Seymour had been any more relaxed, he would have been horizontal. In fact, he remained horizontal throughout their visit. Rumours of Damo's heroics had travelled at speed through the active village grapevine, and this clearly had pleased the Texan. It was clear to him that the Australians had already developed a good connection with the villagers, and this would make the job run more smoothly. From the stories already circulating, the Australians were enjoying legendary status. This had to be a good omen. Hearing Seymour's effusive assessment of their start was music to Earl's ears. From that point on, he felt confident that the Texan was unlikely to be an obstacle to their plans.

Dwelling on the positive start of his new team, Seymour surmised and hoped that the impact on the project would be positive. Enthused by the success of the soccer team, he hoped that the villagers would work at a faster pace. A pace closer to what he was more accustomed to in his own homeland. His previous experience on other jobs was that African time runs much slower than American time and this did not suit his current agenda.

Beneath the relaxed demeanour he portrayed, swinging lazily in the hammock, the American's underlying motivation became obvious during their conversation. He expressed his desire to expedite the construction. An absence of available surf was beginning to get to him. He was homesick, desperate to return to California to get into the water, push the tail and catch some big sea. Earl, Damo and Boof all nodded empathetically and assured him that they were also keen to progress the work quickly.

They all clinked their beer bottles with the Texan, who gave them a toast. "Good to be on the same page and here's to a quick build and getting back to the surf."

* * *

Much to their surprise, as they watch the villagers down tools and leave the building site on Friday, it occurs to them that their first week has flashed by in the blink of an eye. Hours on site had quickly passed each day as they became embroiled in the infectious enthusiasm of the local workers who sing, laugh and joke throughout each day. Always a smile on their faces and a willingness to please. More used to an atmosphere of robust banter and occasional obstructiveness when supervising Australians back home, Earl finds the attitude of the locals a breath of fresh air.

With lower expectations than Australian construction workers, the villagers are grateful for solid, well-paid employment. Their eagerness and willingness to please came as a surprise to Earl, particularly given the often challenging, primitive working conditions. Even when assigning the most arduous of tasks on a scorching day, Earl would be greeted with several smiles and eager nodding heads.

In his daily meeting with Seymour, Earl reports progress and praises the attitude of the workers. He learns from Seymour that the pay rates on American funded projects are astronomical compared to other jobs in the region. Paid work is hard to come by generally, and employment on USAID projects are like gold dust to the locals. They are good people, willing workers and determined not to do anything that would put their position at risk. When Damo asks about their wages, he is stunned at how meagre they are and shocked at the gulf compared to the level of pay back home.

Friday night is frothy night, and it is beer o'clock. After a quick clean up in their cabin, they wander to the only bar in the village. Tired after a long week, they decide that a quiet beer locally will suffice for their first Friday night in the village. All being well, they plan to explore the more extensive Kabale nightlife on Saturday. As it turns out, they get a better and unexpected offer.

A colourful hand-painted sign above the door welcomes them into the village bar. It has green lettering on a yellow background with a tall thin black bird at either end indicating they are about to enter 'The Happy Crane.' Negotiating their way around four unoccupied tables set up outside, they walk through the entrance into the bar. Once inside, they find that the 'Happy Crane' is far smaller than they expect, with only six more tables inside. A small wooden drinks counter occupies a corner of the room accompanied by a rickety high stool that stands at one end. Behind the counter a smiling host waits expectantly for their order. Across the room, three villagers stare at them from the only occupied table and, recognising Damo, they raise their bottles of beer and give him a muted cheer. Once he waves back in acknowledgement, the second cheer is much louder.

Damo's request for Nile Golds is answered with a shake of the head by the host, who explains that they only stock Bell lager. Ordering six bottles, Damo hands over two bundles of shillings, tightly wrapped in elastic bands. Each bundle supposedly contains ten thousand shillings, not that it would ever have been unwrapped and verified. He carries three bottles over to the men at the table who cheer once more in appreciation of his generosity. Gesturing to go outside, Earl leads Damo and Boof to a table.

"Didn't want to sit in there with the others," explains Earl, "need a little privacy."

"Twenty thousand shillings for six beers!" exclaims Boof, taking his first sip.

"Mate, that's not even ten dollars. Yer need to get your head round the local currency," replies Damo.

"Never mind worrying about the price of a beer, we've got bigger fish to fry. We've had a week here already and it's time to get serious about what we came for. I want to work out a plan," says Earl, in a slightly irritated tone.

"Okay, chill out mate," says Damo, leaning back into his chair.

"Mate, I don't want us to get too comfortable here. The longer we leave it, the greater the risk that the cash will be discovered. So just shut up and listen. I don't know about you two, but I don't want to spend the rest of my life in Uganda."

Both Boof and Damo give Earl a nod, encouraging him to speak.

"As I see it, we're nicely settled in, and they all seem to like and trust us."

"Yep, especially me," jokes Damo.

Ignoring him, Earl continues. "So, we now need to find out where the books are stored."

"No worries, I'll just ask one of the workers when we're back on site," offers Boof.

"We're not going to just fucking ask, you idiot," says Earl tapping his left temple. "We need to use our brains, which I know in your case is in short supply."

"Steady on Earl, yer need to calm down. Have another beer," says Damo.

"Mate, just shut up and let me think. But whilst I am, why don't you go and get us another beer," barks Earl, tossing over a bundle of ten thousand shillings to Boof. Staring across the street, Earl is deep in thought, so Damo decides to keep quiet until Boof returns.

"Here's yer beers. I'm a poet and I don't know it," says Boof.

Pointedly looking at Boof, Earl says, "Okay, listen up. I don't want either of you asking them about the books and certainly not bloody well asking people where they are kept. Leave it to me to find that out. Once we know, we can firm up on timing to get the money. We're gonna need to check it out first, make sure the cash is there and decide when it is best to take it."

"Why not just take it as soon as we find it?" asks Boof.

"Because we've nowhere to store it. We don't want it lying around in our cabin, do we? We just need to make sure it is there in the crate. Then, when we're ready, we grab it and run."

"Sounds good to me," says Damo.

"Oh, I forgot to mention, we have just under three weeks."

"Three weeks? How come?" asks Damo.

"Because whilst you were busy messing around on site chatting and taking selfies with everyone in the sodding village, I've been talking to our mate Seymour. He's arranged for us to have a break back up in Kampala at the end of the month. I think he just wants to keep us sweet and on board with the job. He's happy. No I take that back, he's not happy, he's ecstatic with the progress made in the short time we've been here."

"Good one," says Damo, already feeling a little homesick now that a timeline seems to have been set.

"So, we don't want to mess this up. That means no suspicious questions or interest in the books. You two just keep doing what you are doing."

"How are you gonna find out then," challenges Boof.

"Using my brain. I'll work something out."

"Could take a while then," jokes Damo, "you've only got three weeks."

"Yer right. It may take a while," replies Earl, ignoring the sarcasm.

"Right ho! But … we've got a bigger more immediate problem," announces Boof.

"Which is?" asks Earl.

"Food. I asked for a bowl of locusts to nibble on, but they don't serve them in this splendid establishment. And I don't know about you two but I'm bloody starving."

Pointing over his left shoulder with his thumb, Damo says, "Well you've got a choice of one eatery and it's part of the 'Crane' chain of establishments." Looking over Damo's shoulder, Boof and Earl see another sign which is identical in design to the one over the bar door except that the word 'Hungry' is painted on the sign instead of 'Happy'.

Unusually, Damo's reaction is the most positive when presented with the menu. One of the handful of dishes in the world he is willing to eat is on offer, sausages. Inevitably it comes with matoke, which he picks at, and unidentifiable greens which he pushes aside. When the waitress comes to clear the plates, Damo asks what was in the sausages and receives a short and direct response. "Meat". His erstwhile confidence in what he has eaten is shaken and he decides not to delve deeper for the sake of his digestion and gastronomic sanity.

Pointing to Damo's plate, the waitress says, in a challenging tone, "You do not like Sukuma Wiki?"

"Eh!" replies Damo, unused to being interrogated on his dietary habits by restaurant staff.

"These," she replies, pointing to the untouched greens. Not bothering to wait for an answer, she walks off huffily with the plates.

Making their way home they all decide on one thing. Where meals are concerned, they need to stick with Namona. Having sampled food at the 'Hungry Crane', they have a newfound respect and appreciation for her culinary skills.

They return to their cabin with slightly unsettled stomachs. Lying in their beds, sleep does not easily come, each wrestling with the growing queasy feeling in their bellies and gurgling intestines. An hour later, their feelings are replaced with a very physical manifestation and Damo leads a parade to the toilet. Drifting into sleep after his third visit, Damo's last words float into Earl's consciousness before he visits the sanctuary of dream land.

"I hope to God it doesn't take you too long to find out where those books are stored. My stomach can't take much more of this."

The stars align and Damo gets his wish the following day.

* * *

Having spent the morning in bed, with occasional trips to the toilet, the three men slowly turn the corner on the path to recovery. Which is just as well given the news that Seymour brings.

Having knocked on the cabin door, Seymour tentatively opens it after failing to elicit a response from within. He pokes his head into the room and surveys the damage. Although the cabin smells as though someone had poured the contents of the local latrine into it, the inhabitants have all progressed from a deathly pallor to a mildly healthier, if not entirely normal, glow.

"You guys look as though you've all had a big night," shouts Seymour, unconsciously sniffing the air.

Pulling on his shorts, Earl says, "It's not what you think mate. We only had a couple of beers but dinner at the 'Hungry Crane' didn't agree with us."

Laughing, Seymour replies, "Lesson learnt gentlemen. You stray from Namona's cuisine at your own risk. Talking of dinner, you've been invited out this evening." Switching his native Texan accent to a passable impression of a

New York Italian gangster, he adds, "And it's an offer you can't refuse."

"Oh yes we can mate, especially if it's at the 'Hungry Crane.' And that's for certain," replies Damo.

"I don't think a refusal would go down well with Chief Masika. He's back down from Kampala and wants to see you. Don't worry, with one or two caveats, the food and drink at the Chief's place will be good."

"Caveats?" asks Earl, suspiciously.

"Just a couple, nothing to worry about."

"Well, I guess we'll see you later then."

"Good, that's settled. Mukasa will pick you up at around five. It's not far but, by the looks of you three, you'd appreciate a lift," says Seymour cheerily and leaves, closing the door behind him.

* * *

Five minutes early, Mukasa waits outside the cabin, sitting in his Hilux. Having seen him arrive through the cabin window, the three men trudge out in single file and climb into the car giving Mukasa a muted 'hello'.

Partially refreshed from an afternoon nap, they are all over the worst but not particularly relishing the idea of more beer and food.

"Did you gentlemen have a long night?" asks Mukasa.

"Not really, but we went to the Hungry Crane," replies Damo.

"Oh!" says Mukasa. His momentary silence is, like the proverbial picture, worth a thousand words. "Perhaps it's best you stick with Namona."

Assuring his sickly passengers that their journey will be short, Mukasa sets off and less than a kilometre down the road turns into a private compound through a white stone arched gateway. Kicking up red dust from the driveway, the Hilux progresses toward Masika's residence which is partly obstructed from their view by an acacia tree. Once they negotiate a bend, the full magnificence of the building can be appreciated. It is a picture of colonial splendour. The expansive single level white building has a large veranda which spans its whole frontage. In the middle, a small group of people stand conversing and laughing. They each hold a glass of champagne in their hand and a waitress circles them offering a tray of canapes. Each guest examines the tray, selects a piece, and pops it into their mouth, before resuming their animated conversation.

Slowing the car as he nears the house, to avoid kicking up dust over the guests on the veranda, Mukasa gradually brings the vehicle to a halt allowing his passengers to get out.

Climbing the stairs up to the verandah, they are greeted at the top by Chief Masika. "Welcome gentlemen, so nice to see you again. Come. Follow me and I will introduce you to my other guests."

Introductions are made and many hands are shaken. Damo and Earl immediately engage in small talk after taking a glass of champagne from the tray on the table. Distracted, Boof instantly forgets all the names of the guests he has just been introduced to and focuses on the food offered by the waitress. He helps himself to a handful of canapes, prompting her to return to the kitchen to replenish the empty tray.

Drawing the men to one side, Masika tries to make a final introduction to the guest of honour, but the Chief's attempt is preempted. Addressing them in a booming baritone voice which oozes an English private education, the guest says, "Welcome to Uganda gentlemen. I trust you have settled in. My name is Oswald Digby-Jones."

With a vigorous handshake, he gives each of them a beaming smile as they introduce themselves. They try to get the measure of the very tall, bear-like man, in his fifties. His expanding paunch, which hangs over the belt of his khaki chinos, fills his crisp white shirt. Receding at the temples, his blond hair is swept back into a widow's peak and his blue eyes twinkle, mischievously.

"Now gentlemen. Forgive me, but it has become a tradition here that newcomers must sample my homemade wine," says Digby-Jones, gesturing for the waitress to bring a bottle sitting on a nearby table. She carries it over and pours three generous helpings. Boof, who is served first, takes a hearty swig of the deep red beverage. To Earl and Damo's horror, Boof turns away and spits it over the verandah balcony, spraying the lawn below. Masika, and his guests who watch the exchange expectantly, burst out laughing whilst Boof coughs, splutters, and attempts to clear his throat. Holding a glass of water that she had ready, the waitress offers it to Boof who snatches it from her and drains it in one gulp. Digby-Jones's complexion turns purple with suppressed jocularity until he can no longer contain himself and his bulky frame reverberates with laughter.

Earl and Damo place their glasses, untouched, on a nearby table. Masika, explains what has transpired. "I am terribly sorry gentlemen, but this has become a bit of a tradition here, whereby all newcomers to our little community are put to the test. Mister Boof here has just sampled Oswald's much celebrated home-made wine, which is distilled from chilli peppers."

"Did he pass?" asks Damo, smirking at Boof who was still recovering from the shock.

"I'm afraid not," interjects Digby-Jones, who had managed to regain his composure. "Only one person has ever passed the test. His name is Advik Chopra, the Indian ambassador who hails from Andra Pradesh. It's the region that prepares the hottest curries in the country. I must say that not only did he have a second glass, but he had the impudence to ask to take a bottle of my plonk home." Once more Digby-Jones bursts into uncontrolled laughter.

"Now give the poor man a cold beer," says Masika, to the waitress nearby. Patting the Digby-Jones on the back, Masika addresses the group. "You must forgive me, gentlemen, for indulging Oswald, but he is an important and generous man. He owns several farms and is a great supporter of the village. In addition, of course, to being an amateur vintner."

"A what?" interrupts Damo.

"A winemaker," explains Digby-Jones.

"He is patron of the project you are working on," explains Masika.

"I thought the yanks funded it," says Earl.

"Not all of it. To get these projects funded and across the line, they expect to see some sort of local financial commitment. It proves to them that we are genuinely committed rather than just going for a money grab. Oswald here," says Masika, putting his hand on the Englishman's shoulder, "provides his land and the Ugandan Government also put in a small financial contribution."

"It was nothing," purrs Digby-Jones, modestly, "it was good to put that old plot to some use."

Proceedings at the party remain informal and the three friends have an unexpectedly pleasant evening having recovered from the previous night. The beers prove to be the hair of the dog. Guests help themselves at the buffet, which is laid out enticingly, and take their plates onto the verandah to sit at one of the tables set up for dinner. It was the best food they had eaten since entering

Uganda. Ghostlike, the waitress unobtrusively floats in the background plying drinks. At the end of the evening, when the last of the other guests are waved off, Masika invites them to stay for a nightcap before Mukasa takes them home.

Sitting around a dinner table, which had been cleared of plates, the three friends enjoy the cool night air accompanied by Masika, Digby-Jones and Mukasa. The waitress appears with a tray of generously filled brandy glasses and places one in front of each man at the table.

"I take it that this isn't chilli brandy," says Earl, only half-jokingly.

"I assure you it isn't," laughs Digby-Jones, who takes a sip from his glass to prove it.

"I think a toast is in order, well two toasts." Masika raises his glass towards Damo. "To the Lion Slayer of Kikungiri. Mukasa, here, gave me a full match report and you're now a legend in the village and beyond." Damo smiles with strained modesty, avoiding eye contact and what he knows will be a cynical glance from Earl. They drink, and the second toast is made to the success of the project.

"I just want to thank you Chief," says Earl. "You've been very hospitable."

They make small talk whilst they finish their brandy, allowing Earl to ask a question which he had been itching to ask all evening. "Chief, I noticed on the way to your lovely home, that there are three sheds on the side of your drive, near your gate. Is that where you store the schoolbooks you were telling us about when we met in Kampala?"

"Very observant Mister Earl, you're very astute. Why do you ask?""

"No reason really. I guess I was just thinking ahead, for when the college is built. Can't teach without books, can you?"

"No Mister Earl, I suppose you can't," replies Masika, with a raised eyebrow.

Noticing that the silences between the small talk were becoming progressively longer, Masika brings the evening to a close. "Once more. I want to thank you. I can see you are all looking tired, so Mukasa will take you back to your cabin."

"Thank you," says Damo.

"Thank you," echoes Boof.

Watching them from the verandah, Masika shouts a final goodbye. Focusing on Earl climbing into the Hilux, his eyes narrow slightly.

PHOBIAS

TEN DAYS HAVE passed, and they are on a mission under cover of darkness.

It is not the best laid plan and each of them is in their own personal living hell.

Scrambling through the claustrophobic blackness of dense bushland is making Earl increasingly anxious as the minutes pass. He is rapidly regretting his insistence that they approach their target under cover of the bush, rather than using the main dirt road. Concerned that the more direct approach would draw the attention of villagers or, as they drew closer, anyone in Masika's house, he had brushed away the protests of Damo and Boof. Now the complaints are coming thick and fast, not least from Earl himself, as he comes to the realisation that the moonlight fails to penetrate the tree canopy.

Through the impenetrable darkness, a slapping noise is heard. "What was that?" whispers, Earl, slightly unnerved.

"It's me, I'm being eaten alive by mosquitoes. I hate mosquitoes, but they love me," moans Boof, now scratching his arm vigorously.

"Shit!"

"What's yer problem?" whispers Boof, to Earl.

"There's no streetlights."

"Yeah mate, we're not in Sydney, it's darkest Africa, and it's the bloody jungle. Whaddya expect?" asks Boof.

With no response from Earl, Damo explains.

"I've told you before Boof, our Earl is frightened of the dark. It's his kryptonite."

"Piss off Damo," snaps Earl.

"Earl, if yer afraid of the dark, why don't you switch on yer torch?" asks Boof.

"Because, you idiot, I don't want us to be seen," replies Earl, pointing to Masika's residence through a gap in the trees. "I'll use it when we get inside those sheds. There aren't any windows, so once we're in, our lights can't be seen from the house."

Rustling on the ground nearby causes Damo to jump and yelp. "What's that?" asks Damo, with panic evident in his voice.

"Ha! Looks like the resident smartarse now has a problem. It's probably just a snake," suggests Earl, mischievously taking an opportunity to get his revenge. "Not sounding so brave now, are you?"

"You wanker, you know I hate snakes," complains Damo, edging away from the source of the noise.

With mutual relief, they all break through the perimeter of bushland and creep up the edge of the driveway towards the sheds. Despite the increased risk of being spotted, they welcome the respite from the horrors of the bush. Security lights at the side of the house provide sufficient ambient light to allay Earl's fear of the dark. For Damo, there is no undergrowth for snakes to rustle through, just the red dirt of the driveway. Even the mosquitoes refuse to venture beyond the lush vegetation, to the relief of Boof who still scratches furiously but no longer needs to slap away new attackers.

They seek cover by crawling behind the nearest shed. Peeping around the side, Earl studies the house. Although the veranda is unoccupied, there is a light on in the living room. No-one can be seen through the window.

His frown turns to a grin, when the door handle of the shed turns freely and the unlocked door opens. Giving the thumbs up to the others, Earl leads them inside. Once the door is closed behind them, the gloom is vanquished by Earl's torch.

Examining the wooden crate, Damo is surprised, and pleased, to find it intact. "Can't believe it," he whispers, "they haven't even opened it to check the books."

"Books. Good point Damo," replies Earl. "We'd better check that it contains books. It might not be a book crate."

Using a crowbar borrowed from the construction site, Earl jimmies open the wooden lid then uses his hands to pull it gently free of the nails. Another smile slowly grows across his face. He can see books through the clear industrial vacuum wrapping. 'Basic primary level mathematics' is printed along the spines.

"Is this the crate?" asks Boof, with urgency and excitement in his voice.

"Dunno yet," replies Earl, sweeping the beam of his torch around the crate until he finds the customs manifest document taped to its side. Squinting as he reads the cover, he shakes his head. "No, this is dated from over three years ago."

They check the other two crates in the shed and it becomes clear that they were both dropped at the same time as the first one they had checked. With the assistance of Damo, Earl places the lid back to its original position on the opened crate. It is not perfect, but unless it is subjected to a careful examination, no one will notice. Judging by the dust and cobwebs, nobody had been inside the shed for months, if not years.

Edging out of the first shed, Boof is last out and carefully closes the door to avoid making a sound. In the second shed, which contains three more crates, the search is much quicker. Now confident that the crates in the sheds do contain books, Earl checks the manifest on each. Expectant looks from Damo and Boof are met with a shake of the head. He tells them that the crates were delivered just over a year ago. So far they have drawn a blank.

Once inside the last shed, Earl takes a deep breath, and switches on his torch with a mixture of hope and trepidation. It is 'make or break' time. This time they see that the shed contains only one solitary crate. Fearful of disappointment, Earl approaches it reticently. Shining his torch on the manifest, he squints, re-reads it, and then stands motionless.

"What?" asks Damo, desperately.

"Come on Earl, what does it say?" asks Boof, getting increasingly nervous.

Turning to face them, they see the familiar gap in his teeth as he grins. Immediately they know that the news is good.

"Fuck me!" exclaims Boof.

"Jesus," says Damo.

"It's a bloody ripper," says Earl, pumping his fist.

They jump around and fist pump, releasing muted squeals of joy. Gesturing for them to calm down, Earl's expression turns serious.

"What's wrong?" asks Damo.

"Nothing yet mate, we know all the crates have books, but we don't know about the cash. We need to check the middle."

Immediately their mood sobers, and they look on anxiously whilst Earl jimmies off the lid. He shines his torch onto the clear wrapping and reads the spine of the books.

"Whaddya see?" asks Boof.

"At the moment the only thing I can see is 'Introduction to Economics.' Pass me your knife, I need to cut through the plastic so I can look underneath the books."

Once Earl has climbed on top of the crate, Boof hands him the knife. He carefully slices through the plastic until he has a big enough opening to allow him to remove the books. He grabs a few and passes them down. Gradually the pile of books that Boof sets aside increases, as does Damo's concern that they have hit another blank.

Slowly passing down yet another handful of books, Earl pauses, whilst Boof puts them aside on the pile. Torch in hand, Earl shines it into the opening he has created.

"What do you see?" asks Damo, with butterflies in his stomach.

"Yeah, Earl, whaddya see?" asks Boof, feeling nauseous with nerves.

"I can see some old bloke with a moustache."

"What?" asks Damo.

Lowering his head further into the hole he created, Earl gets a closer look. "Yep, it's an old bloke with a moustache and a picture of soldiers behind a cannon. And it says his name is John Monash."

"What the hell are you talking about?" asks Boof.

"Yep. And next to him there is a number. Hang on the number iiiissss … one hundred," chuckles Earl.

"You've gotta be kidding me!" exclaims Damo.

"What?" asks Boof.

"It's a one hundred dollar note you idiot. Earl's found the money."

Immediately Earl jumps down, they form a huddle and dance around in a circle, kicking up dust in the shed. Hot, sweaty, and exhausted, they collapse onto the floor, overcome with emotion.

Once they have calmed down, Earl sits up and puts on

his game face. "Right, first things first. We know where the cash is, so we can sort out what we need to do and when we collect it."

"Collect it? Why don't we take it now?" asks Boof.

"Because mate, we don't have any transport and we don't have anywhere to hide it. I have already explained to you, at length. You're the expert on the weight of money. What is the weight of a few million dollars?"

It's about ten kilos per million."

There you go, we can't lug that around the village. Can we? Tonight is just a scouting mission to see what we find."

"Well we found it, didn't we? Can't we take a little bit?

Exasperated, Earl says, "No mate. If anyone checks the crate and finds a bit of a dip in the middle, they're gonna get suspicious, aren't they? Anyway, what the hell are you going to do with it whilst we're in the village."

"Well, I …"

"Well I, nothing mate. It's a 'no'. We stick to the plan. We've got time off and an all-expenses paid trip back to Kampala in less than two weeks. By the time they discover we're no longer in Uganda, you'll be sucking tinnies on Bondi beach. That's the ideal time to get out of here and, to be honest, the cash is safest if we leave it right here for the time being."

"Yeah, but what if they insist Mukasa drives us? Ain't he gonna notice a few million in the back of the car," replies Boof, sarcastically.

"We'll tell them that we want to hire a vehicle and do a bit of exploring on our own. To be honest, I wouldn't be surprised if they lend us a project vehicle."

Becoming increasingly exasperated, Damo is keen to get them on the move. "Earl's right Boof, so let's just do what we planned. It's been a successful night. We should be celebrating, not arguing. I vote we go for last orders at the 'Happy Crane' for a quiet celebration."

Carefully replacing the books and repositioning the lid, Earl climbs down. Conscious of noise, but not wanting to leave any indication that the crate had been tampered with, he carefully straightens the bent nails and hammers them gently back into the crate using his crowbar.

Once more they brave the dark, snakes and mosquitoes but, this time, in a far happier mood and a much more positive state of mind. The trip back to the village seems much quicker.

Sitting outside the 'Happy Crane' with their beers, they joke and banter, not quite believing that their bizarre escapade is coming to fruition. They do not notice Masika approach them until his deep voice greets them from behind.

"Hello gentlemen. I hope you've had a good evening."

Startled, Boof knocks his beer bottle, but Damo catches it before it spills. Brushing a little liquid off his shorts, Boof thanks Damo.

"We have Chief," replies Earl, "would you like to join us? Let me get you a beer."

'Oh, no thank you. I called in at your cabin, but you weren't there and then I came to the village earlier in the evening, but still couldn't find you. I was a little concerned. Not to worry, here you are now, safe and sound."

"Yeah, sorry Chief, we weren't expecting you or we'd have waited in. We just went for a stroll."

With a smile that seems to hint that he knows more than he is saying, Masika replies, "I hope you enjoyed your walk, but you must be careful. This can be a dangerous place, especially for mzungus. There're robbers and poachers here, you know."

"Really,' says Damo, "I've found the villagers very friendly and welcoming."

"They are Mister Damo. But the Rwandans, Somalians and Congolese are less welcoming, and they're armed. You could be shot."

Despite the messaging of the words spoken by the Chief, Earl could not shake the feeling that the tone was almost threatening rather than one of concern. Probably just his imagination.

"Thank you Chief, we'll take care. But what was it you wanted to talk to us about?"

"Sorry?"

"You said you were looking for us. That you called by the cabin and then the village," explains Earl.

"Did I? Oh yes. Nothing much really, just wanted to catch up and see how you were. I can see the construction is progressing rapidly and I wanted to make sure you've everything you need." Staring at the face and arms of Boof, the Chief gives a sympathetic tut. "Dear me, Mister Boof, look at those lumps on your face. You're badly bitten. Anybody would think you've been tramping through the bushland."

"Mosquitoes. They love me," replies Boof.

"Indeed," says Masika non-committedly. "In fact, you all look as though you've been tramping through the bush," he adds, plucking a small piece of barbed vegetation off Damo's shoulder.

"I appreciate your concern Chief, but we're doing fine."

"Yes, well, have a good evening gentleman. I'll jump in my car and go home, it's late. As I say, please be careful on your way back to your cabin."

With a final wave through the window of his Mercedes, Masika drives away.

"What the hell was that all about?" asks Damo.

"Probably nothing much. Just keeping an eye on his flock, I guess," replies Earl, with a frown.

"You don't think he suspects, do you?" asks Boof.

"I doubt it. But it's a good reminder that we can't be too complacent. Best not to be taken in by the smiles of this lot. They're a lot smarter than you think."

"True Earl," replies Damo. "It's a bit of a wakeup call. But, if we keep our heads down, we shouldn't have any trouble. No-one suspects and everyone is friendly."

"Yeah, there's no sign of trouble. Nothing to worry about," agrees Boof.

No sign of trouble. How wrong they were.

A LITTLE RESPECT GOES A LONG WAY

TROUBLE IS COMING and it is travelling at breakneck speed; around nine hundred kilometres per hour, reclining in the comfort of business class. The expense is of no concern, but the travel arrangements are a matter of necessity. Ahmet will not fit into an economy class seat. In the fourteen-hour leg from Sydney to Dubai, Kemal and Ahmet barely exchanged a word. They have entirely different and opposing perspectives regarding their forced partnership.

Kemal considers Ahmet to be his uncle's mindless pet gorilla. Just brainless muscle. Physically strong but psychologically weak. Every time he leans over to sneak a peek at Ahmet's screen, there is either a nature documentary or some old kids film. *What kind of adult watches ET?* he wonders. With disdain Kemal settles back to continue watching his 'John Wick' box set. In between meals and sleep, he has managed to see the first three films in the franchise and can see a lot of similarities between the titular character and himself.

The disrespect is mutual. Hakan's enforcer has no respect for his boss's nephew, judging the young hot head as weak, entitled, and stupid. Worse still, a bully and a coward.

With a brief stopover in Dubai, the relatively short five-hour flight to Nairobi passes quickly. Having negotiated their way through passport control and customs, they are ushered into a black Toyota Landcruiser and driven to an exclusive suburb, Muthaiga. Two guards nod in recognition of the driver who slows the car so they can check out the passengers. Large, automatic wrought iron Gates swing open giving access to the compound, where a colonial style mansion sweeps into view.

They are ushered into an ante room and told to wait. Twenty minutes later they are escorted into the main living area where a well-groomed man in his forties, wearing an Armani suit, is speaking animatedly on a mobile phone. He ends the call as Ahmet and Kemal take their seats opposite him. Introducing himself as Mugo, he offers them a drink, which they both accept. Their escort leaves to fetch the drinks, leaving Mugo, who starts to read a message on his phone, alone with Ahmet and Kemal.

No niceties are exchanged by the host, not even an enquiry about their flight. Once the lemonades are placed in the hands of the two guests, Mugo finishes messaging and places his mobile phone on a side table before getting straight down to business.

"Mister Muchai has spoken with my employer, Mister Gitau, who had agreed to assist you during your time in Uganda. Unexpectedly, he has been called away on urgent business in Dar es Salaam. However, I am authorised to assist you and have instructions from Mister Gitau."

Affronted by the long wait and the perceived snub of Gitau's absence, Kemal pointedly asks Mugo about his status in Gitau's organisation. Inwardly wincing, Ahmet tries to gauge the reaction of Mugo, but his host's eyes give nothing away.

"Ah, I assume looking at your young smooth skin, you must be Hakan's child. For your information, although I live in Nairobi I am Ugandan, not Kenyan, as is Mister Gitau. We are Mister Muchai's partners. We do not work for Mister Muchai, we work with him. It is only as a favour to him, that Mister Gitau agreed to deal with the likes of you."

Seething, Kemal edges forward on his seat to respond, but pulls back when Ahmet puts a hand on his shoulder. This elicits a slight smile from Mugo, enjoying the fact that he easily got a rise out of Kemal.

Grinning, he leans forward in his seat and looks directly into Kemal's eyes. "Let me answer your question. My role is in my name. Mugo means a 'healer'. So you see, young man, my role is to mend things that are broken. To heal any injury to Mister Gitau's, or in this case Mister Muchai's, interests. Recent dealings with your uncle have been financially damaging and therefore Mister Muchai seeks redress and we have been asked to assist. The wounds must be healed so to speak. Your presence here is part of that healing process and I have been given the responsibility to ensure that the outcome of your visit meets the requirements of Mister Muchai. I hope that clarifies."

Rarely did Ahmet presume to speak at meetings of this nature. This occasion merited his intervention to try to recover some lost ground and respect.

"I would like to convey our respect and thanks, Mister Mugo, and we too have been instructed to assist in rectifying the problem. I understand you have information and contacts to help us in this task."

"I do and to ease your journey we have booked you into the Nairobi Serena Hotel for one night and on a flight to Kampala tomorrow afternoon. Now, before you are taken to the hotel, let me brief you."

* * *

Wisdom and common sense prevail following Ahmet's unwelcome counsel. Kemal spends a quiet night in the hotel instead of following through with his original intention to find a good nightclub, a drug dealer, and a prostitute to make the most of his brief stay in Kenya. Sitting at the hotel bar with a beer, before retiring to bed, they discuss the briefing. It is the most words they have exchanged in one sitting since leaving Sydney.

"How long do you think we will be in this shithole?"

"It depends," replies Ahmet.

"On what?" asks Kemal.

"On the accuracy of the information given to us by Muchai. And, equally as important, your attitude."

Bristling, Kemal snaps back, "What do you mean?"

Before responding, Ahmet takes a long drink from his glass and slowly puts it back down on the counter, before looking directly into Kemal's eyes. "Things will go smoother if you refrain from calling the places we go to 'shitholes'. We need cooperation not antagonism. I've no less desire than you to do whatever it is we need to do as quickly as possible and return home."

"But Mugo was disrespectful, I wanted to punch the shit out of him."

"The likes of Mugo and Gitau are not to be messed with if you want to get home in one piece. Besides, your uncle won't be happy if relations with our African partners are damaged unnecessarily."

"Well, I'll bow to your wisdom, old man," says Kemal, snidely. "So, what's the plan?"

Ignoring the jibe, Ahmet responds evenly. "Once we land in Kampala, we'll meet with Mugo's contact, and we'll get what we need."

"What, the guns?"

"Yes, and a car. I don't want to waste any time, so we'll

drive directly to Kabale. Let's hope Muchai's contact is well informed, and the books were dropped in that area."

"Do you think Mugo's men know where we are going and can be trusted. What's to stop them going there and taking the money themselves?"

"Even Muchai doesn't trust the Ugandans. Muchai told your uncle that he instructed his men to put them off the trail. They purposely went to Kasese to direct their attention away from Kabale, knowing the Ugandans would have eyes on them wherever they went. Mugo is obviously a smart man but, thanks to Muchai's cunning, I assume that they don't know where and precisely what we are looking for."

"It'll be good to get the guns and sort matters out."

"The guns are precautionary. We are in unknown territory; we need to approach this with subtlety. Our reputation holds no weight here and life is cheap, so we must tread carefully. Aside from the threat of Mugo's men, there are rebels, poachers and many others who will not hesitate to deal lethally with anyone who opposes them."

Draining his glass, Kemal gets off his stool. "I'm tired and going to bed."

"Good idea," replies Ahmet, "and, Kemal."

"Yes."

"I will take the lead from now on."

With an expression that falls between a smile and a sneer, Kemal leaves without acknowledging Ahmet's statement. Ordering a nightcap, Ahmet ponders the future. He did not normally get feelings about future events. He just did what was required, pushed it from his mind and then moved on to the next task given to him by Hakan. It did not pay to overthink issues in his line of work. That said, he had a bad feeling in his bones about this one.

With long haul flights behind them, Ahmet welcomes the short hop between Nairobi and Kampala. A bonus for Ahmet is that his companion is sullen and moody after their discussion last night, thus avoiding the need to make conversation.

Passing through the arrival barrier, they are greeted by a tall, skinny, nervous looking Ugandan in a cheap, ill-fitting suit. Pleasantries are cursorily exchanged as they are led to his car and driven to a small unassuming house in the outer suburbs of the city. Their new host clearly wants to conduct his business as quickly as possible and wave goodbye to his visitors. The briefing is short and to the point, before he leads them outside to a battered, old white Mitsubishi Pajero, at the rear of the house. They learn very little additional information from this contact: other than how to get onto the main road to travel west; the location of the handguns, which were in the glove box; and where to drop off the vehicle when they return.

Having insisted on driving, Kemal snatches the key fob from the hand of the Ugandan and jumps into the driver's seat. Hauling his heavy frame into the passenger seat, Ahmet is happy to let Kemal have his way. Give the kid small victories and keep him happy as well as occupied. With a rev of the engine, the car jolts forward but Ahmet puts his muscular arm across Kemals chest, indicating he wants him to stop. Looking into the rear-view mirror, Ahmet sees the Ugandan waving and running towards them. Ahmet opens his window allowing the now breathless Ugandan to give him a box. It contains ammunition for their guns.

"Fucking morons, let's hope it's the right bullets. We're lucky he didn't give us a fucking spear instead," snarls

Kemal, as he accelerates away from the Ugandan, who gives a halfhearted wave.

"What did I tell you about respect? Are you clear where you are going?

"Yes, we need to be on the road to Masaka," replies Kemal, pointing at a road sign.

"Good, and keep the racist shit to yourself."

Drawing breath to respond, Kemal is prevented from speaking when Ahmet holds up his hand. His mobile is ringing. The conversation is largely one way, with Ahmet saying three short phases. "No, I don't think they do"; "it's not us" and "I understand." Intrigued, Kemal asks who called.

"Muchai wants to make sure we've got what we need. He also wants to know if we thought that the Ugandans suspect where we're going. Also, it's probably nothing, but he's been told that there are some other Australians that have already arrived at the location we're travelling to."

"Where, Kabale?"

"Yes. Apparently, there is some confusion. When his contact learnt this, he wondered if it was us and we were already there. And, if so, he wanted to know why we hadn't been in contact with them. It's all cleared up now." A frown on Ahmets forehead reveals his uncertainty, which Kemal verbalises.

"It's a bit of a coincidence that there're other Australians there. Even suspicious. I reckon we need to get down there pronto and sort it out," says Kemal. He picks up his handgun from the central console and waves it towards Ahmet, to indicate his intention.

Scratching his ear worriedly, Ahmet realises that this is a rare occasion where he and Kemal agree. "It could be just a coincidence, but you're right. Best we get down there quickly, to make sure."

Kemal replaces his handgun on the console, stares at the road ahead and sets his jaw. A heavy foot rests on the accelerator.

BAMBI BOTH DEAD AND ALIVE

AT THE PRECISE moment Ahmet and Kemal leave the outskirts of Kampala, Damo wakes up in his cabin four hundred kilometres away. Yawning and stretching, he walks to the door to let in some fresh air. Sharing a space with Earl and Boof usually means that the morning atmosphere in the room is a little funky. Swinging open the door with gusto, he looks out, shouts 'what the fuck' and immediately slams the door shut, which wakes up Earl and Boof.

"Jesus Damo, you bloody idiot, I was asleep," moans Earl, rubbing his eyes.

"Yeah, what's going on?" asks Boof, sitting up.

"There's no way I'm going out there. It's a bloody monster."

"What the hell are you on about? A monster?" asks Earl, as he pushes past Damo and grabs the door handle.

"Well not a monster, but a sort of deer."

"What? A deer … as in Bambi? For god's sake Damo, get a grip. Whaddya expect, we're in bloody Afri—" Earl stops in mid-sentence once he opens the door.

Staring back at him is a large, spiral horned, reddish-brown beast, measuring almost six feet at the shoulders. A loose flap of skin hangs from its neck to its chest which swings as it turns to face him. Its head towers above Earl, who looks up to make eye contact. Holding Earl's gaze, with large brown eyes, it chews disinterestedly whilst nonchalantly flicking flies away with its pointed ears. Earl slams the door shut.

"Fuck me, that's one hell of a deer," says Earl.

"How are we gonna get out," moans Damo. "It's blocking the door and I'm not asking it to move."

"Me neither," says Boof.

Outside they can hear Seymour shouting "shoo, shoo", which prompts a reluctant clicking of hooves away from the cabin door. After knocking, the American opens the door and pushes his head through the gap. He gives them a smile and says 'hi'.

"Jeez, Seymour, that is one big motherfucker of a deer," says Damo, mimicking an American accent.

"Actually, it's an antelope. Perfectly harmless, well mostly harmless. It's an Eland. They're the largest breed of antelope in the world. They feed in the morning and evening when it's cool. Your new friend at the door is almost one of the family. The boys on the construction team have named him Sanyu. It means 'happiness'. He comes to visit every so often."

"Why?"

"Not sure really. I guess he's become quite domesticated and likes the company of humans. Apparently some of them can be a bit bad tempered if you invade their space. Sanyu probably popped in to beg for food," jokes Seymour. "Speaking of which, I came over to invite you to my place for breakfast if you've not already eaten. I'll give you a lift."

Having taken up Seymour's offer, they sit round the table in his cabin eating scrambled eggs and sausages. Watching Boof eat his second helping with gusto, Seymour raises his eyebrow and comments, "Wow Boof, for a skinny little fella, you can sure pack away the chow."

"Cheers mate, it's bloody good tucker," replies Boof, through a mouthful of sausage. "They're really tasty, what's in them?"

"Not wishing to upset you Boof, but one of Sanyu's relatives. Antelope is extremely popular here and in good supply."

Unmoved and undeterred by the revelation, Boof clears his plate. In contrast, Damo puts his knife and fork down. Preferring his sausages to contain beef or, at a push, pork, Damo looks warily at the remnants of his breakfast. Subconsciously, he rubs his stomach. *Bloody hell, I've just eaten Bambi*, he thinks.

Replenishing everyone's coffee, Seymour joins them at the table, his broad smile showcasing his perfectly capped teeth. His facial expression radiates positivity, indicating that he is the bearer of good news.

"Christmas has come early for you gentlemen. There is a public holiday coming up and Chief Masika decreed that the villagers working on the project should have a long weekend with a couple of extra days. He has never seen them work so hard and fast, so he wants to reward them. And you three, for that matter. He thinks your presence here has been incredibly positive."

"What's the holiday?" asks Earl, struggling to think of holidays in Australia around this time.

"Independence Day."

"Independence from what?"

Smiling, Seymour says, "From one thing we Americans have in common with the Ugandans."

"Sorry, you've lost me. What do the Americans have in common with Ugandans?" asks Earl.

"Independence from British rule. They achieved it in the early nineteen sixties I think."

"Bloody POMs," says Damo.

Seeing the look of confusion on Seymour's face, Earl explains that POMs are the English.

"But I don't understand. Why do you call them POMs?" asks Seymour.

"Not sure why we call 'em that. They're just POMs. Pale, whinging POMs," replies Damo.

Momentarily nonplussed, Seymour stares at Damo but quickly regains his train of thought.

"Anyway, setting our language barrier aside, the bottom line is that with Independence Day plus the weekend and two extra days offered by the Chief, then it would be a suitable time for you to take your break in Kampala. It'll mean taking it a little earlier than planned."

"Sounds good," says Earl. When is Independence Day?"

"In four days. Next Friday. I suggest you travel on that day, have four nights in Kampala and you can come back refreshed and ready to kick on. How does that sound?"

"Sounds a ripper," says Boof, giving the others a knowing glance. They were all thinking the same thing. They could bring their plan forward and be back home in just over a week.

"Good. I'm sure Mukasa will be happy to take you."

"Err, no mate, I don't think so," says Earl.

"What do you mean?" asks Seymour, a confused frown wrinkling his tanned forehead.

"He's done a lot for us, and we don't want to impose and drag him away from his family. He seems to spend a lot of time apart from them. We'd prefer to either borrow one of the project vehicles or, if not, we can hire one."

"Sure, no problem. That's very decent of you Earl. You're a good man and you're right. His job does require a lot of time away. So, he'll appreciate the thought."

After being dropped back by Seymour, they discuss their plan freely in the privacy of their cabin.

"That's a bloody result," says Damo.

"Yeah, and good thinking about refusing his offer of Mukasa ferrying us around. It could have got awkward trying to hide a pile of money," says Boof.

"Not to mention trying to scoot off to the airport after a day or so," adds Damo.

"Well, once we have the cash, it should be an easy run. Nothing much to stop us," says Earl.

***

Unbeknown to Earl, and the others, the 'nothing much' that could stop them is only hours away. Ominous black clouds hang over the mountains surrounding Kabale like a cosmic harbinger of doom. Blissfully unaware, the Australians are oblivious of the danger speeding towards them.

Having received news that other Australians had taken up residence in the vicinity of the drug money, the urgency of Kemal's and Ahmet' mission has ramped up. Discussing the new development in the car, Kemal offers alternative theories. It could be entirely coincidental. Just a bunch of tree huggers doing something to feel good about themselves. Ahmet wants to believe that scenario, so charitably expressed by Kemal, because it would simplify their task. And it could still be the case. But Ahmet's gut instinct is telling him that the presence of fellow Australian citizens spells trouble or, at the very least, it complicates matters.

Pointing to a rare sign at the side of the road, Kemal raises his voice above the sound of the engine. With one eye on the fuel gauge, he says, "We're making good time, looks like we're only twenty kilometres from Masaka. I think we need to stop and fill up the tank, we don't want to get stranded, stuck in the backwoods, miles from civilization with no fuel."

Glancing at his watch, Ahmet nods in agreement and they pull into the first petrol station they see, which rests forlornly on the eastern outskirts of the city. It looks the worst for wear, with just two pumps, both with chipped paintwork, which look barely capable of doing the job they were designed for. Behind the pumps, a small semi-dilapidated building stands, where customers pay for the fuel. Ahmet remains in the passenger seat, whilst Kemal pays and exchanges a few words with the owner, who nods and points.

Jumping back into the driver's seat Kemal speeds off. The rear wheels kick up dust and gravel towards the owner, who stands impassively outside his office, watching their departure.

"What were you saying to that man?" asks Ahmet.

"Just making sure we were on the right track. He said to continue into Masaka and the road forks at the western end. He told me which one to take and that we should head for Mbirizi."

"Good. So I take it that you're clear where you're going?"

"Yes Ahmet, I'm not fucking stupid."

Driving through Masaka, Kemal tuts at the brown, poorly maintained roads of compacted dirt and the filthy, poorly maintained buildings. Every shop front looks as though it needs a hose down with a high-pressure cleaner. Looking skyward through his windscreen, Kemal shakes his head. An untidy morass of drooping power lines all lead to a semi rotted pole, strengthened by rusted metal supports.

"Look at that, it'll collapse any minute and half the people in the street will get electrocuted. Wouldn't be a bad thing. It'd put them out of their misery, living in a hovel like this."

Ahmet ignores Kemal's vitriolic remark, deciding he needs to pick his fights with the young fool rather than be in constant conflict. There are likely to be far more important times ahead when he will have to butt heads to pull him into line. For the moment, he decides to put up with the outbursts where they can do less harm, in the privacy of their car. The stick will need to be wielded later when they reach Kabale.

* * *

After a busy morning on the construction site, all the workers are sitting in the shade of three acacia trees enjoying their lunch. A buffet, prepared by Namona, has been laid out on two trestle tables for everyone to help themselves. Easing himself onto the ground, whilst trying not to spill food from his overfilled plate, Boof sits next to Damo who is resting against the trunk of one of the trees. Once settled, he looks up to Earl, who is standing, hands on hips, staring at the half-completed entrance of the building.

Through a mouthful of food, Boof says, "Hey Earl, grab some tucker and come and join us. Yer deserve a break."

Still transfixed on the building, Earl keeps his back to Boof but still answers him. "There's something bothering me. Something's not right."

"Looks good to me mate, we've made good progress I reckon," says Damo.

"It's the shutters on the windows by the main door

that you've installed," replies Earl, still trying to pin down the problem. Realisation dawns and he turns to Damo. "Mate, you've put them in upside down, you bloody idiot."

"Have I?" asks Damo.

"Yes, you have. Yer gonna 'ave to take them out and start again. For fucks sake."

"Easy mistake. Wouldn't worry about it," mutters Boof, shovelling in a mouthful of matoke.

With serendipitous timing, Damo is rescued from Earl's wrath by the intervention of Mukasa.

"The men are going to have a quick kick about," says Mukasa, pointing to a patch of clear land with make-shift goals, each comprising of two poles pushed into the dirt. "They would be honoured if you'd join them. I have told them, with your permission, that they can play a short game of ten minutes each way. We can play five a side. I will go in goal for your team."

Still fuming at Damo's mistake with the shutters, Earl agrees to take part. The game is good natured but the three Australians struggle against the speed and skill of their opponents. Three of them play for Kikungiri Rovers.

Having joined the game already angered by the shutters faux pas, Earl's mood worsens. Increasingly irritated at his young opponent, who repeatedly leaves him looking flat-footed to the amusement of the other players, Earl's face turns a familiar red. Too late, Damo sees the warning sign and gasps when Earl's challenge sends the young player spinning into the air. Fists clenched, Earl stands over the prone youth and is about to vent his frustration verbally when the calming hand of Damo presses on his shoulder.

"Now, now. C'mon Earl. It's just a game and he's just a kid."

Earl stares down at the young player whose eyes have widened in fear. Seeing the expression of his young opponent, Earl's body relaxes as his anger dissipates. Apologising, he offers a hand and hauls up the player who, once on his feet, warily retreats away from Earl.

"There you go Earl," murmurs Damo, in a calming tone.

Loud clapping of hands brings the game to a halt. Whilst staring pointedly at Earl, Mukasa announces, "Break over men, back to work."

"Yer need to watch that temper of yours, mate," whispers Damo into Earl's ear, as he walks back to the site.

"What fucking temper?" snaps Earl.

22

TEMPERS CAN BE EXPLOSIVE

TEMPERS HAVE BEEN simmering in the car but are yet to boil over. With the bigger picture in mind, Ahmet is holding his anger in check. Next to him Kemal is distracted by a more pressing matter, his prejudice of Ugandan's and their capabilities has come home to roost. With this negative mindset, Kemal had dealt with the garage owner in Masaka dismissively and this was proving costly. Driven by his own arrogance, he had barely paid any attention to the garage owner's instructions. Now he desperately trawls his erring memory for the directions he was given and, having reached the southwestern outskirts of Masaka, he has a decision to make. The road splits into two main highways. Does he take the left fork or continue straight?

Scrambling in the recesses of his brain, he attempts to recall what the garage owner had said. Pride, and slight trepidation at the reaction he would get from a sullen Ahmet, prevents him openly admitting that he is not sure which road to take. But the Gods are on his side, and he gets an epiphany. He is a hundred percent certain that the next town on their route begins with an 'M'. Certainty is momentarily clouded with nagging doubt.

Didn't half the towns in this shitty little country begin with an M? But then a more helpful recollection came to mind.

It began with M, but I think it also had a Z in it. Can't be too many places that have a Z in their name.

More mental scrambling. Then a moment of false serendipity presents a road sign, which appears as he reaches the brow of a hill.

Bingo. I'm right.

Kemal's vexed frown turns to a triumphant smile, which elicits a quizzical glance from Ahmet who is staring at him, wondering why he had slowed down. Ahmet tries, without success, to interpret what is going through Kemal's mind.

Switching on the indicators, Kemal takes the left fork to Mubanzi.

Had he continued without turning left, he would have passed another sign three hundred metres further down the road. The name of the town it displayed may have jogged his errant memory. Gesticulating with great care, the garage owner had indicated that the road would fork and that he should continue straight which leads to the town of Mbirizi.

With great purpose and increasing speed, Kemal takes them directly south, in the wrong direction. Blissfully unaware, Ahmet closes his eyes to take a nap. He had not slept well the night before and wants to be on his A-game when they reach Kabale.

* * *

Concerned at the reaction of Earl during the impromptu lunchtime football game, Mukasa sidles over and taps him on the shoulder.

"Is everything okay Mister Earl?"

"Eh! Yeah, fine. Why do you ask?"

"You are holding a great deal of anger within you. You could have hurt young Ochen, and he is one of my rising stars. I confess, I am not happy."

Seeing that Mukasa is upset, Earl puts an arm round his shoulders.

"Look mate, I'm very sorry. It's nothing personal, just a bit of white line fever."

Pulling away, Mukasa says, "A fever, are you not well? Are you infectious?"

"No, no mate. Nothing like that," replies Earl, laughing. "It's an Aussie expression."

"I don't understand."

"It's when someone gets overly aggressive when they play a sport."

"But why white line? Why fever?"

Seeing Earl struggle to explain the concept to Mukasa, Damo ambles over.

"What he means, Mukasa, is that once they cross the white sideline of the footy pitch, they transform from a normally gentle bloke into a madman," says Damo, patting Earl on the back. "Or in Earl's case, from a misery to a nutbag. They get, how should I say, overly competitive."

"Yeah, that's it," confirms Earl.

"Oh! I understand. Mind you, fire and passion are not necessarily bad things. One or two of my players could do with that," replies Mukasa.

"Maybe. But maybe not quite as much fire as Earl has," says Damo, smiling disarmingly.

"Well, that's okay. Perhaps your break in Kampala is coming at a suitable time. You've all been working hard and maybe you need to relax for a few days."

"Yeah. You're probably right," replies Earl.

Sympathetically, Mukasa asks, "Are you sure you don't want me to drive you? The journey itself is long and will be tiring. I'd be more than happy to be of service."

"Aw, naw mate. It's all good. We want to do a bit of exploring of the country on our own and you've done enough for us."

"Yeah, Earl's right. You've done enough," adds Damo.

Walking away, Mukasa calls back, "If you change your mind, let me know."

"No worries, mate," shouts Earl.

Once Mukasa is out of earshot, Damo leans over to Earl and whispers, "Mate, I know you've got anger management issues, but you need to keep that temper in check for a few days."

"Mate, I am keeping it in check."

"What about that kid you took out?"

"Mate, if I was seriously angry he'd have been carried off on a stretcher."

"I'm just saying we need to keep calm and keep a low profile. We'll be gone in a week. Keep the red mist in check. Keep those anger issues under control."

"Mate, if you keep going on about it, you'll find yourself with broken jaw issues."

Shaking his head as he walks away, Damo replies sarcastically, "Glad you've taken my advice on board. Mate, you need to take a good look at yourself."

* * *

Woken by the jostling of the car, Ahmet sits upright and rubs his eyes.

"Potholes! They can't even make decent roads here," complains Kemal.

"You could try driving around them, rather than through them," says Ahmet, irritably.

"Can't help it. There're hundreds of them."

Ignoring the excuse, Ahmet examines his watch and

realises he has slept for an hour. He squints out of the window trying in vain to get his bearings, but the lush landscape looks identical to the countryside that surrounded them before he fell asleep after leaving Masaka. Looking across to Kemal, he asks, "Where are we?"

"On the road to Mubanzi."

"How far is that from Mbarara?"

"Dunno, why?"

"Because we were told that Mbarara is the biggest town on the way to Kabale. I thought you knew where we are going," says Ahmet. His confidence in Kemal's navigational skills is beginning to dissolve. No response, and a failure of Kemal to provide reassurance, triggers Ahmet. Growing increasingly uneasy, he demands affirmation. "Are you sure you know where we're going?" His question is met with a curt, 'yes.'

Unconvinced, Ahmet presses the point. "Why don't you check. Switch on the Satnav."

"There isn't a Satnav in this shit heap."

"No Satnav," exclaims Ahmet. "Why didn't you tell me there's no Satnav?"

"Because you never asked. Don't need one anyway. We have directions and there's not exactly a bundle of freeways in this place, is there? There's only one main road to Kabale and it goes through the place you just mentioned."

"You mean Mbarara?"

"Yes."

"So why aren't there any signs for Mbarara?" asks Ahmet.

"Because the fucking Ugandans are useless. Can't build decent roads, let alone put signs on them."

Pointing ahead to the side of the road, Ahmet barks an order. "Pull over near that fruit seller."

With an overly heavy foot on the brakes, the car skids

kicking up gravel on the verge before sliding to a halt fifty metres past the wooden stand of the vendor. Whilst Kemal remains next to the car, stretching his limbs, Ahmet walks back towards the vendor and attempts to strike up a conversation. But it is not his lucky day.

Ahmet addresses one of the many Ugandans, who live in rurally, that are non-English speaking. Ahmet's grasp of Swahili is equal to the vendor's command of English. All Ahmet's questions are answered with an enthusiastic and vigorous shaking of fruit. Both men are equally as exasperated. Unable to communicate his lack of desire for fruit, Ahmet resorts to shouting 'Kabale' repeatedly. Working on the reasonable assumption that the mzungu stopped to buy his fruit, the vendor responds by shouting 'ndizi' repeatedly, whilst waving the banana in his hand. Varying his approach, Ahmet shouts 'Mbarara'. He gets the response 'Embe' as the vendor picks up a mango and holds it in front of Ahmet's face. Ending the impasse with a dismissive wave, Ahmet returns to the car.

"Well?" asks Kemal, intending to be sarcastic rather than inquisitive.

Ignoring the question, Ahmet opens the passenger door, leans into the car and flicks open the hatch of the glove compartment. With a muttered expletive he drags himself out of the car but is empty handed.

"What are you looking for?" asks Kemal.

"A map. But there isn't one and he wasn't much help," replies Ahmet, pointing to the perplexed fruit vendor in the distance.

"Yeah, I could see you were struggling," replies Kemal with a snide grin and climbs back into the driver's seat. "Trust me, we're on the right road."

Without any obvious alternative option, Ahmet climbs onto his seat, moodily slamming the door behind him.

They drive on in silence for the next twenty minutes, but Ahmet's uncertainty continues to nag relentlessly like the buzz of an insistent mosquito. A seed of doubt grows into a melon resting uncomfortably in Ahmet's mind until it becomes too much to bear.

"This cannot be right; we would surely have come across a sign for Kabale or at least Mbarara by now."

Wracked by his own uncertainty, Kemal drives in moody silence. His ego is a barrier to voicing his own disquiet and the opportunity for a reasoned discussion is lost. Ahmet stares but Kemal ignores him and avoids eye contact. The inevitable happens, Ahmet's patience morphs into controlled wrath.

"Listen to me. You need to stop. We need to turn round and return to Masaka. This can't be the right road," hisses Ahmet.

Ignoring him, Kemal drives on. His temper also worsens and rises in direct proportion to Ahmet's insistence.

Getting only a petulant sideways glance from Kemal, with no acknowledgement of his request, Ahmet raises his voice. "STOP THE CAR!"

Avoiding eye contact by remaining fixated on the road ahead, Kemal snaps back. "Fuck off, you don't know what you're talking about."

* * *

"So what's Earl's problem?" asks Boof, when Damo takes a seat on the opposite side of the wooden bench.

"The usual problem with Earl. His temper."

"Yeah, he was a bit over the top when he tackled that kid."

"Bit over the top? That's a bit of a bloody understatement Boof."

"Yeah, I know. Mukasa didn't look that happy about it. Gave him a few funny looks. Yer don't think he suspects anything, do you?' asks Boof.

"Naw. How could he? He's just pissed off that Earl almost hospitalised one of his best players. Luckily, the kid is okay. Our Earl needs to hold it in check, and we all need to keep our heads down for the next couple of days."

Boof nods in agreement. "True."

Placing his elbows on the bench and leaning forward to whisper across to Boof, Damo winks, saying, "We are pretty much in the clear and there's nothing to stop us grabbing the cash and getting the hell out of here."

"Yep, there's nothing much to get in our way now," replies Boof, smiling conspiratorially.

"Yep," smiles Damo, "and in the words of Robert Mitchum ..."

"Who?"

"He's an old movie actor, I saw a doco on him a while back. Anyway, never mind that. He said to his wife that if she stuck with him, she'd be farting through silk."

"Eh?"

"Never mind. I'm just saying we stick to the plan, it'll be okay and we'll be living the life. No one suspects us and there's nothing to stop us." Damo gives Boof a knowing smile, pats him on the shoulder and climbs off the bench seat to join the others. Oblivious to the potential danger in the form of two Turkish gangsters, Damo whistles happily and shares a joke prompting laughter and a round of applause from his co-workers.

* * *

Any humour, good or otherwise, has evaporated in the car. Ahmet's patience has reached its limit, and the fearsome tone of his voice now oozes menace. Wrapping his large hand around Kemal's left shoulder he issues an ultimatum.

"I … said … stop … the … car …and … turn … around."

Inwardly Kemal's heart rate flutters and his stomach churns. He had heard Ahmet adopt this tone before and it never ended well for those on the receiving end. Two years ago, it preceded a fatality and the explosive brute force of Ahmet shocked Kemal, although he did his best to hide it at the time to save face.

Fear wrestles with pride and Kemal's ego wins, so he ignores Ahmet's instruction. A last vestige of rebellion escapes from his mouth, although his petulant tone indicates imminent acquiescence.

"Look, Ahmet, I'm not fucking stupid. I know where I'm go—"

Albeit unfinished, it is the last sentence Kemal ever utters. The front of the car disintegrates from the force of the initial blast coupled with the instantaneous secondary explosion from the ignited fuel tank. Both die instantly. Neither were aware of, nor heard, the explosion, unlike a small herd of Eland grazing peacefully on the nearby savannah. Like a group of meerkats, their heads pop up inquisitively, still chewing, and they stare in the direction of the distant boom. Curiosity satisfied; they dip back into the grass to continue feeding.

Ironically, six months earlier, the President of Uganda hosted a grand ceremony at the State House in Kampala, where he officially declared his country free of landmines. After congratulating the untiring work of the National Mine Action Program in Uganda, he received rapturous applause from the appreciative audience. Years of internal conflict between the Uganda People's Defence Force and the resistance forces, had left thousands of mines littered across the country. Almost fifty former battlefields and countless other areas had been cleared of mines. In his speech, the President acknowledged that no absolute guarantee could be ever given that all mines had been found and de-commissioned. Setting that sobering fact aside, he told his audience with considerable pride that the annual toll of civilian deaths had reduced from several hundred to only three victims in the last twelve months. It was indeed a cause for celebration.

Until two foreign nationals visiting the beautiful south had an unfortunate and freak accident, there had been no deaths since the President's ceremony. With limited resources and training, the investigation by local police is cursory. Since the remains of the car provide no clue as to ownership, they are unable to identify the bodies. What is left of the human remains and possessions in the vehicle, is also insufficient to enable identification. Ahmet and Kemal are recorded in the statistics as 'unknown' and their remaining body parts are stored in a fridge at the back of the local station. There they will remain until the specialist forensics team, based in Kampala, is next in the area.

23

MONEY FOR NOTHING AND THE CAR IS FREE

HAVING DEVELOPED A more cautious approach to opening their cabin door since the Eland incident, Damo is still a little startled when, leaving to go on his morning walk, he is greeted by Seymour who is about to knock.

"Good morning, Damo, trust you all slept well."

"G'day Seymour. Yer took me by surprise loitering outside. To what do we owe the pleasure of yer visit?"

"I know it's your day off and y'all having a rest, but I come bearing gifts. Well at least one gift."

Gesturing for him to follow, Seymour marches up the path. Intrigued, Damo follows him and sees two Pajeros parked. Waving from the driving seat of one of the cars, Mukasa gives Damo a cheery 'hello'. The other car is unoccupied. Damo presumes it was driven by the American who is now reaching into the empty vehicle to extract the key from the ignition.

"There you go," says Seymour, throwing the key to Damo.

Catching it with one hand, Damo says, "Cheers mate."

"No worries, as you Aussies say," replies Seymour, whilst climbing into the seat next to Mukasa. "It's yours for the next week or so to use on your road trip to Kampala. Mukasa filled up the tank."

"Thanks again."

Through the open passenger window Seymour shouts, as the car departs, "Enjoy your break. y'all deserve it."

Damo keeps his hand raised in acknowledgement, until their car disappears out of sight in a cloud of dust. He juggles the car key in his hand, turns around and walks back into the cabin to the snoring and odours within. *Looking forward to my own room in a decent hotel,* muses Damo sniffing the not so fragrant air.

"Wakey, wakey boys. We've had a visit from our mate Seymour who has left us a little present and it's now game on."

Propping himself up on one elbow, Earl says "Wassup."

"Yeah, what's going on? Has he brought us breakfast again?" asks Boof, rubbing his eyes.

"Not food, but it's our meal ticket," jokes Damo.

"It's too early for riddles, just tell us what's happening," mutters Earl, grumpily.

"Our vehicle has been delivered with a full tank and is ready to go."

Smiling, Earl says, "In that case, tonight's the night."

"And this time next week we'll be hitting the surf," adds Boof.

"If all goes to plan," replies Earl.

Tutting, Damo says "Always a downer mate."

"We just need to stay calm, be careful. We'll get the money tonight and set off first thing in the morning."

All that remains to be done is to pack up their belongings and wait. The rest of the day seems to drag on. With little to occupy their minds, each begins to play through impending scenarios and potentially different outcomes, both good and bad. Conversation throughout the day is stilted and as the afternoon sun begins to wane, their nervous anticipation grows. Laying on their beds in varying degrees of introspection, a loud unexpected knock on the cabin door makes their hearts miss a beat. They all sit up simultaneously, but Earl is the first up to answer the door, only to be greeted by the smiling face of Chief Masika.

"Good afternoon Mister Earl. I hope you don't mind me calling by, unannounced."

"Not at all." Earl steps aside inviting the Chief to enter.

Both Boof and Damo stand up from their beds prompting the Chief to gesture for them to sit back down. Pulling out a wooden chair from under the table, Earl invites the Chief to sit, but he politely refuses.

"I will not stay long but I just wanted to thank you gentlemen for everything you have done before you go to Kampala. I know that all the villagers have grown to accept you as one of their own, not to mention the generosity and time you have devoted to their cause. You all have been incredibly altruistic, and I applaud this."

Three separate and quite different emotions are triggered. A wave of guilt rolls through Damo's mind before it breaks on the shore of his conscience and dissipates. Suspicion sparks in Earl's brain seeking out the true meaning and motive of the Chief. Confusion washes through Boof's thought processes as he fails to decipher the meaning of "altruistic."

Trying to penetrate the thoughts hidden behind the smile of the Ugandan, Earl stares back with a wry smile of his own.

"It's no problem, Chief, it's been our pleasure, and we appreciate the hospitality you've given us. But you talk as though we are not coming back. We're just going for a short break."

Narrowing his eyes imperceptibly, the Chief holds his smile and maintains direct eye contact with Earl. "I know Mister Earl. But I wanted to ensure that you all know how much your charitable work has been appreciated." He then looks over to Damo. "Not to mention Mister Damo's heroic exploits for the village on the football field."

Damo nods in acknowledgement and then the Chief turns to Boof. "And you Mister Boof. The way you have embraced our culture, and our food, has been heartwarming."

"No worries, Chief, yer tucker is amazing."

"Quite so. Well, I won't detain you any further. I'll let myself out."

Moving to the window, Earl looks out to follow the Chief's progress to his car. Once he sees the Mercedes leave he turns and sits on the chair with a frown.

"What's troubling you Earl?"

"I don't trust him Damo. There is something about that smile, something behind his eyes. I get the feeling he's up to something."

Waving his hand dismissively, Boof offers an opinion. "You've always been a suspicious bugger. Yer don't trust anybody. That's what 'appens when you spend half your life mixing with wrong 'uns."

"Says the man fresh out of jail," replies Earl, sarcastically.

"I reckon Boof has a point. We haven't put a foot wrong and he's nothing to be suspicious about. He's just grateful that stuff is getting done for his people." Damo looks at Earl with a hopeful, rather than convincing, expression.

"Maybe," says Earl doubtfully. "Maybe not. Either way we need to grab something to eat and prepare for our little night excursion. It's beginning to get dark."

Dinner at the Hungry Crane met all the low expectations of Earl and Damo but at least it filled the gap. For Boof, the meal serves to change his mindset from nervous anxiety to a warm glow of satisfaction that comes with a full stomach. For the other two, little has changed. Damo's feelings of guilt have increased as he converses with other locals who continue to hold him in high esteem following his football heroics. Feeling like a fraud, he smiles uncomfortably at their plaudits. Suspicion continues to lurk in the shadows of Earl's mind, as he contemplates the night ahead.

Midnight has just passed when they leave their cabin and make their way to the Pajero. Earl drives in silence whilst the others peer through the windows into the pitch darkness, pierced only by the car headlights. Driving to the same spot as where they entered the bush before, Earl brings the car to a halt.

Killing the engine, the headlights snap off, swamping them in darkness before they each flick on their torches. Leading the other two through the bush, Earl follows the same route they had previously taken, maintaining a stealthy but quick pace. This time, each keep their respective phobias of darkness, insects, and snakes in check, concentrating their minds on the main prize. Nevertheless, the clicking, rustling, and hissing noises of the bush give them an uneasy feeling. Despite the increased risk of discovery, the sight of Masika's security lights peeping through the trees is greeted with relief by all three. They switch off their torches.

Bringing them to a halt with a raised hand, Earl pokes his head through the tree line and stares intently at the house. Inside, the house is bathed in darkness with no evidence of life or movement, but the veranda is swamped in the luminous intensity of the security lights. Satisfied that the coast is clear, Earl turns to Boof and Damo and points at the shed which houses the crate with the money. He wiggles his forefinger indicating that he wants them to follow. Without hesitation they scamper to the shed, crouching and bent double like mischievous chimpanzees.

Stopping in a tight huddle at the shed door Earl eases it open, but despite his care, it creaks, and they all freeze in response. Hesitating, then glancing nervously at the house, Earl tries to pull the door fully open without making any more noise and they all scramble in. Now able to switch their torches back on, they shine their lights onto the crate. With the lid loosened from their first visit, Earl makes short work of jimmying it off and carefully begins to remove the books. A momentary feeling of panic washes over him after moving the top two layers of books. He cannot see the cash, just more books. Two more layers are removed, and his increased heart rate settles when he sees the welcome and familiar sight of Australian banknotes.

After getting the thumbs up from Earl, who peels the empty rucksack off his back, Boof and Damo follow suit. First throwing his rucksack down to Boof, Earl starts to pass the packages of cash down. Working methodically, they fill all three rucksacks. Securing the straps of the third rucksack, Damo looks up and whispers to Earl.

"Is that all of it?"

"No."

"No?"

"Yeah, no." repeats Earl with slight exasperation.

"Whadda we do now?" asks Boof.

"We need to make another trip."

"Are you fucking kidding me?"

"Do I sound as though I am fucking kidding you Boof?" counters Earl.

"Shouldn't we just leave it?" asks Damo.

"Mate, we've come this far, and you want to leave a couple of million on the table. There must be at least two more full rucksacks still here."

"So, what do we do? We can't carry it in our arms, can we?" asks Damo.

"We go back, empty the rucksacks into the car and come back for the rest. Or at least as much of the rest as we can carry. We don't want to push our luck with a third trip."

"What if someone nicks it when we come back for the rest?"

"Mate. We are in the middle of the fucking jungle. No-one's gonna nick it. Anyway, Boof can stay with the car, and we'll just come back."

"Fine by me," says Boof, relieved that he would not have to make the repeat trip.

They assist each other to put the rucksacks onto their backs and set off. Weighed down by the cash, the trip back is much harder and all three are breathing heavily by the time the car comes into view. With a gasp of relief, Boof eases off his rucksack and it hits the ground with a heavy thump. Working quickly, they empty the cash of two rucksacks into the back of the Pajero and put the third, still full, next to the pile.

Earl and Damo set off back through the bush whilst Boof sits in the car. Alone, Boof feels a growing nervousness in the pit of his stomach and hearing a distinctive rustle in the nearby bush, reflexively presses the central lock button on the vehicle to secure the car.

Making their way along their well-trodden route, Damo breaks the silence.

"How come Boof gets to stay in the car?"

"Because he is a weedy little bugger who'd slow us down. It'll be quicker with us. Yer must have seen him gasping for breath. He almost passed out when we reached the car."

"Fair comment."

Having reached the tree line, Earl, once more, scans the house for any activity. Darkness inside, bright security lights on the veranda and no sign of movement. They scramble to the shed and, this time, straight through the door that was left open. Sat on top of the crate, Earl hands down the cash to Damo who fills the first ruck sack and secures the straps.

"Shit."

"What's wrong?" asks Earl.

"Ssssh, quiet, I can hear something. Sounds like a vehicle. Just stay there."

Crawling out of the shed Damo lays still. Headlights, accompanied by the crunching of gravel under wheels, move slowly up the drive towards the house. Damo closes the shed door with a firm push and dives into the long grass at the edge of the bushland. Luckily, the door to the shed is on the opposite side facing the bushland and cannot be seen from the driveway. Heart and temples pounding, Damo lays still in the long grass watching the vehicle pass by the shed and it comes to a halt in front of the house. Earl opens the shed door, pokes his head out, and glances from left to right. Urged by frantic signals from Damo, he pushes the door shut once he is out and scrambles into the grass next to Damo.

Anxiously, they look towards the house noticing that the vehicle is a white van. On the side panel are the words 'Mbwa Mkali Security' printed in large black letters with a picture of a savage dog baring its teeth. Two men in khaki uniforms and black berets get out of the vehicle and knock on the door. Masika answers wearing a white dressing gown and an angry expression.

"Why are you disturbing me at this late hour?"

The guard nearest to the Chief recoils slightly and apologises profusely. Nervously, he explains that poachers have been sighted in the area and three villagers have been assaulted and robbed. The other guard tells the Chief that they just came to check that everything is secure and well at his house. Mollified by their motives, the Chief's tone of voice softens, and he thanks them for their consideration, assuring them that all is well. Tipping their caps to the Chief, the two guards leave, driving slowly past Damo and Earl lying in the long grass, before exiting out of the property.

Remaining hidden until they are satisfied that the guards are long gone and the lights inside the house have been extinguished, Damo and Earl breathe a sigh of relief.

"Come on Earl, let's head back."

"We can't you muppet. We've a full sack in that shed and an empty bag to get the rest of the cash."

"It's a bit risky."

"Mate, we are here now, and they've all gone. Besides, we need to leave it looking like it's been untouched in case it gets checked."

Crawling through the grass they scramble back into the shed. Minutes later they have filled the second sack and leave the remaining money in the crate. They replace the books, rearranging them to compensate for the gap left by the money, to make it appear as though the contents of the crate are untouched. With a satisfied grunt, Earl presses the lid back on the crate and secures it using a stone to punch in the nails he had removed earlier.

Assisting each other to put their rucksacks on, they creep out of the shed and close the door. They are soon hidden from prying eyes by the sanctuary of the thick bushland. When they break out into the opening where the Pajero is parked they can see Boof in the front passenger seat, but he is looking in the opposite direction. Earl knocks on the window startling Boof, who recoils in fright.

"Open the fucking door you idiot," snaps Earl, pointing to the door handle.

With a visible expression of relief, Boof complies, jumps out of the car, and runs to the back to open the hatch. Damo and Earl wrestle free from their rucksacks and throw them into the vehicle. Back on the road, their brief silence breaks into group laughter and they all joke and talk at once until they calm down..

"Where the hell were you? You took ages," says Boof.

"A bit of a hiccup, mate. Some security guards rocked up," explains Damo.

Joy dissipates to mild anxiety.

"What the hell!" exclaims Boof.

"Nothing to worry about. They were just checking on the Chief. Apparently, there's poachers in the area," says Earl.

"It's no big deal, we weren't spotted," adds Damo.

"How much do you think we got?" asks Boof.

"No idea, but most of what was there, we couldn't carry all of it."

"Yeah, but how much?"

"Mate, you're the big expert on the weight of money. We'll get a hotel room in Kampala whilst we sort out a flight and, if they've got scales in the room, we can weigh it."

Unsure whether Damo was joking or serious, Boof replies, "Great idea."

Back at the cabin they unload the money and attempt to get some sleep. With adrenaline coursing through their bodies, the only sleep they manage is short and disturbed. Morning light brings relief. No-one wants to hang around and by 8am they are on the road to Kampala with an eventful four hundred kilometres ahead of them.

NO DELIGHT FOR THE TURKISH

SEVENTY-TWO HOURS HAVE passed since Hakan last had word from Kemal or Ahmet. Though not a man prone to worry, this rarely felt emotion is beginning to take a grip. Smelling disaster, the situation in Africa consumes him. Dark clouds had gathered in his imagination with no hint of a silver lining. Events are chaotic and everything is disappearing, his best man, his nephew, and millions of dollars. Worse still, he faces the prospect of far greater losses in the future with the African partnership rapidly being flushed down the toilet. Thirteen (unlucky?) thousand kilometres away, somewhere in Uganda, his business is falling apart, and he has no control of the situation. It is becoming increasingly likely that bungling administrators at Sydney airport have achieved what the Australian Federal Police and Interpol could not. Destruction of his hitherto smoothly run empire. Smelling like an act of desperation he hopes, with little confidence, that his call to Muchai might turn the corner.

"G'day Eric, how are you doing? It's evening here so must be lunchtime for you."

"Yes, Hakan. I'm at my club for lunch but they've allowed me to use the meeting room for privacy."

"Is that the Karen Country Club where we met a few years ago?"

"No, Muthaiga. Hakan, what is it you wanted to discuss?" Sufficient niceties had been exchanged as far as Muchai was concerned.

"I just wondered if there was any update from your end regarding Kemal and Ahmet."

"Update? Why would I have an update? We've given them all the assistance promised and we're awaiting word from you."

With his hopes now dashed, Hakan half-heartedly suggests, "I thought your men might have mentioned something."

"I haven't heard anything. It's in your hands. Why don't you call them and ask? In fact, when you do, I'd also be interested to hear what they have to say."

"I've tried, but both their phones are dead."

"Not entirely surprising, I doubt if mobile coverage in Southern Uganda is good. If it exists at all, that is."

"So, no word from your contacts."

"As I said, nothing. And I don't need to remind you that I remain a few million dollars short after our previous transaction. Either your nephew finds and delivers it, or you'll have to make good the difference."

"But without your assistance this could be difficult and, as you say, there is a shortfall to make good. If I send another man, will you assist?"

"You've already had my assistance. It is now your problem, not mine. And … I have been patient, which I hope you're not interpreting as a weakness. I expect my money within the week, whether or not you find your nephew."

Before Hakan can respond, the line goes dead. Overcome with rage, Hakan hurls the mobile phone with venom and watches it smash into pieces against the wall of his office. Hearing a tirade of screamed expletives, his secretary rushes in. She has never seen such a raw display of fury from her boss and trembles anxiously as she awaits his instruction.

"GET ME DEMIR!" he roars.

"B-b-b-b-but I think he has taken his mother to Byron Bay for a few days. She came over to visit him from Ankara. It's h-h-her 60th birthday."

"NOW. TELL HIM TO COME BACK NOW."

She nods and rushes out of the office. Usually, when Hakan calls for Demir there is serious trouble. Very serious trouble. In her many years of faithful service, she had called him to Hakan's office on only three previous occasions. Demir's presence made her feel uneasy. No, not uneasy, more scared, fearful. The first time she met Demir and looked into his dark eyes it made her blood turn cold. On the second and third occasions she avoided direct eye contact entirely. It would be the same this time.

* * *

Having replayed his conversation with Hakan, Muchai concludes that the likelihood of recovering his money is decreasing with each day. Despite his hardline stance with Hakan, he decides he needs to intervene, with no confidence that the Turk's men will succeed.

"Gitau, it's Muchai, I trust you are well."

"I am, what can I do for you?"

"It is about the two Turks."

"Mugo told me he'd done everything as promised," replies Gitau defensively.

"Knowing Mugo, I have no doubt he did and thank you for that. However, I have a further favour to ask. It seems our friend in Australia has lost his two men somewhere in Uganda."

"Well, that's very careless of him. He should take more care. We live on a dangerous continent," says Gitau, sarcastically.

"He'll be sending another one of his foot soldiers, but I've little faith that he'll be successful."

Gitau gives a hollow laugh. "At this rate he'll run out of men."

"I know, but it's no laughing matter. I'm owed a considerable amount of money which I intend to ensure is collected. I'm happy to recompense you for your trouble if you could mobilise some of your own resources in Uganda to find them."

"For you, I'm happy to do this. If I hear anything I'll be in touch. In the meantime, you may give Hakan my details. By the time his new man arrives we should have located the others but, either way, I will assist."

"Thank you, Gitau, this is much appreciated."

Ending the call, Gitau calls out for Mugo who joins him in his office.

"Mugo, I have a little job for you. We need to try to find those two Turks you met. They appear to have gone missing."

"Yes, Mister Gitau. It doesn't surprise me. The younger one had far more arrogance than brains. I'll send Adroa."

"The Hyena. My thoughts exactly."

IS THIS THE WAY TO MBIRIZI?

"DO YOU KNOW the way to San Jose? I've been away so long … "

"Shaaattt up, Boof. For God's sake give the singing a rest. We've only been driving an hour and you're already doing my head in," snaps Earl.

"Yeah, Earl's right mate. I think you've covered every travel song by now," adds Damo.

Sulkily Boof says, "Jeez, party poopers or what. We're bloody millionaires and you two are a pair of miserable sods. It's not as if Ugandan radio beats out the bloody hits. Is it?"

Enduring a series of public health announcements on the danger of AIDS, smoking and excessive consumption of alcohol, Damo had turned off the radio inadvertently leaving Boof the stage. This gave free range for Boof to treat them to his medley of travel songs. He had already covered *'Born To Be Wild'*, *'I'm Gonna Be Five Hundred Miles'* and *'Midnight Train To Georgia'*.

Flicking on his indicators, Earl turns off the main highway.

"What're ya doing?" asks Boof.

"A short detour to the world famous Ntungamo International Resort. I promised Mukasa we'd call in and say 'Hi' to Akello and Auntie Dembe on the way. He gave me a parcel. It's Auntie's birthday today and he's unable to travel to see her. Apparently, the Chief had an urgent job for him."

Pulling up in front of the hotel they are greeted by Akello, who saw them approach from his office window.

"Welcome, welcome gentlemen. Marvellous to see you again. Will you be staying the night?"

Reaching under his seat, Earl extracts the parcel and jumps out of the car as Akello approaches him with his hand extended. They all shake hands and share their news as they stand in front of the hotel reception.

Turning to Damo, Akello pats him on the shoulder and says, "I hear, Mister Damo, that you are the hero of Kikungiri Rovers. They call you the Lion Slayer and the Ugandan Pele."

"Naw mate, it was nothing. Only glad to help."

"You are too modest."

"No seriously, he's not kidding, it was literally nothing," jokes Earl. "He fell over his own feet and got them a dodgy penalty."

"You're very funny Mister Earl. But you didn't answer me. Will you be staying the night at the International Resort?" Akello moves toward the rear of the vehicle. "Let me get your bags."

Stepping quickly into Akello's path, Earl says, "We'd love to, but we need to press on to Kampala."

Seeing the disappointment on Akello's face, Earl deflects by holding up the parcel. "We just popped by to drop off a present for Auntie Dembe.

A voice from behind causes them to turn, "That is too kind, how did you know?"

Greeted by the wide dazzling smile of Auntie Dembe, they all say 'hello.' Hugging each man in turn, she finally turns to Earl and points to the parcel in his hand.

Smiling, Earl explains. "Unfortunately, I have to admit we didn't know it was your birthday Auntie." Holding up the parcel he says, "This is from Mukasa. He sends his apologies for not being able to visit today but wanted to let you know that he's thinking of you."

Taking the package, Auntie Dembe thanks Earl and invites them to come for lunch. Politely declining, Earl insists that they must continue their journey so that they can get to Kampala before dark. Noticing Akello peering through the side window of the Pajero, Damo addresses him to draw away his attention.

"Is everything okay, Akello?"

"Yes, Mister Damo. I was just intrigued at the number of bags you have. I recall you were travelling much lighter when you stayed here on the way to Kabale. Does this mean you are leaving Uganda for good?"

Surreptitiously, Earl narrows his eyes towards Damo, indicating he needs to respond with care.

"No mate, not at all. Just spending a few days rest and recreation in the big City. Not everything in the car is ours. Mukasa lent it to us for a few days for our trip. Didn't notice all the bags to be honest. Must be footy kit or something, with Mukasa being the coach 'an all."

When Damo falls silent, Earl adds, "yep, Akello, we'll be back and maybe stay over for a night on the return trip."

A broad smile brightens Akello's face at this news. "Excellent Mister Earl, we look forward to seeing you in a few days."

* * *

Back on the highway Earl chides Damo. "Fucking footy kit. Is that the best you could come up with you idiot?"

"What did you expect me to say? I thought it was quite good for an 'off the cuff' effort."

Defending Damo, Boof laughs, "yeah Earl, chill out. I believed him … and I knew the bags were full of cash."

"Hilarious," mutters Earl.

"How about another song Boof," says Damo.

"Noooooooo," moans Earl and switches on the radio. Fast beating music pumps through the speaker.

"Love this stuff," says Boof.

"It's quite good," agrees Damo.

"What is it?" asks Earl.

"It's called Kwassa kwassa. It's African dance music."

"Yer a mine of information Boof. It's quite good. Certainly preferable to yer singing," says Earl, turning up the volume.

With the high energy music, Earl subconsciously puts his foot down on the accelerator which eats up the kilometres. Ahead of schedule, they pass through the streets of Mbarara without incident and are soon back on the open road heading for the next small town, Sanga. Boosted by its proximity to Lake Mburo National Park, the town generates income from tourists and buses which stop over during their journey through the region. Earl suggests that this town is a good place to take a short break. Fuel up and maybe get something to eat. With less than ten kilometres to go, their planned stop comes earlier than anticipated. Earl slams on the brakes bringing the car to a halt a hundred metres in front of a group of four elephants and a calf.

All three stare in awe and disbelief, mesmerised by the majestic beasts which amble nonchalantly onto the road. Playfully, the calf runs around the legs of its mother.

"We appear," announces Boof, "to be held up by a pachyderm roadblock."

"A *Paki* what?"

"A pachyderm, Earl."

"Looks like a fucking elephant to me."

"Indeed, Earl," replies Boof with an air of intellectual superiority.

"So, Mister Paki expert, what do we do now? Drive 'round them? Hoot the horn?" asks Damo, whilst Boof scans the internet on his phone.

"Not a clever idea. It says stop the car at least thirty metres away."

"Done that," says Earl. "What next?"

"If they start to advance towards us, you need to reverse the car away from them."

"Yeah, well they're not moving, they are just stood, waving their trunks."

"All good then," replies Boof.

"Not really mate, what do we do? We can't stay here all day. We've got a truck load of cash and we need to get out of the country, pronto."

Examining the results of his googling, Boof shakes his head. "Sorry mate, it just says we've gotta wait until they move out of the way. Says here, it's a good idea to turn off the engine."

Switching off the ignition, Earl relaxes back into his seat. They sit in silence and stare at the animals. The animals stare back.

"Put the kwassa kwassa on and open the windows," suggests Damo.

"Why?" asks Earl.

"Well, I liked it and it's African, so it might get them moving."

"Didn't mention that on google," says Boof.

Earl switches on the radio and kwassa kwassa immediately pumps through the speakers. The noise is deafening. Tapping him on the shoulder, Damo suggests to Earl that he winds down the windows. Edging the car forward, music blaring across the savanna, Earl looks over to Damo in surprise. Led by the male, the group slowly leave the road and amble onto the grass.

"Told you so," chuckles Damo, triumphantly, "not just a footy superstar but a pachyderm whisperer."

Ignoring the remark, Earl picks up speed once the elephants have sauntered into the bush and switches off the radio.

"What's the next town called?" asks Damo.

"I think we should give Sanga a miss and head on to Mbirizi. It's not far." says Boof, looking at his phone. "I'll sing you a song about it. I'm a genius at making up my own lyrics to songs."

"Go on, let's hear it," replies Damo, which elicits a groan from Earl.

Not needing a second invitation Boof hums the tune to 'Is This The Way To Amarillo' before breaking into full song.

"When the day is dawning,
this U-gan-dan Sun-day mor-ning,
How I long to be there,
Earl's a mis-er-y ev-e-ry where,
Every African town
La la la la
Seems to make him frown,
La la la la
They ain't that pretty
They always get him down.
OOOOOOOOOOOOOOOh

Is this the way to M- bir —riz - i
Africa makes me dizzy
Dreaming dreams of Mbirizi
And sweet Earl who drives me there."

Damo bursts into laughter, congratulating Boof, who beams in a rare moment of glory. Even Earl forces a wry smile.

26

THE HYENA

MUGO HANDPICKED ADROA for the task of finding the errant Turks. Amongst all their operatives he has the reputation as the most cunning and intelligent which earned him the nickname, 'Hyena'. Pondering the nature of the task, Mugo decided a more cerebral, rather than physical, approach is required and the slightly built Adroa is not employed for his muscle. Nevertheless, when he knocks on the door of the tall, skinny man who provided Kemal and Ahmet with a vehicle, his presence strikes fear. Wearing the same ill-fitting suit that he was when he met the Turks, he looks down nervously at the much shorter, immaculately dressed Adroa. It is never good news when the 'Hyena' lands on your doorstep. Everyone knows that. Mercifully, the interview is short, and he feels relieved when Adroa leaves.

Armed with knowledge of the date that the Turks had departed Kampala, a description of the vehicle, its registration, and a clear indication of their planned route, Adroa is confident he can find them. During his briefing, Mugo had voiced his suspicion that the destination of the two Turks is most likely to be Kabale, despite the fact Muchai's men had gone to Kasese. Mugo assumed that Muchai was attempting to misdirect them, aware that the thread of trust between the Ugandans and Kenyans was very thin. Mugo considered the facts. Why would Muchai's men be suddenly interested in crates delivered to Kasese over a year ago and not the ones more recently dropped near Kabale. It made no sense. Enquiries with his men in Kasese consolidated Mugo's theory that the Turks were never intending to go there.

Adroa estimates that, if Mugo is correct about Kabale, the Turks should have entered the town two days ago. Two calls to separate contacts in Kabale draw a blank. It seems that, inexplicably, they never arrived there either. After a moment's consideration, he decides his best strategy is obvious. Follow their trail. He will replicate their journey, making inquiries on the way. They will certainly have been seen when stopping for fuel or drinks. Two Turks, one of considerable size, would have stuck in the memory of whoever had crossed paths with them.

Enquiries at the first two petrol stations are fruitless. No-one recalls seeing the Turks. Pulling up to the third, on the outskirts of Masaka, pays dividends. With enthusiasm, the owner describes his encounter with Kemal. The young man had asked for directions, paid for the fuel, and left. A much larger and older man had remained in the passenger seat.

Having paid for his own petrol and thrown in a tip of twenty thousand shillings, Adroa climbs back into the car with the owner's profuse thanks ringing in his ears. Barely waiting for the owner to finish cleaning his windscreen, the Hyena pulls away on the scent of his quarry. He is on the right track.

Driving to the southwestern corner of the town where the road forks, he surmises that it would be unlikely that the Turks had stopped in Masaka, having just fueled their car. Without hesitation, he starts to take the right fork to Mbirizi and on to Mbarara, but then has second thoughts and pulls the car over to a gravelled area. Reanalysing the conversation he had with the owner of the petrol station, he recalls a throwaway comment that he initially dismissed as unimportant. The young man seemed distracted, and the garage owner felt that he did not listen to the directions he was being given. Adroa pondered on the implications and possible consequences.

Maybe they had taken the wrong turn. Maybe it was worth taking the left turn and exploring that road for a couple of hours.

Swinging the car round in a U-turn, Adroa drives back to the junction and takes the road to Mubanzi. An hour later, he is beginning to doubt the wisdom of his decision. There is no sign of petrol stations or other places where they might have stopped. Squinting through the haze of the heat rising off the road, he spots a figure in the distance and, as he draws near, sees it is a fruit vendor peddling his wares in a shaded area by the roadside. Flicking on his indicator, Adroa pulls up close by the stall.

Thirsty and hot, the watermelons look inviting. Cutting the fruit into segments, the vendor hands two pieces for Adroa to eat and places the rest in a bag which Adroa puts on the back seat of the car before paying. He bites into the watery floral fragrance of the fruit. Throwing the husk into the bush, he greedily devours a second piece.

Striking up a conversation with the vendor in his native language, Adroa's initial disinterested politeness transforms into genuine curiosity. In response to a general enquiry about how business was going, the vendor replies that it has been slow. The other day two foreigners stopped, shouted at him in a strange language but refused to buy any fruit. Throwing away the husk of the second piece of melon, Adroa's interest is aroused, and he fires a series of questions. Taken aback at the renewed intensity of the stranger's interest, the vendor answers hesitantly.

Having been told the foreigners headed south towards Mubanzi, Adroa looks into his rearview mirror as he prepares to pull out onto the road, but the mirror's reflection reveals the vendor running towards him, waving to get his attention once more. Thinking he just wants to sell him more fruit, Adroa tuts, but reluctantly winds down his window, inviting him to approach the car.

The vendor tells him that he had thought of something further that might be of interest. He tells Adroa that he has heard news of an explosion. With piqued interest Adroa switches off the engine and listens patiently to the story. The vendor tells him that two people, not locals but foreigners, had been killed. After being pressed for more information, the vendor explains he did not know anything else, but he wondered if they could be the men he was looking for. He tells Adroa that he had heard that the local police, based in Mbirizi, are dealing with the matter.

Thanking and passing twenty thousand shillings to the vendor, Adroa spins the car round and heads back for Masaka and then onto the road to Mbirizi.

Almost missing the unassuming police station, Adroa parks nearby and eventually finds himself squeezed into a small spartan room with the local police sergeant. Initially wary, the sergeant's manner gradually softens, and he becomes more communicative. Drawn in by the urbane charm of Adroa and a donation of one hundred dollars (American) to the local police fund, the sergeant becomes loquacious. Pocketing the two fifty-dollar bills, he explains that the bodies, or what remains of them, are yet to be identified. He confirms that the victims are of European skin tone and that there are two of them. A small remnant of the cover of a passport, possibly Australian, was also found.

Poker faced, Adroa listens to the sergeant until the well of information runs dry. Assuming Adroa still has an interest in his story, the sergeant asks if these could be the men he is looking for. If so, he asks Adroa if he would be willing to identify them. Dismissively shaking his head, Adroa dashes the hopes of the sergeant.

"I'm afraid not sergeant. The men I seek are both Asian, from Seoul. I am, of course, happy to have a look in the unlikely event that I know them."

Surprised at the willingness of his visitor to examine the gruesome remains of total strangers, the sergeant narrows his eyes. "Yes, of course, you can follow me into the back of the station. Facilities are poor here. Unfortunately we have had to put the body parts into a freezer until the investigators from Kampala are able to make the trip. I should warn you that they died from an explosion, so their bodies are not whole."

"Quite so," replies Adroa, aware of the sergeant's suspicion.

Opening the lid of the freezer, the sergeant moves aside. Adroa peers in and finds the head of Ahmet staring back at him, minus the jaw. It is sufficient for Adroa to mentally match the macabre vision in front of him to the photos he had seen which were supplied by Mugo. Stills were taken of the two men from the video security system when they visited Gitau's residence for the briefing. Displaying no emotion, he turns back to the sergeant, who is quietly impressed at the fortitude of his visitor's constitution.

"No, not the men I am looking for, but thank you for your time. I wish you luck in your investigation." Handing an extra twenty dollar note as he leaves, Adroa adds, "Thank you once again, please accept a little extra for your police fund. Keep up the excellent work officer."

27

A BRIEF ENCOUNTER

BUOYED BY THEIR own good mood, Damo, Boof and Earl laugh, joke and banter all the way to Mibirizi, where they decide to stop to refuel and have a short rest. Peering from their car window, they soon decide that the options for refreshments are limited and just agree to grab a quick coffee before continuing their journey to the capital. As they amble down the main street, Earl spots a small café which is set back from the main road. It is half hidden behind an imposing Uganda Telecom building, whose large blue sign dwarfs the neighbouring café's entrance.

They sit at the wooden table outside the café and are shortly welcomed by a small old man who takes their order. Returning with the drinks, the man smiles and welcomes them, for the second time, to Mbirizi. He asks where their journey is taking them, and Damo tells him that they are visiting the capital. Once they finish their coffees, Earl goes inside to pay and tries to buy bottled water. The man shakes his head, explaining he does not sell water and points down the main street. He directs them to a store just beyond the Police station where they can buy water and other refreshments to take on their journey.

They pass a row of ramshackle shops as they wander down the main street. All the signs are written in English. A prominent dirty yellow one has the words 'Sleeping Baby' in orange letters and the shop sign next to it is more a statement than a business name. It reads 'Give your cooking that Midas touch'. Approaching the Police station, Boof, who is walking in front, turns to ask Earl a question.

"Hey, Earl, how far do you reckon it is to Kamp … oww, jeezus."

Accidently barging into a small well-dressed man leaving the Police station, both grunt but manage to retain their balance.

Straightening his jacket and making a show of brushing himself down, Adroa fires an angry glance at Boof. "You need to watch where you are going, you fool."

"Yeah, sorry mate, it was an accident," apologises Boof.

Unappeased and glowering, Adroa snaps back, "Keep your eyes ahead of you or you might get hurt."

Angered by the tone of the stranger, Earl steps forward but his progress is blocked by Damo who places a hand on his chest. Knowing that once Earl gets involved it is unlikely to end peacefully, Damo steps in front of him. With open arms he attempts to placate the angry stranger.

"We're very, very sorry my friend, no harm intended. Please accept our apology."

Purposely ignoring Damo, Adroa brushes past Boof and strides down the street.

"Should've decked him. He's obviously an arsehole," mutters Earl, scowling at Adroa who is now getting into his car.

Pointing at the sign of the Police Station, Damo replies, "Mate, not a good idea to draw attention to ourselves, now is it?"

"Fair point," replies Earl

After grabbing bottles of water and a few snacks from the store next to the Police station, they return to their car and continue their journey to Kampala.

"About three hours," says Earl.

"Sorry," replies Boof.

"Before you walked into that idiot, you were about to ask how much further. It's about a hundred and fifty kilometres. It'll take us about three hours on these roads."

"Oh, yeah, right," replies Boof.

"In the meantime, try not to assault any of the locals."

* * *

A few kilometres ahead of them, Adroa is driving on the same route to Kampala, his speed well above the speed limit. Tapping the screen on his console he makes a call, a loud ring tone booms through the car speakers followed by the voice of Mugo.

"Yes Adroa, I assume you are calling me because you have some news."

"I do."

"Well, don't keep me waiting."

"I've located the two Turks."

"Excellent news. I knew I could rely on you. Are they with you now?"

"No, they are in Mbirizi."

"Mbirizi?"

"Yes, in a freezer."

"A freezer? What are you talking about? Is this some kind of joke?"

"No joke. It appears that they drove over a landmine and what is left of them is in a freezer in Mbirizi Police Station. The local police are waiting for an investigation team from Kampala to come and assist with the process of identification."

"Are you sure it's them?" asks Mugo.

"Yes. The photos you gave me left me in no doubt. There was no mistaking the larger one."

"Did you identify them to the police?"

"Of course not. I told them that they weren't the people I was looking for."

"Not good news, but well done for finding them. I knew I could rely on you. Where are you now?"

"On my way back to Kampala. I take it you'll be informing the interested parties. Or do you want me to?"

'No. I'll tell Gitau. He'll decide what to do with the information."

* * *

Flicking his hand dismissively towards a young woman, Muchai waits for her to leave and close the bedroom door before answering his phone.

"Gitau, nice to hear from you, how are you doing?"

"I am well Muchai. But I have news of the two Turks you're looking for?"

"That was quick. Excellent, I cannot thank you enough. Where are they? In Kasese?" replies Muchai, under the illusion that the Ugandans were fooled by his misdirection away from Kabale.

"In Mbirizi."

"In Mbirizi?" asks Muchai, unable to process the information he is being given.

"In a freezer," elucidates Gitau.

"A freezer. Is this some kind of joke?"

"No. What's left of them is being kept in a freezer in Mbirizi Police station. According to the local police they drove over a landmine on the road to Mubanzi."

"Mubanzi, what were they doing on the road to Mubanzi?"

"I have no idea. I assumed that was your business, not mine, so I didn't enquire. However, whilst I don't feel overwhelmed by your show of gratitude, I have done what you asked of me. I presume that the favour has been fulfilled."

"Yes. Of course," replies Muchai, distractedly. He adds, "I'm sorry that I was abrupt, but I wasn't expecting this. And thank you Gitau."

Gitau ends the call leaving Muchai to ponder on the news he had received. Sitting in his dressing gown on the hotel bed, Muchai gathers his thoughts.

My missing millions are probably somewhere in Uganda. Recovery of the money rests with Hakan. He has taken responsibility so maybe I should leave him with the problem? Afterall, he's shown good faith by sending his nephew and one of his most loyal foot soldiers. But they have failed ... dead. An accident or murder? Was it a mine or a bomb? If a bomb, who is responsible and have those responsible taken the money? Will Hakan suspect foul play or accept that it was an accident? Either way, the death of his nephew will distract him from his efforts to recover my money. What to do? Perhaps I keep this close to my chest. Possibly I encourage Hakan to send more men to search for his nephew AND the money. Or maybe I give Hakan the unwelcome news to demonstrate my good faith. Proof that we have worked hard to find them. I could suggest we work together to investigate the deaths and recover the money. Pool resources. Or do I just show respect for his loss but demand payment of what is owed. Business is business.

Mmmmmm. I need to give it more thought but, for now, say nothing.

Making a call, Muchai barks into the phone. "Send me up another woman ... yes, NOW."

* * *

What Muchai has not yet factored into his thinking is that, without knowledge of what has happened to his nephew, Hakan had already acted by deploying Demir. Had Muchai been aware of this then he would have approved. Demir and his fabled reputation is well known to the Kenyans. They saw him in action firsthand, when Hakan sent him to work with the Mungiki to resolve a mutual problem three years earlier. A high-ranking politician, who was becoming too vocal in his desire to stamp out the burgeoning Nairobi drug trade, had an unfortunate 'accident'. This removed a mutual obstacle and cemented the partnership between Muchai and Hakan.

Seeing Demir in action three years ago reminded Muchai of a passage from his childhood bible teachings. Most of the bible bored the young Muchai, but one passage remains engraved in his memory. It is in the Book of Revelations. Even now, he can recite most of the text which describes the four horsemen of the apocalypse. It has always held a strange fascination in the recesses of Muchai's dark psyche. One sentence could have been written with Demir in mind.

Behold, an ashen horse; and he who sat on it had the name Death.'

Demir's current ashen horse takes the form of the pale, light grey livery of Qatar airlines, which is speeding him towards the African continent. Reclining in his business class seat with eyes closed, he is unaware that the two air stewards are staring at him from the opening to the galley. It is nothing he said or did. Nothing they could put their finger on. But they did not like this customer. There is something about him which gives them the creeps.

* * *

Speeding along in their own pale ride, a white Pajero, Damo, Earl and Boof are blissfully unaware of events unfolding. Their destination, at least the main one in the African leg of their long journey, is ending. In a country not overly endowed with road signs, they have the comfort of finally passing the first one which indicates that they are heading for Kampala. The city is less than one hundred kilometres away. They have booked themselves back into the Sheraton and are all looking forward to a decent shower and a dip in the hotel pool. Not to mention a celebratory beer or two. Within two hours they reached the outskirts of Kampala.

Pulling the car up to the front of the hotel, they all jump out to stretch their legs. A valet opens the back of the vehicle intending to unload the bags but Earl waves him away indicating that they will carry their own. They each put a cash laden rucksack onto their backs and carry the other bags by hand to the reception desk. Meanwhile the generously tipped valet parks the Pajero in a secure area. Smiling, the receptionist welcomes them back, remembering them from their last stay at the hotel. Once she has all their details, she hands over three keys. With a frown she comments on the amount of luggage they are carrying and offers the services of the valet which, once more, is politely declined.

Luggage safely stored in their rooms; they all agree to meet by the pool. When Damo approaches the pool bar he is greeted by Boof who is lounging in the water at the shallow end with a bottle of beer in his hand. He points to nearby seats, where he has left the towels and Damo sees two bottles of Nile Gold resting invitingly on the table in an ice bucket. He grabs one and eases himself into the water beside Boof.

"It's not a bad life, is it?" chuckles Boof.

"Not at all," replies Damo, "any sign of Earl?"

"Not yet. He better come soon 'cause his beer's getting warm."

An hour, and three further beers later, they are joined by Earl, who sits on the pool lounger, after grabbing a bottle from the ice bucket.

He nods to them, holds up the bottle and says "Cheers."

"Where've you been mate? We were wondering if you'd done a runner," says Boof.

"Been busy sorting out the flights. There are none available until the day after tomorrow, so it looks as though we'll be here for a couple of nights."

"No worries," replies Boof, "we can chill out for a couple of days."

"Yeah," adds Damo, "we're not expected back at Kabale for another four days anyway."

"Yep, by which time we should have landed in Sydney," says Earl, with a smirk. "Anyway, we are booked in First class on Emirates."

Giving a whistle of surprise, Damo says "Jeez, no expense spared."

Grinning, Earl says, "Let's face it, we can all afford it. Besides you get a bigger luggage allowance, and we can carry our rucksacks on to the plane. I want them close to hand. Don't want any nosey baggage handler having a peep and helping themselves. Stuff goes missing in airports, especially in countries like this."

Boof raises his bottle and tips it towards Earl, "Good thinking mate. Ripper. Bloody good thinking."

"Sounds good," says Damo. "Let's just keep our heads down and stay anonymous. There'll be no-one here who knows us. We're practically invisible, so let's keep it that way."

As it turns out, they were very soon reunited with two familiar faces. Both prominent and very visible members of the community.

28

KANT RECANTED

HAVING STAYED THE first of their two nights in the hotel without incident, Earl, Damo and Boof are feeling relaxed as they sip their beers poolside. A group decision not to venture into the city seems to have paid dividends. The finish line is in sight and more of the same is agreed for their last night on the dark continent. It is a matter of sitting out the last twenty-four hours and there are few better and safer places in Kampala to do so than the Sheraton.

All three are dozing on sun loungers when a gentle soft-spoken voice caresses their ears. They open their eyes to find the waitress smiling.

"I am sorry to disturb you, but I was wondering if you gentlemen would care for any lunch. I can take your orders here or escort you to La Terrasse Garden Lounge."

"Actually, I'm a little peckish," says Boof. "What about you boys?"

Nodding in agreement, Damo says, "let's have a change of scenery and eat at La Terrasse."

"Excellent, please follow me," replies the waitress leading the way.

After delivering their drinks, the waitress hands them each a menu. They decide quickly and the waitress leaves.

"Impressive," says Boof.

"Yeah, she's a bit of a looker," replies Damo.

"No mate, I mean the way she took our order without

writing it down. If it was me, I'd have forgotten it by the time I'd reached the kitchen."

"Mate, we ordered three burgers and chips. It wasn't exactly complicated." scoffs Earl.

A voice from the neighbouring table grabs their attention.

"Why, it's Mister Arkins, isn't it? Boof Arkins?"

Squinting at the man addressing him, Boof's eyes widen in recognition and surprise.

"It's Governor Hanson, isn't it?"

"The very same. I know it's a small world but never in a million years would I have expected to see you here. May I join you? I'm keen to hear what you are up to now."

"Er, sure Governor," replies Boof, shifting his chair sideways to accommodate his surprise guest.

Looking expectantly at Damo's smile and Earl's semi scowl, the Governor waits to be introduced. Boof obliges. Nodding in acknowledgement, the Governor turns his attention back to Boof and asks him what he is doing in Uganda. Five minutes later, following Boof's sanitised and abridged version, the Governor leans back and says, "Well, well, well. Who'd have believed it."

Who indeed, thought Earl.

Who indeed, thought Damo.

The burgers and the Governor's drink are delivered to their table and, clearly, their guest has settled in for a big chat.

Chewing on a mouthful of burger, Boof attempts polite conversation, "So what about you Governor?"

"Oh me. Well, I've been here at a conference run by the International Alliance of Prison Authorities. I was invited to give a talk on recidivism and the causes of re-offending."

Fearing the topic had already lost Damo and Earl, Boof dredges up a memory.

"Oh, is that the stuff you used to lecture us about? Immanual Kant and all that."

Clapping, the Governor responds, "Oh well done, Boof. Well … done. You remembered. And I have to say when you told me your reason for being in Uganda, I was profoundly moved that my little talk had such a profound impact on you. Not only have you turned a corner away from crime, but you are devoting your time to a truly worthwhile cause. I'm very impressed. As for our mutual friend, Mister Kant, you will recall that he said that goodwill should drive our actions. It is the principles behind the actions that count, not the actions themselves."

"So, are you still big on the fella Kant then?"

"Well, if I am honest, I've had a slight change of heart. My thinking has altered. At least to some degree."

"Really?" replies Boof, feigning interest whilst polishing off the last three chips.

"Look, Kant said you should act in a way that your principle behind such action might safely be made a law."

Earl glances over to Damo, whose eyes raise to the heavens. The exchanges go unnoticed, and the Governor pushes on with his theories, impervious to the disinterest around the table.

"I think my view now is that Kant's approach to morality is flawed. There is evil in the world and sometimes the consequences of an action can be just as important as the intention behind it." Leaning forward to drive home his argument, the Governor's voice drops an octave to give his statement gravitas. "You see, Kant's focus on intention alone does not, in my opinion, provide sufficient basis for determining the moral value of an action."

"Oh! I understand," replies Boof. Both Earl and Damo

didn't, and they seriously doubted that Boof did either. Unaware of his friends' thoughts, Boof presses on with the conversation.

"Interesting, Governor. May I ask a question?"

"Of course, fire away."

"Take a hypothetical example. What would you say if a person committed a crime but in doing so punished someone who had done something much worse?"

"You mean like a vigilante?"

"Not exactly. Say someone stole money from a person who had got that money through an evil deed."

"Such as?" asks the Governor, clearly enjoying the impromptu debate on moral philosophy.

Pretending to think and formulate an example, which was already embedded in his mind, Boof finally responds to the expectant Governor. "I don't know. Maybe, stealing money from a drug dealer who has got his money from people whose lives he has destroyed."

"Interesting. In my old way of thinking I would reference Kant's moral imperative. That you should act only in a manner that your action could become a general law. If stealing became a general law, then it would mean anyone could steal and therefore you are creating a law where you think it is okay for people to steal from you. Does that make sense?"

"Sort of," replies Boof, which Earl translated, in his private thoughts, as *'not at all, I don't have a fucking clue what you're talking about.'* Keeping his own counsel, Earl stares incredulously at the two men engaged in the discussion.

"To answer your question, which is an interesting one, it highlights the intractability of Kant's thinking. If the intention was to steal money for personal gain, then the intention is clearly not moral, therefore Kant would say the act is immoral." Pointing a finger directly at Boof to emphasise his argument, the Governor continues his speech. "If the intention is to punish the drug dealer, then an argument might be created to consider the act moral. One could make a general law specific to this case. That rationale being that it is okay to steal from a person who has acquired that money through evil means and therefore punish them. Where I now disagree with Kant is that even if the intention was not altruistic, the consequence of the action itself can still have a positive moral outcome. Namely, that there is a moral outcome that the drug dealer has been punished and has less resources to sell more drugs and cause more misery."

After a dramatic pause, the Governor drives home his decisive point. "Therefore, Kant's argument that it is only the intention behind the act that determines the morality of the action is flawed. The consequences of the action also must be considered."

Watching the Governor smugly finish his beer with evident self-satisfaction at his own logic, Damo and Earl remain speechless.

"Yes, I understand, Governor. Thank you for clarifying."

"A pleasure Boof. And once more can I say how marvellous it is to see you, particularly in such edifying circumstances." Rising from the table he says, "And now I must leave you gentlemen. I have a plane to catch."

"Oh! that's a shame," says Damo, rising to shake the Governor's hand. At the opposite end of the table Earl remains seated but waves goodbye.

Patting Boof on the shoulder, the Governor says, "And keep up the good work."

Once the Governor has left the restaurant, Earl turns to Boof. "What the fuck was all that about, you idiot?"

"Whaddya mean?"

"Stealing from drug dealers. Why didn't you just tape a sign to your head which says, 'I'm talking about me', you idiot."

"He'd never have made that connection. He just likes a good chinwag on philosophy over a cold frothy. Besides I was getting a little nervous at all his questions about what I was doing here, so it was good to change the subject. These Governors blokes are nosey, they make me nervous. Think about it. If I was in his shoes, and I was spun a story about working for a charity out of the goodness of my heart, then I doubt if I would believe it. Don't forget, he knows my past."

"Boof has a point," says Damo, keen to diffuse the situation. "Let it drop. Remember Earl, keep a low profile like we agreed. Only one more night here and we're off back to Oz."

"Fine … I suppose. But let's avoid getting into any more conversations with the law," replies Earl looking pointedly at Boof.

"Yeah, let's hope there are no more surprise meetings," says Damo.

Petulantly, Earl agrees. "Let's hope so."

Had the philosophical Governor been party to the conversation, he would have quoted Aristotle. 'Hope is a waking dream.' They did not know it, but they were due for a rude awakening.

29

DO YOU WANT THE GOOD NEWS
OR THE BAD NEWS?

IT WAS TURNING out to be one of their best days in Uganda. Relaxing by the hotel pool, ordering drinks, soaking up the sun, taking an occasional dip to cool down. In Boof's case, also ordering a club sandwich to see him through until dinner time. Even Earl manages a smile or two as the three friends converse. Together, they present a tableau which is the very picture of conviviality. One night left, then on their way back to the land down under.

With the equatorial sun beginning to wane in the early evening, they decide to shower, change, and have dinner in the hotel. They were so close to the finish line they could taste it and the mantra of keeping their heads down is constantly echoing through their minds. Earl and Boof go straight to their rooms but Damo detours to the reception desk and waits patiently as a customer is being checked in. He can hear the exchanges between the new guest and the receptionist. Warm and friendly comments from the receptionist are met with cold, monosyllabic responses from the guest who is tall and slim, sporting close-cropped jet-black hair.

He's a barrel of laughs, thinks Damo, who sympathises with the plight of the receptionist.

Her final words "I hope you enjoy your stay at the Sheraton, Mister Demir," are greeted with a grunt. Turning from the desk, Demir brushes past Damo and they make brief eye contact. Damo tracks Demir's movements across the reception area, then turns to the receptionist and smiles. Pointing to the elevator as the doors close, Damo jokes, "He's a pleasant little soul, isn't he?"

Smirking, but keeping her comments neutral, the receptionist asks what she can do to help. Damo tells her that they are leaving tomorrow on an evening flight and requests a late check-out. Once she has finished tapping on her keyboard, she smiles and confirms that his request is approved. She offers to book transport to the airport, which he accepts with thanks.

Meeting up in the main restaurant, the three friends are relaxed but excited at the prospect of leaving. Damo tells them the hotel has agreed to a late checkout of his room, so the bags can be kept safely stored in his room until they depart to the airport later in the day. Eating, drinking, laughing, and joking they have an enjoyable evening, oblivious of those around them. So much so, that they do not notice a familiar face sat in the corner quietly eating dinner alone. He occasionally looks over to their table.

Replete, they leave the dining area and return to their rooms to get a good night's sleep. Shortly afterwards, the lone diner, after seeing the three Australians leave the restaurant, answers a call on his mobile.

"Yes, I'm just finishing dinner. Our friends are still here, which is good, but I'm tired so I'm going off to bed now to get a good night's sleep. We can speak tomorrow, call me in the morning."

Cutting the call short, he gestures to the waitress to bring the bill which he signs and scribbles details of his room. It is the Club Suite.

* * *

In a more modest room on the third floor, Demir is talking on his mobile to Hakan.

"I'm in Kampala, it's late so I'll hire a car and drive to Kabale tomorrow."

"Good work Demir. I hope that you find them quickly and the only reason for their silence is poor network coverage. Call me when you find them."

"That may not be possible. If they've no coverage, then neither will I."

"True, but there may be landlines you can use at a local hotel."

"If they're in Kabale and I make contact, shall I assist them with their search?" asks Demir.

"Let's deal with one problem at a time. Find them first and then we'll see what progress they've made. I assume they haven't located the money because Muchai is still demanding payment."

"Maybe. But have you considered the possibility that they've found the money and paid Muchai, but then he disposed of them. If he's demanding payment from you, could it be he's looking to profit twice from the transaction?"

Laughing, Hakan says, "Sometimes Demir, I wish I could take a trip through the dark catacombs of your twisted scheming mind. But, of course, you are right to consider this. I concluded that this is possible but unlikely. We've had many years of mutual profit together. There is too much to lose. So, I put myself in his shoes and have thought through what I would have done."

"And your conclusion?" prompts Demir.

"I would take the money and send Kemal and Ahmet home safely. Why risk everything for the sake of one payment when he can look forward to many more in the future. I have also drawn another conclusion."

"Which is what?"

"That I should have sent you, Demir, in the first place."

* * *

On his way to breakfast, Damo goes to reception to check that the arrangements for a taxi to the airport had been made. Anxious to avoid any hitches now that the end is so close, he seeks reassurance that everything is in place. Once again, the receptionist is dealing with Demir who is in the process of checking out of the hotel. She bids him a safe journey which he ignores, and he turns to leave but stops abruptly. Damo, who is daydreaming, is standing a little too close behind and almost gets bowled over.

Those eyes, thought Damo, who moves to one side and apologises, but no acknowledgement from Demir is forthcoming. Having held eye contact long enough to intimidate, Demir pushes past Damo and leaves the hotel.

Addressing the receptionist, Damo says. "Nice. Bet you're glad to see the back of him!"

Professionally non-committal, the receptionist smiles and asks how she can be of assistance.

Having been assured that all the arrangements are in place, Damo joins Boof and Earl at the breakfast table. Boof has already made substantial inroads into his cooked breakfast whilst Earl is sipping on a coffee. After the waitress takes his coffee order, Damo grabs a couple of croissants from the buffet table and rejoins them.

"What're the plans for today then?" he asks.

"Stay in the hotel by the pool, keep our heads down, soak up the sun and then get the hell out of here when it's time," replies Earl.

"I was thinking of going for a wander," says Boof.

This is met with a reproachful look from Earl. "Yeah,

I'd re-think that. We don't need you getting into any bother. Yer can just stay with us in the hotel. You've plenty of time to go wandering when we get back home."

Getting up from the table, Boof grabs his plate and says, "Whoa, take it easy mate. Just a thought. May as well get some more tucker then if we're not going anywhere."

Marvelling at the stack of food on Boof's plate when he returns from the buffet, Damo whistles in surprise. "Jeez mate, I'll never cease to be surprised at the amount of food you can demolish for a scrawny little ticker. Yer must spend half the day on the dunny."

Chewing a mouthful of food, Boof says, "Mate, it's all free, best to make the most of it."

***

By the time Earl, Boof and Damo have finished breakfast and spent the morning lounging by the pool, Demir has passed through Masaka, then Mbirizi and is well on his way to Mbarara. Unlike Adroa, he had not pontificated on what may have happened to Ahmet and Kemal on their way to Kabale. He assumed that they would have made the straightforward journey without incident and would be dealing with matters in Kabale. This being the case he will never cross paths with the petrol station owner on the outskirts of Masaka nor the fruit vendor selling his wares on the road to Mubanzi. When he drives past the modest police station in Mbirizi, he does not register its existence, let alone speak to the local sergeant who has recently come into an unexpected windfall of American dollars, courtesy of Adroa.

Unfortunately for Demir, he neither possesses the local knowledge nor the contacts that Adroa has at his disposal. A couple of calls to contacts in Kabale quickly enabled

Adroa to discover that Ahmet and Kemal never arrived, therefore his search focussed on the journey they made. Not the destination. Operating at a disadvantage, Demir focuses on the destination, harbouring a false assumption that the journey was as straightforward for them as it is proving to be for himself.

Stopping off in Mbarara to re-fuel, he sees a café across the road from the petrol station. Parking his hire car in front of the café, he orders a small beer and a glass of water and sits at a table near the entrance. Habitually, he digs out his mobile phone from his back pocket and checks for messages. Then he decides to ring his mother to check in on her welfare, feeling the guilt of a son who has been called away on business during her 70th birthday celebrations. A short but chatty phone call later, he is satisfied his mother is well and happy, having assured her he will be home soon. Starting to slide the phone into his back pocket, he frowns, hesitates, and has an epiphany. Glancing at the phone screen he stares at the connectivity bars. He has a signal and one strong enough to allow him to call home. Although he still has some way to travel to Kabale, a seed of doubt is planted. Hakan had proposed a theory as to why there had not been any contact. *Was the theory that Kemal had not called due to poor phone coverage incorrect?* His expectation of a quick resolution to matters begins to waver. He jogs back to his car, keen to continue the journey.

* * *

Glancing at his mobile, Damo reports the time gleefully. "Less than four hours from now and we'll be on our way to the airport."

"Excellent," says Boof, halfway through a small bowl of French fries that he has ordered from the poolside bar.

"Yep," agrees Earl, "we're pretty much home and dry." His smile fades and his brow furrows when he sees the hotel manager approaching them, carefully edging his way around the perimeter of the pool.

"Good afternoon, gentlemen, I trust you are enjoying the facilities?"

Warily, Earl responds. "Yes, thank you. Is everything okay?"

"Oh yes, fine. I didn't intend to interrupt you, but we have a guest who has asked me to invite you to his suite for an afternoon cocktail."

"I think there must be some mistake," says Earl.

"Not so. Chief Masika says he knows you all well. He told me that you've been working in his village."

"Chief Masika?"

"Yes, indeed. And, if I may be so bold as to suggest, perhaps you can change into something more suitable," says the manager, eyeing up the assorted swimwear they are wearing.

"Okay, thanks. Tell him we'll meet him in about thirty minutes once we've showered. Where did you say he is?"

"The Club Suite. It's on the ninth floor. Thank you, I'll pass on your message." The manager turns and briskly walks back to the main lobby.

"Shit," says Boof, "what do you think he wants?"

"No need to panic, he probably saw us in the hotel and just wants to catch up. Mukasa will have told him we're on a break in Kampala and he's probably up here on business," replies Damo.

Rubbing the small scar on his left eyebrow, a habit he has when he is concerned, Earl says, "You could be right.

He seems to spend a lot of time up here. We just need to play it cool and act natural."

* * *

At the same time as the three friends leave the pool area to shower, Demir puts a call through to Hakan. In the space of two hours since arriving in Kabale he has matters to report.

"What news do you have, Demir?" asks Hakan, eager for information.

"As you can hear, I am in Kabale and the first thing I must report is that there are no issues of phone connectivity here. In fact, I've not had any issues anywhere. It's unlikely that the lack of contact from Kemal is due to that."

"Clearly," replies Hakan impatiently, moving the conversation on.

"My other news is mixed. All my inquiries here have drawn a blank regarding Kemal and Ahmet. I've asked around and I'm sure that neither of them ever arrived here."

"How can you be so sure?" replies Hakan irritably, having heard the unwelcome news.

Keeping his voice calm and business-like, despite Hakan's angst, Demir replies. "This place is small, and they have few foreign visitors. Those who do visit would be noticed."

"But how can you be so sure?"

"Those I questioned all refer to three 'mzungus' being the only recent visitors they know of. Tourists are rare here and so foreign visitors, especially mzungus who stand out in the crowd, are big news."

"Mzungus?"

"Yes, their word for white people."

"Why couldn't two of these be Kemal or Ahmet?" asks Hakan, with hope dwindling rapidly in his mind.

"From the descriptions given, I am certain."

"You said you had mixed news. All you've told me is bad news."

"I enquired about the three visitors and, to be sure it wasn't Kemal and Ahmet, I went looking for them. They're here working on a project to build a school. I couldn't find them because, apparently, they've left town for a few days, but would soon be back."

"So?"

"When they talked about the school build project, it was a chance for me to ask about the books. I said I'd heard that Americans send them to areas like Kabale. I made small talk and asked if they'd ever got books. They told me that there'd been books dropped by aircraft and that the last drop was as recent as a few weeks ago."

Good news at last, thought Hakan. "Really?"

"Yes, I've also found out where they are stored. Do you want me to check them out and see if the cash is there?" Busy processing what he has been told, Hakan does not respond. Demir prompts Hakan for an answer. "Well, Hakan? Do you want me to check it out or just to focus on finding Kemal?" Demir waits and receives the answer he is expecting.

"If my nephew is still alive, then it will do no harm for you to have a look at the books before we continue the search. He may even turn up whilst you are in Kabale. If he's dead then it also doesn't matter if there is a short delay in the search. Dead is dead."

"You sure boss?"

"Yes, go ahead, make your enquiries but make sure you don't arouse suspicion. I assume the money hasn't been discovered. If it had, discovery of several million

Australian dollars would've been big news in the village.
I expect that would've come up during your cosy little
chats with them."

"I'll get on to it," says Demir, before ending the call.

A QUOTE FROM THE GODFATHER

ONCE THE ELEVATOR door closes and they are alone in the lift, the three friends resume their conversation.

"I think you're over reacting Earl. He's probably seen us in the hotel and just wants to say hello and have a quick drink to see how we're getting on," says Damo, hopefully.

Boof is equally as hopeful, "Yeah Earl, Damo's right."

"Let's hope you both are," replies Earl, doubtfully.

With a cheery 'ping', the lift draws to a halt and the doors open. On the wall facing them they see a sign indicating that the Club Suite is to their left.

Inside the suite Chief Masika and Eze are finishing their conversation before their guests arrive.

"Once we have concluded our business today, we'll return directly to Kabale."

"Yes, Chief," replies Eze.

Hearing a tentative knock on the door, Masika says, "Well that's agreed then and it sounds as though they are here."

Masika remains seated near the French doors which lead onto the balcony and gestures for Eze to let the guests in.

"Welcome, welcome, gentlemen, so nice to see you again." Pointing to three chairs around a large coffee table, Masika smiles and invites them to sit down and take a drink. Six open bottles of beer rest in an ice bucket at the centre of the table. With a nod of thanks, they each take a bottle and a tentative swig, whilst Eze stands beside the Chief.

"Nice little set up you've got here Chief," says Boof, sporting an affable smile.

"It suffices Mister Boof. One must have one's luxury when on business. It compensates for being away from home."

Small talk within the group is stilted. Eze remains silent during the polite exchanges but seems to be carefully appraising the reaction of their guests.

Earl's eyes meet Eze's. *There's something on his mind*, thinks Earl.

This one's in charge, thinks Eze.

Those snacks look tasty, thinks Boof, as he dips his hand into the bowl.

Right, it's time to go, thinks Damo. They finished their beers and the polite conversation is stuttering to a halt. A distinct feeling of awkwardness is evident in the room and he is beginning to get the same uncomfortable vibe as Earl.

Rising from his seat, Earl had also read the room and clearly felt they needed to leave. "Right Chief, thank you for your hospitality, we'll leave you alone. I'm sure you are a busy man."

"Yeah, we'd best get going," adds Damo following Earl's lead and nudges Boof who is emptying the snack bowl.

"Going?" asks the Chief, "I didn't realise you were leaving us."

"Gotta pack before our taxi comes," adds Boof, instantly realising his mistake when he is admonished with a sideways glare from Earl.

For the first time in the meeting Eze speaks. "Yes, I understand Mister Boof. You don't want to miss your flight, do you?"

With a crocodile smile, Masika says, "No indeed they don't Eze, but don't rush off just yet gentlemen. Please sit back down. There's something important I want to discuss, and it will only take a few minutes. Don't worry, you won't miss your flight."

Fuck, thinks Earl as he sinks back into his seat. The identical thought passes through the minds of the others, as they slowly lower themselves back into their chairs.

* * *

Sitting in his own hotel room, less grandiose than that of the Chief's, Demir makes his plans for tomorrow. Although the Kigezi Gardens Inn in Kabale does not offer Sheraton's luxury, it provides a comfortable, conveniently placed base for his mission.

Further enquiries around the village reveal that the books he is looking for are stored in sheds at the edge of the local Chief's property. He is told that he would, of course, need the Chief's permission if he wanted to see them. Keen to allay his concerns, a local shopkeeper tells Demir not to worry, the Chief is due back soon. On the contrary, news of the Chief's absence is not bad, but good news and learning that the property is currently uninhabited is music to his ears.

His strategy is simple. Once he gets a good night's sleep he will seek out the Chief's property during the day to pin down its exact location and double check that the house is empty. If it is all clear, he will return after nightfall to search the sheds under cover of darkness. Room service delivers a meal which he picks at whilst sitting on his bed looking at a hand drawn map. Obligingly, the hotel manager has sketched out directions to the Chief's property which arrived on the tray with his food.

Confident of success, he expects to be able to bring Hakan some more welcome news in the next twenty-four hours. What Demir does not know is that, although the house would be empty when he visits the property during the day, the Chief has planned to travel back to Kabale having successfully conducted his business in Kampala.

* * *

"We have a little business to conduct gentlemen and I am hopeful," says Masika whilst glancing back at Eze, "that it will not take up too much of your time."

"Oh! I see," replies Earl, who did not know exactly what the business could be but was beginning to suspect the worst. Combining hope with a bluff, he adds, "We're more than happy to give you a progress update on the build."

"Perhaps after our other business is concluded."

A perceptible shift in the mood of the room becomes evident to all.

"And what business would that be?" asks Earl.

"Where is the money?"

"What money?"

"Is it still in the rucksacks in your room?" asks Masika, whose manner had shifted from convivial to brooding. Staring intently into Earl's eyes he adds, "the hotel manager kindly allowed Eze, to have brief access to your rooms whilst you were enjoying the sunshine and pool."

Damo whispers "fuck" to himself, unintentionally revealing his state of mind..

"Fuck indeed, Mister Damo. I take it you assume we're all fools. I saw you creeping around my property the night you were having your little adventure in the book sheds."

"How do you know it was us?" asks Boof.

"I couldn't be sure at the time, of course, but things gradually became clear when Eze and I searched the sheds the following day."

"A bit risky wasn't it. Leaving all that cash in an unlocked wooden shed?" asks Earl, with bitterness and anger in his voice.

"Oh! you misunderstand. We had no idea that there was money amongst the books. It was more the case that we were confused as to why anybody would have such an interest in our schoolbooks. So much so, that you would try to steal them in the middle of the night."

"Our first thought is that it was poachers," says Eze, joining the conversation.

Masika laughs sardonically. "Eze is correct, that was our first thought. But we did wonder why poachers would be so desperate to educate themselves with schoolbooks and risk imprisonment over them. They are not known for their thirst for academia and knowledge. So, we dismissed that thought, especially when we found that the crates had been disturbed and one seemed to have a lot of books missing. Imagine our surprise when we found a significant amount of cash in Australian dollars resting underneath a few books that had clearly been removed and hastily put back."

"How come you didn't think poachers had stolen the money?" asks Boof. Earl remains silent, glowering at the Chief.

"I suppose a few things. No local people would invade my house or enter my property without my permission. Afterall, I am the Chief. Secondly, it is Australian currency and who, may I ask, around the village is Australian. Lastly, if poachers are bold enough to enter properties where they risk getting caught and shot, then they are likely to invade the house to steal whatever valuables they can find. Not break into a glorified garden shed."

"And even if they did," adds Eze, "they wouldn't leave two hundred thousand dollars behind."

"So, what is it you want to do now," asks Earl, through gritted teeth.

Masika gives a hollow laugh. "Ah! That's the spirit, let's get down to what my English student friends used to refer to as *'brass tacks.'* In the words of Marlon Brando in that marvellous film; *'I want to make you an offer you can't refuse.'"*

"Go on," replies Earl.

Masika glances over and points to Eze. "Eze here, counted the money and there is close to two hundred thousand dollars which you left in the crate. Incidentally, it now rests somewhere far more secure. Now my thinking is that if you left behind such a large amount of money, it must have been because you could only carry so much. I also deduced that what you have taken must be a significant enough sum to satisfy the three of you. Certainly, significant enough to leave two hundred thousand dollars behind. Therefore, the cash in your possession must be in the millions."

"Which I assume you intend to try and take from us," snaps Earl, knuckles white from gripping the arms on his chair.

"Oh! There's no 'try' about it. One word to the authorities and you'll all be spending the rest of your life in a Ugandan prison and, believe me, they don't measure up to the Sheraton. Unless of course you have a plausible explanation which accounts for the large amount of money you are smuggling out of the country. Do you have a plausible explanation?"

"If we give you the money, what's to stop us reporting it to the authorities. Then no-one benefits," counters Earl.

"That is a good point and one I have carefully thought through, unlike your good selves. You seem to have given the whole affair extraordinarily little forethought. What pray do you think would happen when the baggage going through the airport gets scanned. I mean, no offence, but you don't exactly present as jet-setting business executives. You may find it hard to explain what you are doing with that amount of cash. Am I not correct?"

No response is forthcoming from Earl, Damo or Boof.

"I take it from the silence that I am. Correct on all counts that is. What were you thinking, I wonder. Trying to get millions of dollars in cash through airports and into your country."

Resigned to the inevitable, Earl asks, "What do you propose? Our flight is in a few hours."

"I want you to understand that these funds will be invaluable to the project and the development of more infrastructure in and around Kabale. We can now also afford to attract leading educationalists and put the training school on the map. So, in contrast to your own motives, it is not for my personal gain. However, I believe in being fair and suggest you take a small amount of the cash between you. I propose around fifty thousand dollars and I will sign a paper confirming this is a payment for the work on the project. The amount may raise some eyebrows, but if it does, you'll have my backing to support what is a credible story."

"Fifty fucking thousand!" exclaims Earl.

Wagging his index finger to signal a further proposal, Masika hushes Earl. "That is not all. I will also electronically transfer a further sum of three hundred thousand to a bank account of your choice, giving you each a nice even sum of money to share which compensates for your time and effort. Think of it as a 'thankyou' from me, on behalf of the village."

"And what guarantee do we have that you'll transfer the money?"

"You have my word." Waving towards the balcony, Masika says, "I suggest that you go and discuss my proposal amongst yourselves. It will give you some privacy."

Closing the French doors behind them, the three friends convene in a huddle. Damo glances through the glass and sees that the Chief and Eze have retreated further into the lounge area, to give comfort that they are out of earshot.

"We're fucked," says Boof, opening the discussion.

"Helpful," replies Earl. "On the other hand, we could just tell him to fuck off and take our chances that he won't follow through with his threat."

Tutting, Damo leans closer to Earl and speaks in a hushed voice. "I don't want to take that risk. Anyway, he'll do it in my opinion. He's not gonna pass up this opportunity. It's a no brainer for him. No risk but a large reward. Even if we avoid prison and they let us through the airport, they're going to confiscate the money. We'd go back empty handed. This way we get something. On the bright side we get a hundred grand each, plus a share of the fifty."

"If, and it is an 'if', he transfers the money," replies Earl, bitterly. "And we've gone from a couple of million each to a hundred grand."

They argue back and forth between them but eventually all agree that they have no choice. Reluctantly they re-enter the lounge area of the suite and return to their seats. Eze's expression hides all emotion, and the Chief raises his eyebrows to prompt them to speak, which they do.

But all efforts to negotiate a higher figure fail.

"Okay Chief, we have a deal. But if we don't get the money, we'll be approaching the authorities ourselves," says Earl, acutely aware that his threat was empty.

"Point taken," replies Masika. "You know of course I am well respected. It will be your word against mine and I doubt that what you say will have much sway with the embassy in Australia. I have no idea about your connections and standing, but I would be willing to bet the two hundred thousand we already have, that you are unlikely to have any success."

Subconsciously Earl glances over to Boof. The Chief has inadvertently hit the nail on the head. Any scrutiny of their background, particularly Boof's recent history, would not bear scrutiny. They would have zero chance of getting support from the embassy for keeping the amount of money they had in their possession without a very convincing story. They simply did not have one.

Pleased that the tone of the Australians suggested their compliance, Masika's mood becomes more conciliatory and reassuring. "Once again, you have my word and despite how this has ended for you, I want you to know that we're grateful for all you have done for the village. The payment, that I will transfer to you without delay, is well deserved."

"I don't have a bank account," says Boof.

"Unusual," replies Masika, unaware of Boof's series of stints in prison. "But my intention is to transfer all the money to Mister Earl and he can pass on your share, as well as Mister Damo's." Flicking open his laptop, Masika says, "If you give Eze your room key, he will collect the rucksacks whilst I transfer the three hundred thousand."

Once Masika has accessed his own account and set up a transfer payment, Earl dictates his account details. Masika chats genially whilst happily tapping his keyboard, but the conversation is one sided, with the three friends sitting moodily, in sullen silence. By the time Masika has pressed 'Confirm', Eze returns with the room key and nods to Masika to indicate he has the money.

"Where are the bags with the cash?" asks Earl. Seeing that Eze is empty handed.

"I've put them somewhere safe," replies Eze, enigmatically.

The deed was done. Masika had one further question before they left for the airport. Where did the money come from? Giving an abridged version of the story, Earl, Damo and Boof leave Masika's suite. Congratulating the Chief on the coup he has pulled, Eze's smile transforms into a frown once he reflects on what they have learnt.

"I think, Chief, we need to stay alert. If Mister Earl's story is only half true, we need to be wary of strangers in the village. If the cash really is drug money, then there will be serious and dangerous people involved and looking for it."

"What's a few gangsters compared to the war and civil strife our country has endured. Who are they compared to dictators like Idi Amin Dada? I agree that we need to be careful and vigilant, but we fear no one, especially criminals."

Walking over onto the balcony they look down to see the three Australians climbing into their taxi. Shaking his head, Masika says, "These mzungus need to take a good look at themselves." Eze responds with a chuckle, nodding in agreement.

DON'T SHOOT THE MESSENGER

HAVING DRIVEN PAST Masika's property that morning, Demir noticed that two gardeners were busy working on the grounds. His previous experience in Kenya, when he was sent to assist Muchai, was that the wealthy often have domestic staff and gardeners who live in quarters on the compound. They had their truck parked on the driveway indicating they lived elsewhere. With no sign of life within the house and a clear sight of the storage sheds, he is confident of success.

When he returns after sundown, the whole property is shrouded in darkness. Labouring for over an hour in the three sheds proves to be more arduous than he expects. It is hot, dusty and ultimately fruitless work. All he has found is books, no sign of any money, not even a single banknote. Another dead end. Another piece of negative news to convey to Hakan.

Frustrated and angry, he thrusts his fist against the partly opened door causing it to slam against the wall of the shed as he exits. With the compound isolated from the main village and uninhabited when he arrived, he is unconcerned about making noise. He has searched all three sheds, top to bottom. *'Nothing but fucking books,'* he thinks, as he reaches into his back pocket for his phone. Musing on his options, he decides on the best course of action. *'Better call Hakan with the bad news and check that he still wants me to continue his search for Kemal.'* Peering at his mobile screen, he starts to search under 'Recents' to make his call.

A rustle near the bushland startles him.

"It's a trifle late in the night to be visiting our little library. May I ask which books you're looking for?"

Masika and Eze see the stunned expression of their intruder which is illuminated by the ambient light from his mobile phone screen. Struggling in the darkness to see the faces behind the voices, Demir strains to discern the features of the two men addressing him. There is no mistaking the object being pointed at him. Stabbing the rifle towards Demir to show they mean business, Eze raises his voice, "You heard the Chief, answer him?"

From the expression on Demir's face, Masika can see that the intruder is neither scared nor intimidated by them or Eze's weapon. Warily, he takes a step forward. "Be so kind as to speak up. Looking at you I'm guessing you're not a poacher. What's your purpose here?"

Taken by surprise, Masika gasps when their adversary dives to the ground and somersaults towards Eze. Aghast, Masika calls out a warning too late and Eze's legs are swept from under him. Momentarily airborne, Eze hits the ground and the jolt dislodges the rifle from his hands, which skids along the dirt. In one fluid movement Demir rises to his feet, sprints away and disappears into the bushland under cover of darkness. The sound of rustling and footsteps quickly receded into the night.

Swearing, Eze scrambles to his feet, grabs his rifle and aims it in the direction that Demir escaped. Masika holds up his hand, as Eze fumbles for the trigger.

"Leave it Eze, don't fire. He's gone."

Ignoring the order, Eze fires a shot harmlessly into the sky and turns to Masika. "Sorry Chief, but I want to discourage him from coming back."

"Good thinking Eze, now let's go into the house. I think our friend got the message. I just want to ensure he didn't break in, and that our other money is safe."

* * *

Back in his hotel room, Demir lays on his bed. With a towel wrapped round his waist after a shower, he picks up his phone and makes a call. It has been a hot and dirty night's work which has left him empty handed. Prior to the evening's escapade, he was confident he would be able to report good news. Even though the actual news he had would be unwelcome, he decides it is best to rip the bandage off and tell Hakan what he has found. Or rather what he has not found.

"You're certain the money was not there," barks Hakan.

"I searched every crate. If the money was ever there, it isn't now."

"If it was, either Kemal and Ahmet have taken it, or it has gone forever."

"My enquiries confirm that they never arrived here, so that can be ruled out. What do you want me to do?"

Situations outside his control rarely occurred, but this was one such situation. Uncertain as to the best course of action, Hakan processes his thoughts before replying. Knowing how his boss's mind works, Demir waits patiently until Hakan's voice filters through his earpiece.

"If there is no money with the books and you are certain that Kemal and Ahmet never made it to Kabale, there is little point in staying. All you can do is make your way back to Kampala. Take the route they would have used and make enquiries along the way. Stop everywhere. Someone must have seen them. No-one would forget Ahmet with his build. If he'd passed through anywhere,

288

he'd have been remembered."

"Okay boss, I'll get on to it tomorrow."

"If you hear anything, call me immediately," says Hakan, then ends the call.

* * *

Demir is characteristically thorough. He left Kabale after breakfast and decided to stop off at every town and every village, no matter how small, on the way. At the first village, Rubaare, he drew a blank. Its size alone convinced him that he is wasting his time, but he is determined to leave no stone unturned.

His second stop, Ntungamo, is equally unproductive, even though he spent part of his visit at the Ntungamo International Resort. In normal circumstances Auntie Dembe and Akello would have happily welcomed a visitor from Australia. Since Earl, Damo and Boof visited, they had developed a soft spot for Antipodeans. From the moment Demir uttered his first sentence, they were guarded. They had a bad feeling about this stranger. Even though he spoke in an Australian accent, he oozed trouble. Normally they would have chatted happily about the other Australians they had befriended, but they decided that discretion is the better part of valour.

Driving out of the small town, Demir has a slight nagging feeling they knew something more than they had told him, but by the time he reaches the outskirts of Mbarara he has shaken these thoughts off. He remembers Mbarara on the way down to Kabale. It is much larger than the other places he had passed, and he is hopeful that, if Kemal and Ahmet had stopped off anywhere, it would have been here. One hour later his hopes are dashed. Nobody in the town remembers seeing them.

Having quickly investigated Sanga, the next small settlement after Mbarara, he arrives at Mbirizi. Enquiries at cafes and shops draw a blank but as he opens his car door to leave, a sign up the road catches his eye. Normally, it would signify a place that he studiously avoids, but he wrestles away his reticence and decides to test the water. All other options had been exhausted.

He finds himself sitting opposite the sergeant in the smallest, most spartanly decorated police station that he has ever had the misfortune to enter. With no expectation of any success, Demir describes Kemal and Ahmet, explaining that he is searching for his friends, but they appear to have gone missing. With a mixture of surprise and confusion at the odd response, Demir witnesses an ever-widening smile, packed full of yellowing teeth, which lights up the expression on the sergeant's face. Mentally rubbing his hands with glee, the sergeant knows that the mystery of the identity of the bodies in his freezer is about to be solved.

Reflecting that his revelation will be unwelcome to his visitor, his smile morphs into a carefully crafted expression of concern, which is more appropriate in the circumstances.

"I am sorry to say that the description you have given matches that of the bodies of two men."

"Bodies? Are they dead?"

"Yes, I suspect that these are the men you are searching for, Mister Demir. I'm very sorry. But to be certain, would you be willing to identify them?" asks the sergeant.

"What … you have them here?" replies Demir, looking around the station with growing incredulity.

"I have. They are in a freezer at the back of the station."

"A freezer?"

"Yes sir. But I must warn you that they are not whole."

"Not whole?"

"Yes sir. They drove over a landmine."

Demir's incredulity levels rise further. "A landmine? You have open roads with landmines lying around?"

"I can assure you that it's a very rare, almost freak occurrence. There's been a program of clearing landmines for many years in Uganda. But unfortunately for your friends, this is what happened. Now, perhaps if you could please follow me."

Leading Demir to the back of the station, the sergeant approaches the freezer.

In disbelief, Demir says, "What, you've got them in there? That's a food freezer! How can you fit them in there?"

Carefully lifting the freezer lid, the sergeant says, "I should warn you, once more, that they are not whole. But we have their heads. It should be enough to identify them."

After Demir has had sufficient time to identify Ahmet from the remains of his head, the sergeant moves it to one side to reveal Kemal's face. Unlike Ahmet, Kemal's head is whole and still attached to his shoulders. A sight that would be challenging for normal people, has negligible impact on Demir's psyche. He returns to the office to make a formal statement of identification.

Placing the completed forms and statement into a file, the sergeant informs Demir of the protocol. "Once the investigation is completed, the bodies can be passed to the family."

"I will inform his relatives," says Demir.

"It may take a few weeks. This will be dealt with in Kampala. I will give you the contact details."

Driving away in a reflective mood, Demir considers the mixed results. He did not find the money but, there again, he was not sent to find the money. That was Kemal and Ahmet's job. On the other hand, he has done what he was asked to do.

He found Kemal and Ahmet, well, he had found most of Kemal and Ahmet. This was the reason Hakan had sent him to the back end of the world. Mission accomplished, but not with an outcome that Hakan will welcome. In fact, reflecting on every call he has made since landing in Uganda, he has been the consistent bearer of bad news. To cap it off, his final call would be the worst of all.

Three things occurred to Demir once he had finished his call. Surprisingly, Hakan remained calm as if he was already resigned to the fact that Kemal and Ahmet would be found dead. But of a greater surprise to him was that, if any emotion could be perceived from Hakan's stoic responses, it was that he was more regretful of Ahmet's demise than of his nephew's. What Demir did expect was that Hakan would quickly fall into damage limitation mode. They were no nearer to locating the missing millions and the natives were getting restless.

Hakan had to strategise. Distilling the problem down to three options, there is work to be done.

Option one, Hakan rationalises, is to write off the millions as a loss and send another payment to keep the African's sweet. A short-term loss for a longer-term gain with continued business and a workable business relationship. Aside from the financial pain, Hakan's ego was at risk. Was Muchai making a fool of him, having found the cash himself? Afterall, Demir had found the books and there was no cash. Who had taken it if not Muchai, was the question to which he had no answer.

The second option considered by Hakan, is to refuse any further payment. A short-term win but a longer-term loss of significant future revenue streams as well as acquiring a lifetime enemy. Unless he persuades Muchai to swallow the loss (highly unlikely) or he finds an alternative partner (unlikely, as he will have gained a reputation for double crossing Muchaï) the future is very uncertain.

Hakan decides there is a further option, which is painful, but less painful than option one. Negotiate a reduced payment thereby sharing the loss between them. Unless of course, reverting to Hakan's egoistic insecurity, Muchai had already found the first payment and was playing him for a fool.

IF AT FIRST YOU DON'T SUCCEED ...

IT IS A lazy Tuesday afternoon in Randwick. Caressed by the spring sun, the Dog is practically empty. Being a workday there are only a handful of punters drinking in the bar, mainly bored retirees discussing the outcome of their latest golf round. Sitting at a table in the corner are three men who had early retirement in their grasp only for it to be snatched away by an African Chieftain. Neither Boof, Damo nor Earl, had slept much during their fourth night back. All three finally passed out around dawn only to wake two hours later.

"So, this is what they mean by jet lag, it's worse coming back than it was going," says Boof, taking a half-hearted sip of his beer.

"Yep," replies Earl.

"How long will it go on before things get back to normal?"

"It varies, maybe a week," says Damo, yawning.

"Anyway, I've got some news," announces Earl. He looks at the expectant but fatigued glazed expressions from his friends. "The money came through. The funds Masika transferred have cleared. Three hundred thousand, as promised."

Putting his beer glass back down on the table, Damo frowns, "You sound surprised. We saw him process the transfer on his laptop."

Sardonically, Earl responds. "What, me? Surprised? Well yeah, a little bit. He double crossed us, stole our money, and sent us packing."

"Yeah, but," says Boof, unable to develop his thoughts into a logical statement.

Glaring, Earl says, in a sarcastic tone, "Of course he wouldn't cancel the payment. Oh no, not our Chief. Afterall, he had a few days before it'd hit our account, didn't he? He's, no doubt, got friends in high places. Some probably at the bank. Friends who'd do him a favour. Y'know, like blocking the money transfer. So yeah, I would have been far from surprised if it hadn't cleared."

"Such cynicism from one so young and innocent," replies Damo, returning the sarcasm. "The bottom line is that he's been true to his word."

Turning to Boof, Earl asks, "Have you set up a bank account yet, like I told you to?"

"Nah! Not yet. Haven't had time. No worries, no drama. Yer can just give me cash."

"I can't take a hundred thousand dollars out in cash you idiot. Banks don't do without a bit of a drama and I don't want to draw any unwanted attention. Get a bloody account set up, give me the details and I'll transfer the money."

"Okay mate. Yer pretty tetchy for someone who's just come into a lot of money," replies Boof, shovelling a handful of nuts into his mouth.

"Might be something to do with the fact that it's a hundred grand rather than over two million," barks Earl.

"Now. Now. Boys," interjects Damo. "What's done is done. No point crying over lost millions. To be honest I agree with Earl. I wasn't convinced, either, that we'd get it. All things considered, I'm happy."

With a bitter tone in his voice, Earl says, "Yeah well. It's back to fly in and flyouts for me. Can't retire to Bali on a hundred grand." Looking at Damo, he adds, "And you won't be able to either."

"What about you Boof?" asks Damo. "What're you gonna do?"

"Probably gonna end up back in the pokey," says Earl, snidely.

Shaking his head and smiling, Boof dismisses Earl's suggestion. "Not me mate. Now this may not be the best time to mention it … but … I have another proposal."

"You've got to be kidding," replies Damo, assuming it is a joke.

"If yer have, then forget it," says Earl, "yer last one didn't go to plan. Did it?"

"It sorta did, mate. The money was there, and we got it. Wasn't my fault that there was a crafty Chief in the mix."

With his interest piqued, Damo sniggers. "He's got a point, Earl. And we still ended up with a hundred grand each."

"So, do yer want to hear it or not?" asks Boof.

Conspiratorially, they all lean in. Satisfied he cannot be overheard, Boof rubs his hands gleefully and begins his story.

THE EPILOGUE

GREED TRUMPS EGO and Hakan's third option becomes reality. At a face-to-face meeting on neutral territory (Dubai airport) Muchai and Hakan iron out their differences and agree to share the loss equally. Hakan arranges a second payment equivalent to half the money originally dispatched, but this time not using Ugandan schoolbooks as the delivery method.

Neither party wants to jeopardise far more significant future income for the sake of one errant payment. Each kept their own counsel and did not share the thinking behind their decisions. On Hakan's part, he knew the delivery had been botched and the fault lay entirely at the door of his Sydney operation. Demir had found the books but not the money and confirmed that the crates had already been opened. Hakan had enough respect for Muchai to conclude that if he was responsible, he would not have left loose ends. The money would have been taken and the books destroyed to hide any evidence of their existence.

It was clear to Muchai that the books had been delivered, albeit to the wrong location but who was at fault and how they ended up in Kabale was unclear. He had not entirely dismissed the possibility that the cause may be from within his own organisation, but the torture of those he suspected most, did not reveal any new information. He also recognized that Hakan had shown good faith by sending his nephew and one of his most trusted foot soldiers to try to recover the money; and he lost both in the process. If Hakan had tried to dupe Muchai, he paid for it through this loss.

Business continued as normal between Muchai and Hakan. Each a little more wary of the other. Both keen to avoid any repetition of events, both ignorant of what happened to the money.

* * *

Chief Masika proceeded with due care. Cash was released slowly and spent gradually to avoid any suspicion or attention. Each time the windfall funds were accessed he pedalled various theories and spread rumours that the World Bank, USAID, and other international funding agencies had been generous. Able to attract and employ qualified teachers, his project blossomed, and a stream of impressive alumni made their successful way as teachers in the Ugandan education system.

More facilities are constructed and infrastructure for the Kabale district is enhanced and modernised with the addition of various community assets. One being a modest, small football stadium for Kikungiri Rovers FC, along with new kit and a small gym. Mukasa is given the funds to achieve a five-year plan of getting the team into the higher leagues. Masika saw the impact that Mukasa had on the local players and how the success of the team re-invigorated the community. Kikungiri Rovers had made the cup final for the first time in their history but lost one nil to Busheyni United. Many believed the only goal of the game should not have been allowed. A penalty awarded in dubious circumstances. Post-game rumours that the

Bushenyi Chief was seen handing cash to the referee before the game started, were never proven.

* * *

Governor Hanson took advantage of his accrued long service leave and used the time to complete his Post Graduate Thesis entitled 'A Modern Critique of Kantian Philosophy'. In doing so he studied one of Kants' critics, Friedrich Nietzsche, and became a supporter and proponent of the controversial German Philosopher's ideas. Increasingly disillusioned with the modern world's culture of entitlement, instant gratification and dumbing down of intellectual thought through social media, he related strongly to Nietzsche's work. On his lecture tour he became increasingly evangelistic, preaching Nietzsche's idea that mass culture led to conformity and brought about mediocrity thus leading to the decline of the human species.

Some of his audiences challenged his obsessive love of Nietzsche, referencing the association of the philosophers' ideas with Hitler and Nazi Germany. On occasion he was laughed out of the lecture theatre, especially when confronted with the latest generation of young 'intelligentsia'.

Lecturing at Keele University in Northwest England, most of the audience were members of the Socialist Workers Party society, despite their comfortable, privileged backgrounds. Catcalls of "Nazi, Nazi" echoed round the theatre. Trying to counter mindless chanting with reasoned discourse, Hanson referenced Nietzsche's famous letter, which commanded the German Emperor to go to Rome to be shot and summoned European powers to act against Germany. Unfortunately, Sebastian Harcourt, son of a wealthy landowner in Lincolnshire and President of the Social Worker Party society, was front and centre in the audience. Sebastian was familiar with the letter referenced by Hanson. Rather than shout abuse, he raised his hand seeking permission to speak. Encouraged by the more civilised politeness of Sebastian's engagement, Hanson invited him to speak.

"Yes, young man, what are your thoughts on Nietzsche's correspondence?"

"Yeah mate. I've read it and he does say that stuff that you said, but he also claims that he created the world. Basically, he was going through a mental breakdown at the time."

Renewed laughter and guffaws from the audience drowned Hanson's, now futile, attempt to argue that the letter proved that far from being a Nazi, Nietzsche was a vocal critic of antisemitism. With a defeated shake of his head, Hanson left the stage and promptly cancelled the remainder of his engagements. Upon resumption of his post at Long Bay Correctional Facility, he never repeated his experiment of philosophy lectures for inmates.

* * *

Due in no small part to the influence and connections of Mukasa, the Ntungamo International Resort had its first ever entry into the African Mecca Safaris guide to Ugandan Hotels, Camps and Accommodation. It was a proud moment for Akello and increased his business twofold in the subsequent twelve months. It was no coincidence that an ex-teammate of Mukasa, from his professional playing days, took over ownership of the online publication and gave the resort a highly favourable review.

* * *

As for Boof's proposal …